RUTHIE
FEAR

RUTHIE
FEAR

a novel

Maxim Loskutoff

W. W. NORTON & COMPANY
Independent Publishers Since 1923

Copyright © 2020 by Maxim Loskutoff

For information about permission to reproduce selections from this book, write to Permissions, W. W. Norton & Company, Inc., 500 Fifth Avenue, New York, NY 10110

For information about special discounts for bulk purchases, please contact W. W. Norton Special Sales at specialsales@wwnorton.com or 800-233-4830

Manufacturing by Lake Book Manufacturing
Book design by Chris Welch
Production manager: Beth Steidle

Library of Congress Cataloging-in-Publication Data

Names: Loskutoff, Maxim, author.
Title: Ruthie fear : a novel / Maxim Loskutoff.
Description: First Edition. | New York, NY : W. W. Norton & Company, [2020]
Identifiers: LCCN 2020008284 | ISBN 9780393635560 (hardcover) |
    ISBN 9780393635577 (epub)
Subjects: GSAFD: Science fiction.
Classification: LCC PS3612.O7733 R88 2020 | DDC 813/.6—dc23
LC record available at https://lccn.loc.gov/2020008284

W. W. Norton & Company, Inc., 500 Fifth Avenue, New York, N.Y. 10110
    www.wwnorton.com

W. W. Norton & Company Ltd., 15 Carlisle Street, London W1D 3BS

1 2 3 4 5 6 7 8 9 0

For the wolves

Approximately seventy miles long and up to fifteen miles wide, the Bitterroot Valley is sheltered by the majestic Bitterroot Range to the west and the Sapphire Mountains to the east. Watered by the Bitterroot River and its tributaries, the valley climate is mild. The valley provides easy forage for bear, elk, moose, deer, mountain goat, cougar, muskrat, and beaver.

Coniferous trees cover the mountain slopes and deciduous softwoods line the valley waterways. Edible plants and berries flourish throughout the valley including bitterroot, camas, huckleberries, chokecherries, serviceberries, and strawberries.

In 1850, Major John Owen established a trading post on the original site of St. Mary's Mission. It was the first permanent white settlement in Montana, and welcomed Indian, Trappers, gold seekers, and settlers.

Long before, the Bitterroot Valley was home to the Flathead Indians, who called themselves "Salish."

—MONTANA HISTORICAL SOCIETY

Since our forefathers first beheld him . . . [the whiteman] has filled graves with our bones . . . His laws never gave us a blade of grass nor a tree nor a duck nor a grouse nor a trout . . . You know that he comes as long as he lives, and takes more and more, and dirties what he leaves.

—CHIEF CHARLO

I

I.

The year Ruthie Fear was born, her father shot the last wolf in the Bitterroot Valley. He strung it up by the hind feet from the peak of his shed. Nearly pure white, it was so big its snout grazed the dirt. It twisted slightly, front paws dragging, in the hot, still afternoons. Ranchers and tourists came from as far away as Ennis to see. They stood in clusters around the Fears' trailer, laughing and spitting and toeing the dirt. They paid a dollar to pose for pictures. Some put their arm around the wolf and grinned. Others stared silently into the camera. All were shorter than the wolf was long.

When the interest waned, Rutherford cut the wolf down, skinned it, and turned it into a rug. He replaced its eyes with pieces of colored glass. He folded its ears back and shaped its jaws into a perpetual snarl. He laid the rug down to fill the trailer's narrow living-room floor.

It looked enraged and confused there, claws still fixed to the ends of its flattened legs, as if wondering where its spirit had gone. Ruthie's mother left soon after, and the only place Ruthie would fall asleep was on the wolfskin rug. With her cheek on its shoulder and her small fingers wound through the white fur on its back. It looked less angry then. She screamed uncontrollably when lifted away, and slept there until she was four years old. Rutherford claimed, for the rest of her short life, that this was what had made her so stubborn and wild.

Ruthie knew it was simply having to live in the world of men.

2.

The first time Ruthie Fear went hunting with her father, she saw a huge winged skeleton flying in from the north. It approached over the dawn-lit mountains, wings stretched across the horizon, undulating on currents of air. Each bone rose and fell discretely, hinged together like vertebra and marked by shafts of light. The skull pointed toward her. Its shadow slid over the earth. An alien, Ruthie was sure, some creature that glided from world to world on gravitational tides and had died in between, the heat of a thousand suns slowly stripping away its flesh.

Only five, she felt the vastness of the universe. Saw herself as a single dot. Imagined skimming through the cosmos beside this hunter, without fear or hunger, passing strange worlds and towering nebulae of green and purple gas millions of miles across.

Her father's Auto-5 shotgun broke her reverie, and shattered the skeleton into a mass of flapping, twisting parts. One tumbled down to the ice-covered pond before them. It landed silently in a puff of snow. The rest of the flock reassembled, carried on, and were lost in the shadow of the Sapphire Mountains. Her father cursed and lowered the gun. White frost clung to his red beard. "Pulled too early," he said. His orange cap was the brightest piece of the morning world. Ruthie struggled to understand: one moment the skeleton, the next a dying goose. Smoke threaded up from the gun barrel in a mirror of her father's breath. The goose dragged itself across the ice with a broken wing, making not for the shore but the center as though it would be met there in safety by a healing force.

The cold air stung Ruthie's throat. Sudden warmth ached behind her eyes. She mourned the loss of the winged skeleton much more than the goose dying in front of her. The impossible distances it had crossed. The freedom to move from galaxy to galaxy, feeding on light, while her own life was confined to the trailer she shared with her father, and the valley that surrounded them. The goose collapsed. Only its unbroken wing continued to beat weakly against the ice in steady, desperate cadence. Her father cursed again. He breached the stock and emptied the spent shells into the snow. Gunpowder's acrid ammonia smell wafted out. "Point away," he said, handing Ruthie the shotgun. "Not at me, not at you." Ruthie gripped the warm barrel to her chest. She wished the skeleton had passed overhead. That it had streamed on to Las Vegas or Cancún or one of the other exotic places, populated by bikini-clad women, on the posters on her father's bedroom wall. He was only twenty-four, not much more than a child himself.

Together they stood before the world.

He turned and picked his way down through the brush to the edge of the pond. He paused on the shore, his eyes narrowed against the cold, his eyebrows drawn together in determination. "Never do this," he said.

He lay down on his stomach and spread his arms. Paused there for a moment, a supplicant flattened with his chin to the snow, then pushed off the snowy bank with his legs and slowly pulled himself over the creaking surface by the elbows. His arms in a crooked V above his head, his body flat, one ear cocked to the shifting sounds beneath. Heat seemed to ribbon off him, an invader on the blank white void, only the goose also moving within it. Willow forest on three sides, and the snowy roof of former country star Wiley King's unfinished mansion—on which Rutherford had found temporary work after the closing of the mill—a white slope in the distance.

The wing beat like a heart, *whomp, whomp* . . . *whomp*, slowing, failing, a bloody motor running down. A trickle of red reached out to meet her father, to guide him, as a serpent to its lair. Ruthie wanted to scream, but she was afraid even that sound would crack the ice. She held her breath. Her father inched farther out. Ten feet from the shore, twenty. His gloved hand reached for the bird's black foot. Nearly touched it, when a sound like another gunshot split the morning and two white walls tipped up to form a canyon, sluicing both man and bird into the dark water below. Then flopping back to horizontal, only the jagged vein between the sheets revealing the break.

For a moment, Ruthie did not move nor scream. She was trapped between reality and her imagination. What had been real? Her father on the ice or lost in the dark water below? The flying skeleton or the flock of geese? Her booted feet in snow or skimming along beside a huge winged creature in the black of space?

The ice violently upended into a mountain and her father's orange hat burst forth. Icy water gushed off his cheeks. He howled. His arm thrashed free from the water holding the struggling bird by the feet. He flung it toward Ruthie. It skidded into the snowbank on the shore. It looked oddly unharmed there, only dazed, with all the blood washed from its feathers and its wound temporarily frozen shut. Rutherford brought his elbows down onto the ice, breaking it again. He twisted his shoulders like a bear and lurched toward Ruthie. She stood frozen in terror holding the shotgun. His approach was relentless, smashing through the ice in the waist-high water, his face contorted. Monstrous, beastly, a killer who would kill again. For an instant, she was so afraid that she thought to level the barrel to her father's chest, pull the trigger, and send him back beneath the ice. Seal it above his head; the massive skeleton once again winging south across the sky.

3.

Ruthie Fear felt the nearness of unseen beings. On fall trips into the national forest to poach firewood with her father, she searched for them in the bushes between the trees. Patches of larch flamed ocher in the midst of the evergreen forest. The smell of butterscotch wafted from ponderosa bark. Ruthie walked carefully, avoiding fallen branches. Like the winged skeleton, the beings seemed to follow her; only their shadows remained by the time she whirled around.

"All this land used to be free," her father said, stopping to appraise the trunks surrounding a small clearing. "Free game, free wood." He'd been a stacker at the mill and now worked whatever construction jobs he could find. He tapped the head of his ax against a young ponderosa, and nodded at the dull *tock*. He stepped back. "Now the government thinks they get to decide who uses it." Ruthie watched him brace his feet and shake loose his shoulders. The tree he'd chosen was twice his height, with a straight, reddish trunk and thin branches growing thinner to the needles at its top. The ax's haft doubled the length of his arm. The blade's concave head gleamed. *A maul.* Ruthie couldn't remember where she'd heard that name, but it seemed fitting. What her father was about to do to the tree was what a bear would to him.

Blisters from previous firewood expeditions marked the palms of his hands. It was their first season harvesting their own wood. They hadn't needed to when he worked at the mill. His eyes fixed on a single point on the bark. "The woods will only be for the rich." He raised the ax and swung it down in a hard, smooth, clean motion. The wedged blade chunked into the wood and he immediately jerked it back, in rhythm, to chunk again. "With them shutting down the mills and the mines." His muscles strained with each successive chop. The wedge deepened; veins stood out on his arms, his body like the piston of some terrible machine. Splinters shot from the trunk and littered the ground around him. He began to sweat. "All these towns are going to die." The violence of the work increased, as if he and the tree were pitted against one another—both could not remain standing. The blisters split open on his palms. The tree began to moan. Ruthie covered her ears. Sap leaked from the scaly bark, like the blood on her father's hands. When the wedge was deep enough, Rutherford circled the trunk, wiped his brow on the shoulder of his T-shirt, spat, and began on the other side. Ruthie watched him, torn between fear and love. His swings slowed, hacking unevenly into the new wedge to create a hinge with the other, but still they did not cease. The treetop swung unsteadily in the breeze coming down from the mountains. It leaned over him.

Ruthie backed to the edge of the clearing. Would this be what killed him? It seemed fitting: a tree he'd cut falling down on top of him. She touched the bark of another ponderosa and felt its rough, steady life. The butterscotch scent had grown stronger, marred now by suffering.

The tree fell with a rending creak. Her father hopped to the side as branches popped overhead. It crashed down beside him and for a moment he was lost in the dust that billowed up from the ground. When the trunk settled, neatly bisecting the clearing, he stood over it. Sweat ran down his dirty cheeks into his beard. Broken branches hung like garlands from the pines around him. Sunlight poured through the fresh space above the stump. Rutherford looked at his bleeding palms. He grimaced. "They always put up a fight."

ON THE LONG WALK HOME, Rutherford knelt beside Trapper Creek. The large bundle of wood on his back loomed over him as he rinsed his palms in the water. Ruthie—her own, smaller bundle chafing her shoulders—watched the blood slip away in the current: two red, ropy fish elongating as they were carried downstream.

RUTHIE, RUTHERFORD, and the dog Moses lived at the mouth of No-Medicine Canyon near the southern end of the Bitterroot Valley. Above them, Highway 93 rose to the hot springs and Lost Trail Pass into Idaho. Their teal trailer was set across the driveway in front of a single acre of barren ground eight miles from Darby, Montana. Theirs was the smallest property on Red Sun Road. In the winter, they slept side by side next to the woodstove, the windows sealed with plastic to hold in the heat, a towel stuffed in the crack beneath the door. The sheet metal siding rattled in the wind. Ruthie was often too cold, or hungry. The Bitterroot Range loomed overhead. Ten-thousand-foot peaks seeming to attack the sky with jagged, glaciated teeth. These were mountains that forced Lewis and Clark a hundred miles north and ended, once and for all, their dream of a northwest passage.

The north entrance to the valley was marked by a sign reading JESUS CHRIST IS LORD OF THIS VALLEY, and the south entrance by a sign advertising Second Nature Taxidermy School, where farm boys with ghoulish ambitions came to learn the modern, fetishized art of embalming. Between these risen corpses, thirty thousand people lived.

When Ruthie pressed her face against the window of her closet-sized room, she could see Trapper Peak, the tallest in the Bitterroots, hooked like a finger beckoning her above the tree line. Circled by bald eagles and white with snow eleven months of the year, it reassured her that men were small scrabbling things, crawling across the ice unaware of the depths below. The boys in her class made each other bleed with straightened paper clips. Her father's friends—Kent Willis, Raymond Pompey, and the Salish brothers Terry and Billy French—drank themselves into stupors of displaced rage and stumbled outside to shoot bottles off a busted washing machine. The glass shards glinted kaleidoscopically in the morning sunlight while the men snored in the living room, their arms sprawled tenderly over each other's chests, showing affection in sleep in a way that would be impossible awake. Tiptoeing around them to the bathroom, Ruthie wanted to fly away. She climbed on top of the toilet and wedged her head through the small window. Her gray eyes had a yellow ring in the irises like the beginning of an explosion, noticed by strangers, that she hoped would allow her to see farther. She tasted a storm approaching in the air. Saw herself zooming over the spent shotgun shells, the glittering pattern of glass, the cannibalized dump truck her father used as a kind of fort—full of discarded whiskey pints and *Bowhunter* magazines—to perch atop Trapper Peak and look back down on her life, free from its bonds and humiliations.

When the storm came, she ran outside to catch frogs in the rain.

As if in opposition to the mighty peak, No-Medicine Canyon was a dark, narrow portal where wind sprang up of its own accord, to scream and rage and then cease without ever leaving the canyon's confines. Ruthie feared it instinctively, as did her father. They never went inside. She was sure that twenty thousand years of spirits lived within, beginning with the People of the Flood, a tribe whose marks were washed away when the ice dam broke at Glacial Lake Missoula fifteen thousand years before, but who remained below the dirt. Her friend Pip Pascal had found one of their fertility icons on the bank of Lost Horse Creek. A plump, headless stone figure of mounded breasts and pubis that caused both girls to look down over their own skinny bodies and think, *No, this could never happen to us.* They found other mysteries along game trails: strange dragging tracks, ancient flint tools, figures with many arms chipped into the west faces of boulders.

"You should be afraid of every canyon," Terry French told her, when she asked. He and his brother were the only Indians Ruthie knew, and she came to them with her most pressing concerns. He smiled and palmed her head. His wide, scarred fingers easily curled over her skull to the nape of her neck. "You're six years old and you weigh forty pounds."

Ruthie stared up at him around his thick wrist. Sleep crust stuck in the corners of his eyes. A red rubber band loosely held his ponytail. He smiled down at her. "Now help me get this meat into your freezer so you and your dad don't starve." The butchered hindquarters of an elk, poorly shrink-wrapped, dripped blood in the bed of his truck. He handed Ruthie a package of steaks. Reluctantly, she lugged it inside, dumped it on the kitchen table, and left Terry in the kitchen talking to her father about where work might be.

She watched the canyon. There was something inside, she could feel it. Water slid down the cliff walls, slicking the granite black as obsidian. Strange ferns and mosses grew along the bottom of what was once a mighty riverbed and now held the low flow of Trapper Creek. Ruthie walked to the edge of her yard and pissed in the soft dirt. She saw the chasm that formed, the power of water. The ferns trembled in the wind. The long shadows held a wet, fecund darkness utterly apart from the dry valley outside. Ruthie shivered and pulled up her pants. She walked as close to the canyon's mouth as she dared. Moses barked and ran across the yard to her side. She touched his ears. He sniffed the air, worried. Bleached skulls were piled in the far corner by the shed. Hunters from all across the valley brought trophy heads to be cleaned by Rutherford's dermestid beetle colony inside the shed. It was his only regular source of income since the mill closed. The fifty thousand beetles lived among wood shavings in three large plastic bins beneath heat lamps. In a constant state of voracious hunger, they could remove every shred of flesh from a bear skull in twenty-four hours, leaving the bone porcelain-clean and preserving all the delicate structures within the nasal cavity. Ruthie sometimes snuck in to watch, transfixed, as the beetles swarmed over the flesh, flooding the orifices, adults and larvae working together with a speed that filled her with dread. On the coldest nights of winter, when the heat lamps weren't enough, Rutherford brought the bins into the trailer and Ruthie had to listen to the larvae squirming over one another as she tried to sleep on the wolfskin rug.

She knew not every girl lived like this. Some had mothers who sang lullabies.

Moses began to tremble. What was in there? Ruthie smelled something from the canyon's depths: a rot, a dead thing come back to life. She crouched beside Moses and rested her hand on the wiry fur of his neck to calm him. He was a Yorkie, always alert, save for in midwinter when he grew depressed. His breath came in quick pants. Together they stared into the shadows.

She probed the darkness. Green blades of grass, tall in the spring, wavered in front of her eyes, dividing her vision by oscillating degrees. Straining to see farther, using the yellow in her irises, she channeled her entire being into the canyon. The sounds of the outside world ceased. The sun was swallowed by blackness. She felt herself standing on the edge of a giant open maw—an abyss of incomprehensible depths into which all previous explorers had fallen. Moses's body shook as if he felt it, too. Only the dark of the canyon remained.

A shadow slid over another shadow. Ruthie froze. She gripped Moses. Something was moving.

The creature took shape slowly, awkwardly. A tall feathered thing, it lurched toward the creek on two long, spindly, double-jointed legs. Each step was tentative, as if it were just learning to walk. Its feathers were gray and slightly iridescent. Its body curved into a single, organ-like shape. A kidney. Misshapen and lumpy, frighteningly perched atop the thin legs—taller than the saplings on the shore. A monster, deviant in its unsteadiness. But what horrified Ruthie, what made her want to scream, was that it had no head.

Its chest continued roundly over its collar and back along the ridge of its spine. Nothing protruded. No way to see nor hear nor smell, no orifices at all. Yet it paused by the creek and leaned forward as if it wanted to drink.

Ruthie felt like she was caught in a dream, unable to run, seeing a future of death. She wondered how the creature had grown. She imagined it wriggling, maggot-like, from the mouth of a dying elk, before growing to its terrible size. It reminded her of the tumor-ridden lamb that Len Law had shown off in front of her school, or the mold that grew around the drain of her shower.

Moses began to growl deep in his throat. His wiry hackles rose. The creature lifted one of its pronged feet and dipped it into the water. It stood like this helplessly. The current rushed around its thin ankle. Ruthie was sure it would be knocked over. She didn't see how it could get up again. Sudden pity mixed with the fear and revulsion in her chest.

The growl in Moses's throat crescendoed to a harsh, hysteric *yap*.

"No!" Ruthie hissed.

The creature twisted toward them. It faced Ruthie with its feath-ered mask. The feathers trembled. Sensing her. Knowing she was there. She wondered if it navigated through vibration, like a bat. She could feel trucks on the highway when she pressed her ear against the dirt. The creature shied backward, stumbled, straightened on its stilt-like legs, and shuddered away into the darkness.

The canyon was empty again. Ruthie parted her lips. No sound came out. Cold sweat ran down her neck. She felt a terrible impor-tance, as if fate were for a moment balanced in her hands. Hers and her father's and that of all the others in the valley. Moses looked up at her with the whites of his eyes showing, frightened and begging for a treat, the way he did when a truck horn scared him in the night.

4.

Rutherford lay shirtless on the couch in the trailer's narrow living room with the cartridge of a freshly oiled Glock on his belly. *Wheel of Fortune* played on the TV at full volume. Terry had gone. The carpet was filthy with crumbs, oil drips, and the wrappers of cheese singles, which Ruthie had planned to eat for dinner. An open beer stood on the table by her father's head. Two empties and a full can were keeled over beside it. Ruthie panted in the doorway, her reddish hair—chopped short to avoid the recurrence of lice—sticking up, her cheeks flushed from the sprint across the yard. Moses charged in past her and shook himself furiously.

"I saw something," she said.

Rutherford's eyes rolled away from the TV but he made no move to sit up.

"A creature."

"A creature?"

She nodded rapidly. "It went up into the canyon."

"A canyon creature. Shoot it next time. We can sell it to the university." Rutherford pronounced all five syllables, as if it were a disease. Hair made a scraggly divide down the center of his belly, and his feet, propped on the couch arm, were frighteningly long and pale.

"It had feathers and no head."

"Sounds easy to shoot."

"*Dad.*" Ruthie hated being a child; no one listened to her.

"I'd do it myself except it ain't headless creature hunting season. But you, you can't get in trouble for poaching when you're six."

More than once, Ruthie had seen the game warden's white truck pull into the driveway and heard the storm of cursing it elicited from her father. On the TV, a woman jumped up and down, screaming at a new car. Rutherford shook his head at the male contestant standing dejectedly behind her. "Damn fool could've kept the Wheel." He reached around on the carpet for his oil rag.

"*Dad!*" Ruthie yelled.

The TV made a brief static crackle when he muted the volume. He rose up on his elbow and turned toward her, jostling the cartridge to the floor. "Dammit, Ruthie, can't you see I'm busy?"

She clenched her fists in frustration, her heart pounding.

"Last thing I need is your bullshit." He took a long drink, shook the last drops from the upside-down can onto his tongue, then tossed it aside. He located the full one behind his head and his mood immediately brightened. "Maybe it was an emu got loose from Del's farm. Remember the one on top of your school last year?"

"Emus have heads," Ruthie said. "And necks."

"Still don't know how it got up there. That beak looked sharp enough to skewer old Del." Rutherford grinned at the memory. He sank back down and popped open the beer. "Fucking dumbass, chasing it around with a net. Supposedly they go for five thousand dollars a pop if you can breed 'em." The gap of Rutherford's missing incisor showed where a snowmobile had tossed him face-first onto a stump when he was in high school. "Don't know why I'm mucking around with beetles."

"It wasn't an emu."

"A deer with mange, then. They lose all their hair and look like demons."

"Deer have heads, too!"

"Keep your voice down. You're making my goddamn head hurt. Hasn't that fool teacher taught you what an imagination is? You don't know what you see when you're six." He looked around the small, crummy room as if to prove his point. "You think you do, but you don't. You'll learn that as you get older. The world ain't all you think it is."

What did he know of the world? Ruthie wondered. Expired hunting tags were tacked to the wood panel wall by his scope and elk bugle. Envelopes from the bank accumulated on the kitchen table until he burnt them with the last wood of the season. The only food they ever had enough of was meat. He was angry at the rich, the government, and Ruthie's departed mother in varying order and intensity. The only cultivation he'd done of their barren acre was to install a meat freezer and gun safe along with his beetle bins in the storage shed, and erect plywood targets at twenty-five, fifty, and one hundred yards, to shred with bullets every summer. "You don't believe me," she said.

"I believe you saw something, but you didn't know what it was, so you made it up. Like the flying skeleton."

Ruthie found herself too angry to speak. She wished she could grow a hundred feet tall and kick Rutherford on his couch into the canyon. Then he'd see. She tried to imagine life with another family in another town. Going out to dinner, shopping at the mall. She stepped back onto the porch, grabbed the screen door with both hands, and slammed it as hard as she could. The hinges rattled. Her father's prone figure was lost behind the mesh.

"You're sleeping outside if you broke that door!" he yelled after her, the TV volume crackling back on. "Goddammit."

THE CREATURE REMAINED in Ruthie's mind like a bruise, aching whenever her thoughts bumped against it. She was determined to see it again. Determined to prove to her father that it had been real. She picked a spot in the trees facing the canyon on the edge of their property and made Rutherford help her build a blind.

"Thank Christ you didn't ask for a dollhouse," he said.

They scavenged wood from the dump and nails from behind Whipple's Feed Store. Len Law watched them from beside his pickup. A scrawny, decrepit man, he owned the town scrapyard and often appeared when Ruthie and Pip were playing on the shore of Lost Horse Creek. Once he'd knelt before her and said, "You know what the Indians used to do with little girls with yellow in their eyes?"

She shook her head.

"Send them off into the mountains."

Now he crossed his arms and called to her father across the lot. "Lean times?"

"We're getting by," Rutherford answered shortly.

"Must be hard on your own. No woman at home. . . ." Len's narrow eyes lingered on Ruthie as she climbed into her father's truck. She clenched the nails in her fists; the sharp points dug into her palms. Her father had told her that Len's grandfather Hark was Darby's first sheriff. Hark Law had done something so bad before he was fired that adults spoke of it only in whispers, and wouldn't tell Ruthie no matter how often she asked. The Montana Café and Sawmill Bar passed by.

Back on their property, with the mouth of No-Medicine Canyon before them, Rutherford built a two-by-four frame. Ruthie held the weathered front boards in place while he started the nails, then they switched so she could pound them home. She banged ferociously, holding the hammer with both hands, gritting her teeth, not satisfied until the nail head was snugged well below the dented wood. She hit one so hard on its edge that sparks shot out.

"That nail do you wrong?" Rutherford asked, grinning. It confused her that her anger always made him proud.

Ruthie glared up at him. She blinked the sweat from her eyes.

"Lord knows what'll happen if you ever hit a knot. Might burn down the whole woods. Blind won't do you no good then." Rutherford nodded toward their cleared yard. The teal trailer was set at the same angle across the driveway where the delivery company had left it, up on cinder blocks. Ruthie's mother had had grand plans for its placement, along with flower boxes, teal curtains, and a welcome mat. The plans disappeared along with her. The canyon loomed behind Rutherford. Dark and menacing even in the summer heat. He knelt to measure Ruthie's height with his hands. "You're getting big now. Longer than a rifle."

Ruthie refused to be flattered. She gave the edge of the blind a final hard *whack* with the hammer. It was a ramshackle box with a plywood roof and floor, but she was proud of it—her first idea to become reality. Her father straightened and hitched up his jeans. "You'll be hunting on your own in no time."

"I'm not going to hunt anything," Ruthie said.

"Oh no?"

She shook her head. "No. I'm going to spring all the traps in the woods."

Rutherford smiled. "All of them? You'll find yourself pulling butterflies out of spiderwebs." His missing incisor, chapped lips, scraggly red beard, and sun-weathered cheeks made him look older than his twenty-five years. Ruthie never knew what to say when her teachers asked what he did. She always lied about his beetle business, claiming he was a builder, and imagining a fridge full of vegetables and chicken nuggets.

Mosquitoes whined up from the water. The creek was high with snowmelt from the mountains. Whenever Rutherford was out—working or using whiskey to get properly drunk—Ruthie would sneak into his room. She'd get down on her knees and look at the guns underneath his bed, including the CMMG Banshee, his pride and joy. A $1,400 piece of machinery with a silenced suppressor and .300 Blackout ammo that shot through walls. He'd bought it with his small severance from the shuttered mill. Some nights he'd sit on the couch with the barrel across his lap, staring at the door as if he hoped for an intruder, so he might prove what the beast could do. A showgirl in gold lingerie was superimposed over the glittering Strip on the poster of Las Vegas above his bed. It reminded Ruthie of the night sky erupting from the ground. A place where man had built the stars. As different from the dilapidated trailer parks and potholes of Darby as the sun was from the moon. "I'm coming," she'd whisper, before returning the gun to its place and tiptoeing out from Rutherford's room.

He took the hammer from her and walked across the yard to the shed where the wolf had hung. Along with the beetles, meat freezer, and gun safe, it held all manner of tools, antlers, shoeboxes full of bones and feathers, wildcat drawings he'd made as a boy, and Indian artifacts he'd found. You could hardly move inside. The rotten smell was enough to keep Ruthie out most of the time. One of his hand-drawn flyers for Bitterroot Beetle Works was nailed to the door. The rest were on bulletin boards across the valley. Ruthie slapped a mosquito on her neck. She looked down at her own blood in the mangled legs on her palm. She imagined splattering the creature like this, squashing it against the face of a rock.

Her father returned with his circular saw, trailing a long orange extension cord. He had a plunging, downhill gait when on his own property, with none of the careful alertness he carried in the outside world. Moses snapped at the cord, then barked outright when Rutherford powered on the saw. Loud noises always made him aggressive. He flung his small body into the air at the blade and Ruthie feared he might get cut in half. "Git!" her father said, and stomped the ground. Moses reluctantly backed away. Using Ruthie's measurement, Rutherford cut a slit for her eyes in the front planks. Sawdust gusted out on the breeze. The blisters on his hands were turning to calluses, rough white patches outlining the ghost of a haft. "There," he said. "Now you can learn how to look."

"I know how to look," Ruthie said.

He shook his head. "All the chain stores and gas stations where everything is the same make your eyes go dull. The mall you're always going on about. You've got to teach yourself how to see again. A tree isn't just a tree. It's a certain tree, with certain sap and certain needles. Certain parts, like a person. Some you can eat, or use to stanch a wound. They might save your life." Sawdust clung to his beard. One shoulder was slightly lower than the other—exaggerated by how he held the saw—from the same snowmobile accident that had taken his tooth. "You thought you saw a creature but you couldn't tell me what it was. Nothing in the wild is ever the same. If you think a rock looks like another rock, you ain't looking hard enough."

"It wasn't a deer," Ruthie said. "And it wasn't a goddamn rock."

Rutherford spat in the dirt. "Learn how to look, then you can cuss at me all you want."

5.

Ever since John Owen's first white settlement at the fort, the valley's inhabitants had done everything they could to domesti-
cate its hillsides and riverbanks. Fence it into squares and pave roads
between those squares. Slaughter the bears and wolves and mountain
lions and bison. Drive out the Salish. Nail crosses to the hilltops. Yet
still the wildness encroached, running in flames down the mountainsides each summer and pushing up in tree roots to crack the sidewalks
each spring.

After the closing of the mill, the Rocky Mountain Laboratories
became the valley's largest employer. Founded to fight the scourge of
spotted fever, it housed a maximum containment facility, one of the
most secure bio labs in the country. The former mill workers hated
the scientists for their arrogance and job security; the scientists looked

down on the uneducated rednecks who bought new machine guns while living in trailers.

With no mother, no church, and no interest in what she was taught in school, Ruthie devised her own morality based on the behavior of animals she saw from her blind. In the passage of deer, coyote, beaver, muskrat, and raccoon, she noted life pared down to the core of instinct. Free from the twin anxieties of past and future. She took no sides in the valley's conflicts, wanting only a house deep in the woods, another dog, a trip to Las Vegas, Len Law's accidental death, and to prove to her father that the creature was real.

To the blind's southeast, Ruthie looked into the mouth of No-Medicine Canyon. The creature taunted her from its depths. Every fern-rustle was a hint. Every moving shadow suggested it would reappear. When her eyes tired of their futile search, she turned her attention north, where the blind looked over the creek into the yard of June and Reed Breed. Trapper Creek swelled suddenly after leaving No-Medicine Canyon and ran along their property line. The water itself was entirely on the Breeds' side, making their land, which was lower, verdant with native grasses and wildflowers, their pine trees taller and more bountifully needled, and their air noticeably sweeter. Their house was an actual house; their truck replaced itself every two years. Rutherford considered them rich, and took every opportunity to urinate on their side of the bank.

On top of this, it was said softly among the older girls at Ruthie's school that June Breed was adventurous and Reed Breed a cuckold. That she enjoyed her adventurousness as frequently as possible, and that he lingered on it in the most intimate, humiliating ways. When Ruthie heard her father howling over the motor of his miter saw, she assumed it was the fault of such dark, incomprehensible aspects of adulthood.

On her second day within the blind, instead of a mysterious headless being, Ruthie saw June Breed strip naked on a beach towel in the shade of her garden shed. Mosquitoes whined lazily above her breasts in the early summer warmth. There were lessons in the parting of her lips, the lowering of her eyelids to crocodile slits, and the slow arching of her back, but they were not what Ruthie had expected to learn. She was frightened and enthralled. She wondered if she could become this kind of woman, half melting in the sun. She hoped so. The future took on a new and dangerous light.

Later in the afternoon, when the sun had finally begun to drop into the Bitterroots, Mr. Breed came out from his office. He looked at his wife, asleep now beneath a horsehair blanket, then punched the trunk of the large ponderosa by their deck. Hard. Twice.

Ruthie was fascinated. She forgot the creature completely as Mr. Breed rubbed his knuckles and returned inside. What had brought on his violence? Ruthie considered the two dull *thocks* his fist had made against the bark. She had a vision of her father and his friends standing in front of a fire, kicking at the logs until sparks whirled up around their faces. Kicking harder so the sparks shot higher, showering their heads as they caught at them with open hands.

Darkness reached down into the valley from the Sapphires. Ruthie left the blind and walked through the yard. She passed furniture that had once lived inside the trailer and now lived outside, including a rickety card table beside the bullet-riddled washing machine, a brown recliner, and a sodden yellow mattress. On summer nights when it was too hot to sleep inside, she and her father used the mattress to watch the stars. Rutherford's rare moments of creativity were spurred by the cosmos and the nearness of wild, killable game. As they were lying on their backs, he told Ruthie stories of planets with forty-point elk the size of school buses. "You hunt them with rocket launchers," he said. "If you miss, they'll skewer you on their antlers and toss you out into space."

How did I end up here? Ruthie wondered. She imagined the giant elk watching the winged skeleton pass overhead. The tines of their antlers so numerous they were like the branches of a willow tree.

As the long hot August days passed in the blind, Ruthie was disturbed to find contradictions within herself. Places of illogic that animals lacked. Just as she had imagined shooting her father in the icy pond, she saw herself dying for him, too. Leaping into the water and heaving him onto the shore with her last breath. Pulling his body from his burning truck only to be engulfed in flames herself. Stepping into the path of a charging bear and beckoning for him to run. Some days she was determined to never hunt an animal as her father did. On others she fashioned guns from sticks and aimed them through the eye slit, massacring every squirrel in the Breeds' big ponderosa.

NIGHTS GREW COLD in October. Ruthie had trouble sleeping in the confines of her closet room. Cloud shadows loomed between the stars through her window. They transfigured into starships, then became malevolent, light-swallowing monsters. In frightening moments, the rumble of trucks on the distant highway went silent. She clenched a flint arrowhead in her palm. She listened to her father's fitful snoring through the thin door. She saw the creature looming over the trailer on its stilt-like legs. Felt it bending down toward her. Faceless, eyeless. Silently calling her into the maw.

Leave me alone, she mouthed.

She wrestled with the scope of existence. The way the dark sky and the dark mountains could make her feel both huge and infinitesimally small. How she could see her shadow stretching across her yard like the black finger of God, or cower in her blind at the sound of a branch snapping a hundred yards away. How she felt like a part of the entire breathing world, yet totally alone.

Rutherford kept a separate freezer full of discarded heads in the bunker beneath the shed. He fed them to his beetles in the winter when business slowed to nothing. Occasionally, overtaken by morbid fascination, Ruthie would descend the ladder and open the lid to find the frost-lashed eyes of deer, antelope, and bear looking back at her. Their implacable wondering reminded her of the wolf's, as if in all animals the body's final question was where its spirit has gone.

She spent most of her time alone. Emotions stormed through her. Cars passing on the road could make her so angry that she wanted to sow the asphalt with land mines, while the flight of a bee, one of the season's last, over the withered plants in the Breeds' flower garden could lift her almost to tears.

At recess, she'd stand on the edge of the playground—a small, solitary figure—and stare up at the tops of the lodgepole pines waving in the breeze. Always in motion, these stationary things. She tried to decipher the messages they transcribed on the sky. Each needled tip writing its story, roots reaching through the ground beneath her delivering messages. She sent herself zooming up the trunks to look back down into her own eyes, and found the yellow rings glowing around the pupils.

Only her friend Pip Pascal seemed to understand. An orphan, also motherless, Pip watched the world with the same intensity. She was the only other person Ruthie told about the creature. They sat together on the pavement in the shadow of the gymnasium and Pip drew it in her notebook, ending with a feathered kidney atop two tall menacing spider legs. The idea of a disembodied organ pulsing with life disturbed Ruthie and delighted Pip, who drew other variations: lungs and hearts and bladders, lurching together across the paper void.

"You think it came from outer space?" Pip asked.

Ruthie shook her head. "I think it came from here." She described how she'd imagined it wriggling out of the mouth of a dying elk.

"They could be coming out of *all kinds* of animals," Pip said, in sudden awe.

When any classmate besides Pip tried to talk to her, Ruthie would hurl their ball over the fence into the woods. She forestalled their

questions—about her yellow eyes or her short hair or her father—
with anger, and was known to bite, scratch, and kick. She didn't own
a single dress. Rutherford bought her jeans and black T-shirts at the
same thrift store where he bought his own. They looked like full-sized
and miniature versions of each other when they were seen together.
The red in Ruthie's hair glowed like the red of her father's beard.
She accompanied him on every errand in Darby and Hamilton, and
on odd jobs after school, to escape the property on Red Sun Road.
She studied each detail in the outside world: the way old ranchers
sucked their teeth in the Montana Café, speaking only of the weather,
how George Whipple watched the stock boys from high behind the
counter of his feed store, Kent Willis doing push-ups on his lawn
while the radio blared conspiracy theories and his neighbor Danette
kept count from her lawn chair.

The teachers placed Ruthie carefully in the back row of desks and
only called her name during roll.

"What do you want to be when you grow up?" they asked.

"A wolf," Ruthie answered.

She inspected the carcasses of dead birds and wondered what they
would look like if she fed them to her father's beetles. The delicate,
almost impossible architecture of flight. When she learned the fate
of sea turtles and the blue whale—choking to death on ten thousand
plastic grocery bags—she felt such rage that she wanted to incinerate
every ship on the ocean.

Rutherford was little use in matters of morality, as he was adrift in
the modern world himself. His conversations with other men in the
valley revolved around jobs, guns, engine parts, dogs, what dogs are
thinking, and everything being ruined by outsiders. He never pun-
ished Ruthie except if she disturbed his things or entered his room
without permission. When she came home with a scraped knee from
a schoolyard fight, he didn't ask her who or why, he simply lifted her
dirty foot to the middle of his chest, held her calf firmly in his callused

hands, and inspected the cut. She could feel his own heart then, as strong as the thud of the ground through her soles. She struggled to keep from flinching as he poured on rubbing alcohol.

The sawdust-and-rot smell from his shirt announced his approach, though generally he left her alone, allowing her to roam free, even as the weather turned cold. His advice was primarily related to hunting and the petty wars he constantly found himself in: with neighbors and the game warden and rich ranchers like the singer Wiley King, whose mansion he'd helped to build. With employers and checkers in the grocery store and tourists who drove too slowly while gawking at the glacier-sheared cliffs of Blodgett Canyon. He defined himself in opposition to the wealthy scientists at the Rocky Mountain Laboratories, and the billionaires building eighth homes on Charles Schwab's Stock Farm Club. He stockpiled supplies, tested his survival skills deep in the woods, and told Ruthie stories of society crumbling, when all the rich and soft—unable to hunt or fend for themselves—would come to him and beg for help.

The only people he trusted were the poor. At the top of a small rise to the south, on land even drier than the Fears', lived the Happels. A family of fellow former mill workers destitute to the point of subsistence living. M. Happel and his nephew poached firewood beyond the national forest boundary along with the Fears, and often the two men, Rutherford and Happel, met by their sagging fence in the evening to look out at the mountains without speaking, as if they owned all that they could see.

HEAVY RAINS FELL in November, delaying Rutherford's annual overnight bowhunt with the French brothers in the West Fork Wilderness. Ruthie spent long afternoons in the blind, watching the water pour down on the mouth of No-Medicine Canyon and make a swamp of the Breeds' yard. The Breeds themselves were gone south to Arizona for the winter. She'd watched them pack up. June humming to herself, barefoot, as she watered the plants in her window boxes one last time. Reed cursing as he struggled to hitch the trailer to the back of their new Silverado. The blind stayed dry but the damp chill seeped beneath Ruthie's clothes and made her want to burrow into the earth. She wondered if the creature had shelter. A den of some kind.

Sometimes Pip joined her, armed with the large hunting knife she carried underneath her shirt. They carved their names into the wood floor as rain splattered the roof. Ruthie carved ROSE, a name she wished for, more beautiful and deadly than her own, and not a mirror of her father's. Pip rolled up her short pants and showed the many-armed figures she'd drawn on her thigh, like the ones they saw chiseled in the rocks. They talked about what they'd do if they caught the creature. How they'd lead it through town for everyone to see, then bring it to a veterinarian to give it eyes and ears and a mouth. The houses they'd buy with the reward, the talk shows they'd go on, all the different foods they'd eat.

But it didn't reappear.

Pip grew bored when the rain ceased, and followed the yellow explosions of larch up into the hills.

Ruthie remained through the first snow and her seventh birthday, held in place by a feeling that she would miss something if she left. Staring out through the slit, waiting, she felt like she could both visit the past—the time of petroglyphs, before highways and power lines and houses like the Breeds'—and prospect the future. When the creature would make its slow, lurching way among grass-covered ruins.

6.

As they were driving home from Darby Elementary on Old Darby Road, Rutherford's truck suddenly dropped hard to the right. It rolled to the left and slammed onto its axle. He wrestled the wheel around. The beer he'd been drinking leapt from the cupholder and spit foam over the upholstery. Power lines whipped overhead, making a high singing noise. Ruthie clutched her backpack and stared up at them. She was only seven and the world was ending. The road jumped and swung. Her lunch came hot and sour up her throat. She tried to focus on the trees. They were jumping and swinging, too.

"Sonofabitch." Rutherford's voice cracked. It was the first time Ruthie had heard him afraid. Even when he'd nearly blown himself up with a scavenged propane grill, he'd simply stared at her from below his charred eyebrows, and told her to go get him some ice. The underpinnings of her existence shifted. Her father couldn't be afraid. He was supposed to know what to do, always, in all situations. What could she depend on if not him or the stability of the earth? They slowed down horizontally but not vertically. Ruthie tried to pray. The only word that came was *help. Help, Dad, help.*

He reached for her, then jerked his hand back as the truck slammed down again. Ruthie's backpack flew up from her lap and hit her in the face. Warm blood trickled from her nose. "Dad, it's a *tornado!*" she screamed. She'd seen a movie on TV where a truck was sucked up from the highway and deposited fender-first in a cornfield. She was sure they were going to die. The only hope was to come down wheels-first on a gentle incline, like the planes she and Pip watched land on the private airstrip at the Stock Farm Club. White-knuckled, her father looked for a place to turn off, but didn't stop.

Across the road, a brick chimney crashed through the roof of a farmhouse and Rutherford said, "Earthquake?" in disbelief.

All Ruthie knew of earthquakes was that they were supposed to happen in California, not Montana.

Mexican workers were huddled in the doorway of Pompey Nursery. Raymond Pompey stood with his arms over his head as flower-pots shattered on the ground around him. Another worker was trying to run from his truck to the door. The truck was dancing around. Ruthie watched until—as suddenly as it had begun—the shaking stopped and the truck went still. The worker fell to his knees. He dug his hands into the dirt and closed his eyes. His lips moved silently.

Rutherford kept driving as if he couldn't think of what else to do. His right eye twitched. For Ruthie, seeing him afraid was like seeing her own hand on fire. "Dad," she said. "Is it over?"

She wanted him to stop the truck. She squeezed her backpack and tasted blood. The pain began: a dull ache spreading behind her eyes. Rutherford nodded. "But aftershocks. There might be after-shocks." He said the words unsurely, as if from a half-remembered source. Later, Ruthie would learn that the Bitterroot Valley hadn't had an earthquake in twenty-seven years, before either of them was born.

They passed Adrian Pascal, Pip's uncle, standing outside the house where Pip often stayed, holding his chest like he was trying to keep his heart in. His neighbor's roof had collapsed. Ruthie wondered if people were inside. Trapped. Dying. She hoped Pip was safe. Distant sirens began to yowl. Sheriff Kima stood outside the sheriff's station holding a cage full of birds.

"Moses," Ruthie said.

Rutherford didn't answer. His eye twitched again. Moses slept in Rutherford's bed most nights, on a pillow by his head.

Two trucks had collided in the Overturf intersection. One of them was on its side. A woman cried inside, belted to her sideways seat, clutching her shoulder. Her bloody hair hung to the road, and her tears and the blood flowed across her forehead instead of down her cheeks. A cluster of people stood in front of Whipple's store with wild eyes, and some others, who'd abandoned their cars and run up the hill, were now coming back down on foot. Rutherford slowed to a crawl and called out the window to Whipple, "What the fuck was that?"

Usually talkative, Whipple only nodded, his face as pale as the ends of Ruthie's fingernails. She dug them into her thighs. She tried to stop shaking. The ground had stopped shaking, so could she. Inside the store, hammers and nails and screwdrivers were strewn across the aisles. The stock boys leaned against the wall in their aprons, looking dazed. Loose grain covered the linoleum. A sheepdog ran across the parking lot, glanced back at her briefly, and disappeared around the store.

"Moses is alone at home," Ruthie said.

"Or wherever he is by now," Rutherford replied. Which made her heart rise up her throat.

THE TRAILERS in Whispering Pines Trailer Park were still standing. The little bridge over the irrigation ditch was still there. Some dirt had splashed across the asphalt, but no trees had fallen over the road. They stopped at Kent Willis's. Kent, Len Law, Len's crippled sister Eleanor, and Eleanor's nurse were in the yard. Kent was squatting like a linebacker, looking crazed, as if he'd wrestle the next natural disaster into submission himself. Eleanor was bright-cheeked in her wheelchair, while her young nurse trembled beside her. Len held a crowbar. His narrow eyes gleamed. "Have you seen Moses?" Ruthie asked, momentarily forgetting her hatred.

Kent blinked at her and slowly straightened from his crouch. "He might've run by."

"You were outside?" Rutherford asked.

"Mowing." Kent nodded to the lawn mower on its side in the grass by his foot. "Near lost my toe." He shook his head in disbelief.

"We were walking," the nurse said. "Thank God."

"God's got nothing to do with this," Len tapped the crowbar against his sister's chair for emphasis. His bowlegged stance gave him the aspect of a lost vigilante. "It's Charlo's curse, same as ever."

"There's people dead," Eleanor said. "I just know it. Can you imagine Missoula? All those big buildings downtown. . . ." Excitement tinged her voice. Ruthie supposed she wanted bad things to happen to other people. She longed for a nation of the legless, in which she, with her years of practice, would be queen.

"What curse?" Ruthie asked.

"They don't teach you nothing in school, do they?" Len said.

"Chief Charlo cursed this valley from up on Lolo Pass when the army finally ran him out. Bad things been happening ever since. Disease. Accidents." He nodded to his sister's legs.

"No, this comes from Yellowstone," Kent cut in. "I heard it on the radio. The government's been doing experiments—all those scientists in the labs. They knew this was coming. The whole thing's liable to blow. A super-volcano, wipe out the entire Northwest."

"Never should have let Charlo go free. That was the army's mistake."

"Oh, Christ." Rutherford shook his head in exasperation. "Just let us know if you see the dog."

They left Len and Kent arguing on the lawn. Ruthie tasted the metallic salt of blood on her tongue. She looked up at Trapper Peak to see if the finger had broken off, but it remained there, beckoning.

RUTHERFORD DROVE OVER the hill past Happel's shack, which was flattened as if a giant foot had stomped it down. The nephew sat dejected on the front stoop. He looked up at Ruthie but didn't wave. The Fears' teal trailer still stood across their driveway but a thin lodgepole pine had fallen on it, and its one sturdy branch was skewered through the roof. It looked funny there, like it had just dropped in for coffee. Ruthie laughed.

"You going to fix it?" Rutherford asked.

They parked and Ruthie stood in the yard calling Moses while her dad went and turned off the gas. She called until her throat hurt. She searched the hillsides for his small boxy shape. She even looked into the dark mouth of No-Medicine Canyon, though she knew he'd only go in there if he was facing certain death. He'd seen the creature as surely as she had. She wondered if the earthquake had thrown him clean off the earth. He was only twelve pounds. She pictured his small body twisting away through the black of space.

Finally, he appeared on the ridge by the Happels' collapsed fence. He approached shamefaced, his head low, stump tail quivering, as if the whole quake had been his punishment for pissing on the bathroom rug, or chewing up one of Ruthie's shoes. She got ahold of his collar and didn't let go. She pressed her face into the wiry fur on his back. He licked her hand. She took him back to the trailer and Rutherford crouched to pat his head. "Good boy," he said.

Ruthie picked Moses up and watched her father clamber onto the windowsill to survey the damaged roof. In motion, his big hands and feet made it look like he still had room to grow. As if he might yet turn into someone else. His face, though, was aging rapidly. The seething, backed-against-the-wall expression he held when observing the new mansions being built on the Mitchell Slough by Wiley King's friends had etched permanent lines in his forehead. His eyes remained so pale as to seem almost unreal.

He balanced his level on the edge of the roof. Ruthie prayed the trailer hadn't been knocked askew. Everyone in the valley knew the story of old man Pascal, Pip's father, who'd gone crazy when he couldn't get his trailer back to level after the mudslide that killed his wife. It was a common problem in a valley marked by hills and defiles. The slant turned him insomniac and he grew paranoid with grief, refusing to leave his property, forgetting to feed his daughter. In the end, he shot himself, and his body slid from his bedroom to the kitchen, ending up against the bathroom door, where Pip found it.

"At least we're flush," Rutherford said, hopping down and going to check on his beetles.

Aftershocks. Ruthie wondered if there'd be any warning, or if they'd come from nowhere like the first quake had. She listened to her father curse inside the shed. She knew she should go in to help, but the idea of the beetles swarming over her bare arms, scurrying up toward her nose and mouth, wanting to feed, was too much for her to bear. Rutherford came out looking pale. "Bins fell," he said. "Most of them are gone."

"Maybe they'll come back," Ruthie said softly.

"They ain't dogs."

All the Fears' belongings were off the shelves inside. The TV lay facedown on the floor. It looked tragic there, like it couldn't get up. Ruthie set Moses in his bed, told him to stay, and ducked around the tree branch coming in through the ceiling. She heaved the TV upright. A large crack split the screen with little spiderwebs coming out on both sides.

"Goddammit to hell," her father said, coming in behind her.

The screen didn't even flicker when she tried to turn it on. How would they eat without its voices in the background? They'd been standing on a bowl of Jell-O the whole time. Why had no one told her? Curses, calderas, government experiments. Already she'd seen a headless creature and felt a mountain rise beneath the road. What else were they hiding?

"Is Charlo's curse real?" she asked.

Her father snorted and sank down onto the couch amid plaster from the roof. He ran his hand over the stubble of his hair. "Hell no. He was just the last Indian around for people to blame. First they blamed him for spotted fever, then crop failures, droughts, and now earthquakes, I guess."

"Bitty Law, at school, said you're an Indian lover."

Rutherford grimaced. "You just stay away from the Laws. They got poison in their blood."

Ruthie paused. "Why do we live here?"

"What?"

"It's . . . it's not safe. The people are mean, there's no work, and we don't even have a house."

"Where should we go? San Francisco? New York? Think I could be a banker there? Suck people dry and live in a glass box while you play with dolls all day?" Rutherford gripped his knees. "I didn't ask for this."

Silently, Ruthie crossed the wolfskin rug to her small room. She straightened her shelves and placed her stuffed eagle back on the bed. She lay on her back and did what she was most ashamed of: she wished for a mother.

AT CHURCH ON SUNDAY, the choir stood up to sing, the organist struck a low note, and the entire congregation jumped from the way the floor vibrated. Ruthie figured instead of a sermon Father Mike should just point at each person and say, "Repent," to save himself a lot of trouble.

Instead, he went with Corinthians. A young priest, he was new to the valley from Boise, and enthusiastic. His voice rose to fervid heights: he knew the sanctifying value of a good old-fashioned natural disaster—the kind you never saw coming—in bringing people back to God. The pews were packed. Rich and poor. White and Salish. The rich families were up front: boys wearing suits to match their fathers', girls in frilly, flowerlike dresses. Rutherford had slicked his hair back and had the stunned, blasted look of three days sober. Ruthie could smell his aftershave from two seats away. Kent Willis—likewise shellacked—sat with his neighbor Danette and her roommate Judy Conklin behind them. All the Happels and Laws and Pompeys were scattered throughout the pews. Ruthie's teacher was there, too, with her children. Pip sat alone in the back by the door. Her notebook was clutched against her chest.

Sunlight streamed through the stained-glass Christ crucified above the altar. It cast a radiant spectrum of red, orange, and gold that shone on Terry French's long black braid. He sat beside Ruthie with his niece Delilah. Both girls fidgeted on the hard wood. Ruthie couldn't remember ever coming to church except on Easter, when they gave away cooked chickens. She'd never seen Terry there before. His brown fingers rested on his knees, notched and busted and perfectly still. He seemed to be in the pew and not in it at the same time. She wished she had this power: to be in one place while her mind occupied another. Delilah had a small bead thunderbird purse in her lap. She was visiting from the Flathead Reservation, where her mother's house had fared worse than Terry's hogan.

"Look for an egg along the river," she said, when Ruthie leaned over to whisperingly ask if thunderbirds were real. "Then you'll know." Delilah gazed up at the heavy beams in the rafters. Ruthie followed her eyes. She was sure she'd seen an egg beside the river before. If these beams came down it wouldn't matter who was rich, none of them would survive. It would be the end of the valley. The thorns on Christ's head had blood on their tips. They looked gruesome. His eyes expressed more misery than salvation. Ruthie decided it was better to die most anyplace besides a church.

After the service, there was a fair in the parking lot, where people had brought clothes, food, and other things to give away. Delilah and Ruthie kicked a rock back and forth while Rutherford shamefacedly took an armful of blankets from Father Mike's pretty young wife. The hole in their roof hadn't fixed itself, and nights were cold, even though summer was coming. Others took mittens and gloves and Ruthie saw a pink bike she wanted but knew her father wouldn't let her have. She asked Delilah how her house was in Arlee.

Delilah shrugged. "It wasn't that good to begin with."

Ruthie had never been to the reservation. Only eighty miles away, it was another world to her. As full of mystery as the sky.

Father Mike parted the men around his wife. "Let this bring us together," he said.

A singing group from Lolo started playing children's songs. Delilah disappeared into the crowd. Ruthie stood on the edge looking after her. Pip had left before the service was over. Ruthie remembered the way Pip's uncle had held his hand over his chest. She hoped he was okay. The band had a hen in a cage. For the grand finale, they let it out and stood it on a bucket. The hen seemed quite pleased and stomped its foot, adding a tuneful *cluck* to the music. Ruthie wasn't impressed. One night through her window she'd seen an owl pass overhead and heard music too beautiful to describe.

Only the mountains remained unshaken, as tall as ever against the sky—seeming to chastise the little crowd beside the church. They formed the edges of a bowl around the valley that could easily be recognized for the lake it once was, fifteen thousand years before, complete with waveforms etched high on the hillsides. Ruthie had found shells there among the rocks and switchgrass. Little mollusks that once trawled the depths. Fragile, impermanent. She'd never seen the ocean but she pictured it as a giant gray animal with eyes of mirrors and a mouth big enough to swallow the sun.

She kicked the rock across the pavement toward the basketball hoop. She wished she could fly away over the backboard, the church steeple, and the mountaintops.

Happel and his wife, daughters, and nephew stood off by themselves. Their arms were loaded with plastic bags full of food. Rutherford led Ruthie over and he and M. Happel began to talk about where work might be, while the nephew looked at Ruthie with hungry, leaden eyes.

"I heard the whole highway slid into the river over by Lee Metcalf. Might be years before they can get traffic through," Rutherford said.

"Maybe they need hands there," Happel answered.

Rutherford shook his head. "State jobs. Contract work. You have to be union."

"Lots of houses here need rebuilding."

"You'd think. But my phone ain't ringing."

Happel looked down at the ground. "It didn't have to sneak up on us like that," he said.

Puffy white clouds moved over the Bitterroot Mountains. The

kind that look solid enough to stand on. Angel clouds, if you believed Father Mike. Ruthie stared at them to avoid the nephew's eyes. She turned to see if Terry was nearby. Maybe he'd known the quake was coming; maybe there'd been some sign that her father and Happel were too blind to see. But he was already over at his truck. Loading the pink bike into the bed, with Delilah up on the wheel well tugging the handlebars.

7.

The screams from Lake Como sounded panicked in the distance. Ruthie sat on the edge of the cabin's back deck. Her scratched legs dangled over the creek. The skin on her ankles was pale where her socks had been. She searched the rushing water for otters and listened to the other children, wishing they would go away. Or at least shut up. She'd seen a show about otters on TV. She knew the only way to see one was to make them forget you were there.

Cleanup crews had traversed the valley and it was hard to find remaining signs of the earthquake. Passing Whipple's store, Ruthie could hardly believe she'd seen a truck overturned in the intersection just three months before. Moses lay beside her in the sun. His head rested on his paws, then jerked up to snap at the fly circling his ears in the August heat. A duck bobbed in a shallow eddy. Ruthie flicked her dirt-blackened toe in its direction. "Git."

The duck looked up at her with brown glassy eyes. A pair of nostrils were carved from its beak. There was something frightening—almost horrific—about them, as though they'd been bored out by a dentist's drill. Its orange feet struggled against the swirling current. Ruthie felt a tug of fear. She decided that otters don't like ducks.

"Go on, now. Git!" She looked around for something to throw, but the deck planks were bare save for a scattering of pine needles.

Lodgepole pines towered above the opposite shore of the creek. A firepit was centered in the clearing beyond. At night, families camping on the lake roasted marshmallows there. The cabin behind Ruthie belonged to Rutherford's former boss at the mill. He'd offered it to them for the weekend while the caulk, glue, and coating dried on the metal patch Rutherford had finally installed on the roof.

The cabin felt like another world from the trailer, although it was only ten miles away. Huge picture windows faced the creek. Lacy dish towels hung by the stove; fluffy mats covered the bathroom floor. It smelled like wood instead of bacon grease, and the shower didn't shriek when you turned it on. There was no mold. All the lights worked; her father's dirty clothes weren't strewn over the couch. Ruthie would've stayed forever.

Discovering a bottle cap in her pocket, Ruthie turned it over in her fingers, found a grip, and hurled it at the duck. "Git!"

The duck didn't move even when the bottle cap splashed the water by its body. It continued to stare at Ruthie, orange feet churning. She scooted her butt forward. She tested the lingering Popsicle-stickiness of her fingers by pressing one of the scratches on her leg, making it sting, and then pulling her fingers away. Her legs were scratched all through the summer from forays into the woods with Pip. The flash of pain shifted her mind. Maybe the duck couldn't move. Maybe it was stuck, struggling to stay afloat. Could it die like that? The possibility opened up a new realm of emotions. Ruthie was sorry about the bottle cap. She wanted the duck gone, not dead. Out of her life, not the world. The same feeling she often had about her father.

She turned and found his figure through the sliding glass door: leaned forward in the recliner in the cabin's main room, watching stock cars race on the fifty-inch TV, a beer in his right hand. His body was tense, his rapt expression on the verge of anger. Ruthie knew he was thinking of Wiley King, even while he followed the cars around and around. In the confusion after the quake, King and his rancher friends had tried to close the Mitchell Slough to hunters. King had set up bait feeders on his property, since it was illegal to hunt ducks that had been baited. "I'm feeding ducks all over my place," he told Lad Pompey at the *Ravalli Republic*. "And I won't stop." Rutherford had stayed out of it at first, until Kent Willis wrote a letter to the editor calling Wiley a "California carpetbagger" and got himself and all of his friends banned from the pond where Rutherford had hunted since he was a boy. This struck Rutherford as an act of tyranny directly in the lineage of King George, and in late-night conversations he could be heard suggesting solutions ranging from tarring and feathering King to burning down his mansion—which he'd helped build. His determination worried Ruthie, who'd seen the furtive, hollow-eyed expressions of the foster children who passed through her classes each year.

Near the cabin, rushes and willows grew along the shore. Ruthie wriggled beneath the lowest rung of the deck's railing and dropped onto the soft dirt. Moses stood at the edge. He looked down over the five-foot drop, across at her, and decided to stay where he was. Up above, the mountainsides were blackened from the Short Draw Fire, which had ravaged the Bitterroots the summer before. The fire had gotten national news coverage when the separatist Mormons in Pinesdale ejected federal firefighters at gunpoint, saying they'd caught them sabotaging a water line. Rutherford told her the Mormons were worried the feds would find all their extra wives and artillery. Ruthie dug her toes into the dirt. She got down on her hands and knees and crawled beneath the low bush branches to the water. A thorn caught her arm and scratched her anew. Sunlight glinted on the creek's surface. Needles drifted past. The algae on the rocks undulated in the current.

Up close, the duck's eyes were nearly black. Its emerald head bobbed as it paddled. The eddy was on the far side of the creek, in a bend where it widened. Pine needles, mossy twigs, and water skimmers swirled around the vortex. It reminded Ruthie of an open mouth. The yawning entrance to No-Medicine Canyon. The duck seemed unable to escape.

"You're not very good at being a duck," Ruthie said.

The duck went still. Their eyes held for a moment and then she watched in horror as it began to swirl faster and faster, being drawn into the eddy, orbiting the churning darkness, its compact body as helpless as a moon. "Dad!" she screamed.

RUTHIE FOLLOWED HER FATHER across the narrow wooden bridge. She kept exactly four steps behind him, stretching her legs to mirror his stride. She landed on her toe in the center of the bridge and paused. On one side, an old wooden water wheel was slowly collapsing. On the other, a metal chute ran down beside the rock dam. Keeping her left foot in the air, Ruthie grabbed the railing and pivoted, sweeping her leg out behind her in a karate kick. She peered down at the water in the chute. Green algae grew on the metal sides. Tendrils reached toward her among the sediment.

"It's for the fish," Rutherford said from the far end of the bridge. She waited for him to go on, to explain what the fish did in there. Why they needed a ramp. His right hand rested on the handle of the knife in his belt loop. After he'd scared the duck from the eddy and sent it winging up the creek, she'd insisted he take her to the lake. She could tell he wished he was still in front of the TV.

"Do otters use it, too?"

Rutherford's brow furrowed. "No. I don't know. Come on."

Ruthie took a deep breath and looked up at the line of blackened spear trees along the ridge. She imagined the flames sweeping down the mountainside. Bears fleeing into the creek. Dozens of them, charging and crashing through the water like Rutherford had done in the icy pond years before. Their brown fur charred, their eyes hooded with ash.

She was so caught up in her thoughts that she didn't notice the children until they were all around her.

The lake was shattered with sunlight. Motorboats knifed across the center. Jet Skis bounded over their choppy wakes. Brightly colored donuts floated aimlessly with sunburnt swimmers in their centers. Directly above the lake's western tip, the familiar shape of Trapper Peak pierced the blue sky. Two canoes moved along the piney shore beneath it. Lake Como had been named by a Jesuit priest who thought it looked like Italy, but now a huge dam blocked off one side. The concrete wall and holding tank, along with the two long docks from the public beach, gave it the odd aspect of blighted civilization on one end and unspoiled natural beauty on the other. A metaphor for the valley. Terry called the lake by its Salish name, Logs-Under-the-Water, which made a lot more sense.

Above, a particularly large and misshapen tree stood alone on a clear-cut patch of the mountainside. It looked like Sasquatch with one knee raised, thundering up to higher ground. Ruthie stared at it, feeling overwhelmed by all the people.

Rutherford followed her eyes. "When they clear-cut, they always leave one tree to tie off their equipment to," he said. "They call it the anchor tree. Usually it's bent or damaged, one they can't get much value out of." He trailed off, as if there might be a lesson in this, but found none.

Together they walked down to the water. The shallows around the dock were roiled with children: splashing, screaming, jumping, disappearing beneath the pylons. Mothers and fathers dozed in angled pairs on the rocks, occasionally jerking awake to shout at a child drifting away from shore. The air smelled of sunscreen. Father Mike and his wife lay beneath a checkered umbrella, looking healthier than all those around them, glowing in their modest swimwear. Father Mike turned toward the Fears. Ruthie noticed that his wife's toenails were painted red. "Some kind of day," he said.

Rutherford nodded, squinting out at the water.

"We've started work on the new church playground. Sure could use some help next week if you have the time." Father Mike raised up on his elbow and faced Ruthie. "Going to be a place for you and all your friends to play."

"I only have one friend," Ruthie said.

"Well, then it's a place where you can make some more." He smiled at Rutherford. "I was glad to hear the patch worked out on your roof. Len came through for a lot of people."

Rutherford reluctantly mumbled affirmation. Len had given him the sheet metal piece from his scrapyard for free, but Rutherford had been somber when he brought it home. "I'll eat shit for this for the rest of my life," he'd muttered.

"The Lord provides," Father Mike said, gazing out at the lake in satisfaction. Rutherford led Ruthie away. He found a secluded spot on the beach and squatted on his haunches. He hadn't brought a picnic or blanket or swimsuit or floaties or anything like the other families. He hadn't even brought a towel. Just his knife. Ruthie wished he were more like the other fathers, joking and laughing in the sun. Cannonballing off the dock. She looked back at Father Mike's wife's red toes, glinting in the sun.

"You see that buoy?" Rutherford said, pointing out to where the water flattened. "Don't go past it."

The orange oval appeared to be floating exactly in the middle of the lake. Past where even an otter would go. Ruthie's palms went clammy. She looked down at the rocks. She didn't want to get in. She only had her underwear to swim in. Watching the other girls in their fluorescent bikinis, she saw how pathetic this was. Why had she insisted they come? She should've stayed on the deck with Moses and hidden food for the otters. Seen if she could find a thunderbird egg by the creek.

A fat toddler ran into a circle of girls all wearing comically large snorkels. His soaked underwear clung to his butt. The girls screamed and shooed him away. He turned to Ruthie and began to toddle up the beach toward her. His skin was so tan it nearly glowed, with a sheen to it, like oil. She hissed at him. He stopped and stuck out his tongue. There was something on it, a piece of candy or pebble or some wicked little talisman. She felt threatened. She searched around her feet for a rock to throw if he came any closer.

All around, people were talking, laughing, tossing neon balls. The snorkel girls watched her. One of them giggled. Their eyes felt hot on her, burning. Ruthie picked up a kidney-shaped green rock striated with pale veins. It was solid in her hand. A hint of the power of holding her father's shotgun. Rutherford absentmindedly flicked the blade of his knife in and out. When one of the mothers caught his eye, he glanced away, reddening. He was shy, too, Ruthie realized. Out of place and embarrassed. Used to his friends in the Sawmill Bar, as unsure of how to talk to the mothers as Ruthie was to their kids. It didn't seem right. One of them should know what they were doing.

The toddler took another step toward her. He grinned, showing little yellow corn teeth. Ruthie looked at her father, now cleaning his nails with the knife tip. She looked down at the rock in her hand. It was shaped like the creature, with the same inscrutable menace.

The boy waggled his belly at her. She could see his penis through his wet underwear. Without thinking, she raised her arm and threw the rock. Hard.

It struck the boy on the shoulder. The grin fell from his face into a blank expression of shock. There was a long moment—as the bruise formed and blood began to seep from its blue-black center—when he and Ruthie simply stared at each other, bound together by an intimacy she'd never felt. One of awe and cruelty. *I am stronger than you.*

He squeezed his eyes shut and his mouth broke open. He began to wail.

Ruthie covered her ears, suddenly afraid.

The rocky beach was swept out from under her feet. Her father slung her over his shoulder and she saw the lake and the boy wobbling upside down as he hustled with her off the beach, away from the other parents, over the bridge, and back to the cabin.

SMALL YELLOW BUTTERFLIES swirled over the creek in the late afternoon sun. Ruthie sat on the bank and watched. They were so delicate and sheer they seemed to be somewhere between matter and air. Their flight had a pattern to it, moments of unison, like a murmuration of swallows controlled by music only they could hear. The susurrus of wings. Ruthie held out her hand, perfectly still, hardly breathing.

She waited a long time, until her hand ached from being out-held and she wasn't sure she could keep it still any longer. Then suddenly a butterfly landed on her fingertip. Its yellow wings stilled like twin sails closing, and she was amazed by the tiny, strong grip of its feet. The pincers were too small to see, yet their hold was unfailing. She concentrated on the feeling. It seemed important: the strength of these delicate creatures, the sure power of their feet, the goodness of being held, and how things that seemed helpless could sometimes be the strongest.

She didn't know if she should be sorry about the boy, or if she'd only headed off his violence with her own.

THAT NIGHT, RUTHIE STAYED AWAKE in bed in the cabin's loft and listened to her father, Terry French, Kent Willis, and Raymond Pompey talk about Wiley King in the living room below.

"He's got his foot on our throats and it won't ever be enough," Kent said.

"I been hunting that pond since I was a boy," Rutherford answered. "And my dad before that."

"My dad's dad before that," Terry said.

"My family used to go there for mushrooms in the spring," Raymond said. "Asparagus, too."

Rutherford's voice rose. "Half-assed country star moves in and puts up a big fence like he owns the entire valley. Starts baiting ducks. It's goddamn low-down. We got rights to that land. We been using it for generations."

"'They're taking your ancestral land?" Terry asked.

"Yes," Rutherford said.

"Land you thought belonged to you by birthright because your people had been using it for generations?"

"Exactly!" Rutherford paused. "Oh, I see what you're doing. Cut the Indian shit. This is serious."

Ruthie peered down from the loft at Terry's face half smiling in the firelight. Kent grunted. "He's got three lawyers in from Seattle, trying to say the slough is a 'man-made feature,' not subject to public access laws. They know people are too distracted rebuilding to put up much of a fight. If he wins, it'll be closed off all the way from Pine Road to the West Fork."

Tense silence fell as this injustice churned through the men's heads. Ruthie wondered if this was part of Charlo's curse, too. She didn't know if it was better to hate the rich or become rich. She stared across the ceiling—the firelight turned the pale wood beams gold—and said a prayer for her father not to do anything stupid.

LATER, AFTER RUTHERFORD's friends had left and he lay sleeping in the twin bed beside hers, Ruthie silently listed as many endangered species as she could: black rhino, mountain gorilla, Amur tiger, bonobo. In her mind, these disappearing animals were enormous, like dinosaurs. Bigger than the cabin, big enough to knock aside trees. She imagined herds of them thundering over the mountains. She wanted to stay awake to see the otters.

Her father wheezed, sweating out the beer he'd drunk. He gripped the pillow tightly with both arms, his thighs clamped together. The pillowcase was damp even though the night was cold. He always sweated and clung in his sleep, traveling the course of his wolf-plagued dreams. One of Ruthie's worst memories was coming out of her room as a toddler to find him passed-out drunk, pantless on the couch, his testicles squeezed back between his thighs like two tor-tured little eggs. The image refused to leave her as she aged. She felt betrayed by it.

They were going home in the morning. Most of the other families had already left. There were no fires across the creek, no marshmal-lows. The stars were hidden by low thick clouds advancing from the east. An armada of them, like a hundred-year wagon train moving west across the plains. Ruthie watched through the loft window, lying cross-wise over the twin bed, her bare feet sticking off the side. She rested her chin on the web of her fingers. She pictured tunnels where the otters lived stretching for miles beneath the cabin. A place where she and Moses could escape. Far from slough wars or corn-toothed toddlers. No shame, no fear. The only thing her father had said to her about the boy was, "If you're going to go after someone, it's best to have a reason."

Wind began to blow in the trees. The tops of the pines swayed deeply. They called through the windows in silence, as if stirred by a noise too huge for her to hear. She sat up. Cones fell and bounced off the deck. Lightning flashed in the distance, but no thunder came, nor rain.

Dry lightning. It would surely start more fires in the tinder of the late summer woods. Ruthie pictured a crackle in the branches, a bang, falling sparks, and a single flame spreading over pine needles, then whooshing up trunks to light the sky orange. Before pouring back down with new strength through the deadfall.

Disaster was always nearby. The quake had taught her that.

The sound of small, scuttling feet wafted into the loft. Ruthie stared at the ceiling, her eyes wide, then slowly, carefully, she dropped out of bed. The feet pattered across the deck. Her heart began to pound. She crept to the ladder and down. The bottom rung creaked. She froze. Her father's breathing paused, then with a hitch resumed. Shafts of moonlight divided the living room. Moses's eyes shone in his bed by the door.

"Shhh," she whispered, coming toward him. Obediently, he set his head down on his paws. A lone ember glowed in the woodstove.

Low dark forms moved outside the glass door. Ruthie bent at the waist, her hair hanging in her face. She held up her hand. The otters went still. Their eyes gleamed in the stormy night. Their flat noses twitched, long translucent whiskers quivering. Their skulls were softball-sized and almost perfectly round. Ruthie wanted to hold one in her hand. Feel its weight, its softness, the gentle tremble of the eyeballs beneath the lids. She counted three of them. Four. She knelt and placed her palms on the cool glass.

"*You came*," she whispered.

They crowded around, staring up at her, before bending to snuffle between the planks for the hamburger she'd tucked away. They gulped the hamburger, chewing with their mouths open, their sleek bodies lost in shadow. They nudged one another as if they had something to tell her. Ruthie stared back. She wondered if they'd seen the headless creature, too. If they knew there was a wrongness in the woods. Their jaws worked. They nodded their heads back to swallow. The clearing across the creek was milky in the moonlight. The towering pines swayed above it. The air was full of restless gatherings, as if a new and inconceivable face were about to show itself. Ruthie touched the door's handle. For an instant, lightning turned the night white. The otters quickened, snuffling and pawing.

Above in the loft, the bed creaked and Ruthie knew her father was awake. That he'd stood and was watching her and the otters at the glass.

8.

The fire that started that August night burned until October. Pushed by high winds, it rushed into the backcountry. Torching over ridges and through canyons, avoiding the places the Short Draw had burned the summer before, it crossed into Idaho where the Selway-Bitterroot connected to the Frank Church–River of No Return Wilderness, and raged there in the roadless woods until it consumed nearly a hundred thousand acres and killed three smoke jumpers.

The same day they died, on the other side of Trapper Peak, Sheriff Don Kima arrested Rutherford for his role in dynamiting Wiley King's duck feeders and a section of his fence. Rutherford pled temporary insanity, due to the pressure the quake had put on him. Unimpressed with this excuse, the judge sentenced Rutherford to three nights in jail. He had to pawn several of his guns to Terry to pay the fines. The chances of ever hunting his favorite pond again seemed as remote as the return of the bison. Ruthie stayed with Terry during her father's absence, sleeping on the small cot in Terry's one-room cement hogan on the West Fork of the Bitterroot River. Pictures of college basketball players were taped to the walls above an array of old bead jewelry from his pawnshop. Things too holy to resell filled most of the shelves: a necklace of bear claws, buffalo-hide war drums covered with blue dogs and running horses, ceremonial corn maidens. A former basketball star himself for the Darby Eagles, he had two TVs angled together so he could watch two games at once. A woodstove sat in the center of the floor, its black pipe reaching up through the roof. Except in midwinter, Terry left the front door open for light and air. Now it was closed against the wildfire smoke. Ruthie kicked the blanket down to her feet in the claustrophobic heat. As she tried to sleep, Terry slowly circled the stove.

"What're you doing?" she asked.

"Walking."

"Why?"

"To relax." He wore plaid slippers, sweatpants, and a T-shirt from a powwow fifteen years before. His long hair was loose and in the dishevelment of his face she saw, just for a moment, a mother.

"I think I'd relax more lying down," she said.

"Why don't you go to sleep?"

"I'm not tired."

"Yes, you are."

"Tell me a story."

The woodstove was empty, cold, but she imagined how the room would feel with its crackling fire. The shadows dancing on the wall. It was the first night she'd slept away from her father, and she was anxious. Terry sighed, still walking. "All right, I'll tell you a story about your dad when he was a little older than you."

Ruthie nodded.

"He used to think he could survive in the woods without any help. During spring break—I think we were twelve—he went up Bear Creek with nothing but his .22. He said he'd stay there on his own for the whole week, killing what he needed to eat and using the furs to keep warm. We thought he'd be back in a day or two at most. But on the third day there was a blizzard, a bad one, you know the kind we get in March, and he was still gone. Twenty inches fell overnight with windchill to twenty below. Me and Billy went looking for him as soon as the sky cleared. We found his tracks a few miles in, full of blood. We thought he must be hurt and started calling him. But he wouldn't answer. Finally, we found him sitting in front of a doe he'd shot. He was covered in her blood and guts, all frozen to him, and her organs were dumped out in the snow. He'd sawed her rib cage open and wedged himself inside to keep from freezing. Lucky he was so small." Terry laughed. "I've never seen a sorrier sight, and he stank worse than his beetles. But he still didn't want to come home. He said he could make it the whole week." Terry paused his circling and pulled the blanket up to Ruthie's chin. She blinked sleepily in the warm, smoky air, trying to imagine her father alone in the cold, trembling inside a fresh-killed doe. "I think he would've, too. He's the stubbornest fool I ever met."

"You think he's okay?" she asked softly.

Terry nodded. "He'll be fine. I've been to jail. It's easier than sleeping inside a deer."

THE NEXT NIGHT, sitting on the edge of the cot, Ruthie noticed that Terry's circling had worn a path in the cement floor. A smoothness lighter than the surface around it. This struck her as madness. How long, how many nights? . . . Why didn't any of the men she knew have a wife? The sound of the river outside reminded her of the sound of the highway, and she felt bad for this, as though she were betraying them both. She looked down at her bare feet on the cool floor. She wiggled each toe in turn. The rhythm of Terry's passage was like the hand of a clock.

"Is this valley cursed?" she asked.

"What?" He slowed. "Who told you that?"

"Len Law. He said so after the earthquake."

"He might be cursed." Terry pursed his lips. "He's all twisted up inside. You know his grandfather was the first sheriff of Darby. They had a big house on the river."

"What happened?"

Terry paused. Ruthie could tell he was editing the story because she was a child.

"Tell me," she said.

"His grandfather did bad things and finally got in trouble for them. He lost his job. Then he killed himself. And his son—Len's father— left the valley. No one's ever seen him again. Len's mom had to sell their house to take care of all her kids, and they ended up where they are now."

"He thinks that's Charlo's fault."

Terry smiled. "He blames it on one Indian or another."

"That doesn't make sense."

Terry gently pushed Ruthie's shoulders back onto the bed so she was lying down. "A lot of men don't make sense. You're going to have to learn that." He patted her arm. "I'm still surprised by the bullshit I hear."

She wondered if he would believe her if she told him about the creature. She was suddenly very sleepy. "Are you lonely?" she asked.

"Not usually. I have the pawnshop, friends, my brother. But yes, sometimes I am."

"You should get married," she said.

He laughed, his large head and chest framed by the dim lamplight, his shadow connecting him to the stove. "You're probably right. Now go to sleep. We'll pick up your idiot father in the morning."

·

RUTHERFORD—SEEMINGLY UNCHANGED by his stint in jail, if slightly more agitated—came home determined to teach Ruthie how to shoot. He'd planned to wait until she was ten, but now believed the matter was too urgent, with Sheriff Kima and the rest of local law enforcement in the pocket of corrupt landowners. As he readied the targets for her first lesson, Ruthie watched the fire planes curve over No-Medicine Canyon and up into the mountains, where they disappeared in the huge plume of smoke that billowed and pulsed as if from a volcano. Wide, heavy-bellied ships of the sky, their twin rotors were so loud they made the ground vibrate. Moses looked up from the antler he'd been chewing and barked. Rutherford had told Ruthie that some of the planes carried smoke jumpers and others the retardant she'd seen them spew over the treetops in great red arcs. She wondered what the animals thought of this sticky red rain. If they knew it was there to put the fire out. If it clung to their coats. If somewhere in Idaho a little girl like her would look up from her homework and see a bright red bear crashing out from the woods.

Moses went back to gnawing. Ruthie's throat burned. Her eyes watered. She wished she was inside next to her fan. Her father's friends argued over whether there had always been this much smoke in late summer. Kent Willis said that a properly managed forest would never burn. When one did, it was because of the liberals who'd killed off the logging industry. "They used to have 'em out by ten the next morning," he said. He'd been a logger himself, until a bucking accident put him on permanent disability.

The smoke trapped the heat in the valley and gave it a hacking denseness reminiscent of humidity. The air felt ripe for destruction and chaos. Rutherford strode across the overgrown yard to the plywood target stand at fifty yards. He used a staple gun to bang a neon-yellow paper target into place. Then he turned to Ruthie and pointed at the black bull's-eye like she might not know what it was. Old bullet shells, the squashed copper nubs of the bullets themselves, and splinters of plywood littered the range. It was his proving ground. His kingdom. Ruthie was surprised by how badly she wanted to do well. She was often embarrassed by her father, and complained bitterly about him in her mind, but there was nothing she wanted more than for him to see her as strong. He smacked the target with the flat of his hand, then went into his shed and came out carrying an old .22 rifle and a box of shells.

"This was my first gun and now it's yours," he said.

Ruthie nodded. He nodded back.

"As long as you ain't trying to stop a bear, it'll do the job. Small-caliber is why, that means low-velocity. When you hunt something big, you'll need a bigger gun, but shooting hasn't got much to do with the gun at all. The gun is just the size of the bang, and any jackass can make a bang. It's about looking with your hands." He leaned the rifle against the hay bale that served as a table behind the firing line. He motioned for her to stand then crouched behind her so they were one height, his knees on either side of her. He held her empty arms and pulled her back gently into his chest, planting them both, as one creature, firmly in the dirt. "First you've got to learn how to look at your target without a gun. Just look. Look and breathe." Ruthie stared at the yellow circles on the black sphere. They seemed to draw her in like the eddy in Como Creek. "Don't see anything else."

The planes and smoke and mountains fell away. The bull's-eye was a void, a pit, the dark center of the universe. Ruthie began to feel dizzy. Gently, Rutherford raised her arms with his and straightened them, palms together, her hands forming a blade pointing at the target.

"Line your top thumb up with your eye and the bull," he said. "Let your eye become your hand. Keep breathing. Keep it still. If you trust your eye, you'll shoot where it's looking." Ruthie sighted over the ridge of her knuckle, and felt her father's whiskers scratch her cheek. She smelled the sawdust in the collar of his shirt, and the beetles—repopulating even at that moment in the shed—beneath it. She felt his collarbone against her shoulder and the way blood and life coursed through him. It was the closest she could ever remember him holding her. She stared into the center of the bull's-eye and felt the power of the smoke and flames overhead. It was a feeling of freedom.

"Don't let that thumb move when you pull the trigger. Breathe into it. Nothing moves—not your eyes, not your arms, not your hands, not your toes. Pretend you have roots and the only part of you that can move is the little twig of your index finger."

Carefully, Ruthie freed that finger.

"Okay," he said, and she pulled the invisible trigger.

At that moment, as if she had fired some kind of magical bullet, a phalanx of planes emerged from the huge plume of smoke above the mountains. Their engines roared. Ruthie and her father looked up. Moses leapt to his feet and turned in a circle, barking. One after another the planes flew east low over the valley. Twelve of them, all sleek and white with gold stripes along their sides. Private jets, emerging like a mirage from the unmapped woods. Moses ran after them yapping, his years falling away in puppy-like excitement.

"Fire must have changed direction," Rutherford said, tipping his head back to follow the planes' flight.

"Who are they?"

"Rich people. Assholes. From Angel's Landing."

"What's that?"

"It's a town for people with so much money they don't want anyone else to be able to find them. You have to have your own plane to get there."

"They live back there?" Ruthie asked, awed by the idea.

He nodded. "Terry backpacked in once. It's sixty miles from the nearest road, the last thirty bushwhacking. He got all the way to the security perimeter. He says they have a man-made lake and a real one, a golf course, a runway, even a little grocery store." Rutherford blew a piece of ash from his beard. "It's a bunch of Russians and Chinese. I hope the whole place burns."

Ruthie watched the planes until they disappeared over the Sapphires. Her cheek itched where her father's whiskers had been. She wondered if the rich were fleeing to another secret hideaway, in other mountains, with another man-made lake. She tried to picture a town so deep in the woods that it had no roads. Was there a school? A restaurant? She saw, vaguely, castles. A drawbridge. She decided she wanted to live there.

Rutherford stood and retrieved the .22. "You ready?" he asked.

Ruthie nodded.

"Always assume a gun is loaded. All the ones in my room are, and from now on you'll keep this one by your door. An unloaded gun is just a stick you can't throw straight. Keep it loaded with the safety on. People will tell you that's dangerous, but they're the ones who want to take them away. You understand?"

"Yes." Ruthie took the gun. She held it, remembering how the skeleton had shattered across the sky. She felt that once she pulled the trigger, she'd leap forward in wisdom and years. The thought scared her.

"Good." Her father knelt again and gently raised the gun in front of them. His chest pressed against her back, shoulders against her shoulders, arms over her arms. He placed the stock into her hands along with his and pointed toward the target. "Hold it here." Ruthie touched the grain. Gripped it. It was like any other polished wood, a banister or cabinet handle, cool and smooth, yet different also. She could feel the bucking explosion that would take place, and the violence it would send forth. "Now put your other finger over the trigger like this. Not on the trigger, just over it. You only touch the trigger when you're going to shoot. That's the most important thing to remember: only touch the trigger when you're going to shoot."

The barrel moved with their hands, steadying toward the target. "The velocity of this gun is low, and the bullets are light, but they can still kill someone." Ruthie imagined the creature lurching and twisting away from the sight, trying to escape up the canyon. She decided the first person she'd shoot was Len Law. Then all the whalers in Japan. "Keep the butt firm against your shoulder. It's going to buck a little, and a big gun would buck a lot, but it'll only hurt if you don't keep it firm. A bigger caliber could break your nose or knock your eyeball out if you flinch." Ruthie's heart started pounding. Knock her eyeball out? It seemed like too much to keep track of: breathing and touching the trigger, keeping the butt on her shoulder and her eyeballs in her head. She struggled to hold her finger over the trigger and not on it. The rifle barrel felt much too long to control.

"Breathe," Rutherford said. He slid his hand over hers and clicked the safety off. The rifle's weight was spread evenly between all four of their hands. His heart beat behind hers. She stared at the target. She willed the rest of the world away. "Now."

She pulled.

With the first shot, she hardly noticed the plywood splinter above the target, she was so worried about the butt punching her shoulder. She felt it, but only a little. Relieved adrenaline rushed through her. She could do it.

Her second shot blew a hole in the target's second yellow ring and she couldn't help but shriek with excitement. Her father laughed. "Look at you," he said, and drew his arms away. Suddenly bereft, Ruthie pulled the trigger as the barrel fell, kicking up dirt ten yards in front of her.

"Careful!" Rutherford said, yanking the gun upright and holding her again. "Jesus, you want to shoot your damn foot off?"

She did not, but nor had she wanted him to let go.

The morning drew on, the fiery light going from purple-red to the deepening orange smoke haze of midday. The rifle steadied in

Ruthie's arms. Her aim improved. Spent shells glinted in the grass around her feet. Her father watched, grunting in appreciation each time she hit the target. An instinctive switch occurred within her. She began firing not for his love, but through it. Channeling his skill, which he'd used to fell the last wolf across two hundred yards of rolling sagebrush hillside, and so many other animals besides, and finding that she could dwell there. The barrel an extension of her eye, the trigger extra length to her finger, the butt molded to her shoulder, and the lines between her and him slipping away. She watched as the target ripped apart.

"You're a natural," he said, crossing his arms and smiling, showing the missing incisor gap he usually hid. His baseball cap was cocked far back on his forehead. Pride crinkled the lines around his eyes. A lone figure in the smoky, apocalyptic light. Warmth spread through Ruthie. She felt at home.

II

9.

Dreaming of heroes, old men filed into the Darby High football stadium. Their lined faces were gold beneath the halogen lights. They wore flannel shirts and canvas jackets. Jeans with bison-skull belt buckles and scuffed boots. Retired from mills now closed: Bonner, Stimson, Darby Lumber. The hulking buildings sagging behind barbed-wire fences. Windows smashed. Ruthie and Pip watched the men from the concrete steps atop the bleachers with a red blanket wrapped around their knees. They sat close together, their arms touching. Gusts of cold October wind ran down from the mountains. The first snow dusted the upper slopes. They were freshmen, but Ruthie didn't feel like they belonged. Her classmates gossiped about senior boys and homecoming, while she and Pip still hunted for the tracks of a headless creature.

Pip thought she'd seen it once near the four-wheel track off Lost Horse Road, but it disappeared before she could be sure. "Maybe it wasn't real," Ruthie said. "I don't know anymore. Maybe I made it up."

"Maybe this isn't real." Pip smirked at the school behind them. Her black bra was clearly visible under her white shirt. She wore short pants through the winter and seemed to hold heat like a filament—snow melted in her tracks. She carried her knife in a purple backpack along with her notebook and a mouthwash bottle full of food-coloring-disguised vodka skimmed from her uncle's bar. She was tough in a way that came through in her shoulders, not wide but angular, taut with budding muscle. The only activity she and Ruthie didn't do together was hunt. Ruthie had shot her first deer with her father when she was nine, slotting the bullet behind its ear with her .22 so it died standing up. Pip refused to even hold a gun, hating all weaponry beyond her knife. She marked herself with the knife's tip, scratching runes in thin trickles of blood on her thighs. Other girls whispered that she was a witch. The principal even had to be called in one day when Len Law showed up at the school and demanded Pip not be in the same class as his twin nieces, because she was trying to pox their wombs. This was doubly ironic to Ruthie, as these were the same girls who slept with dropouts at the kickboxing gym and talked about ways to get rid of a baby if they got pregnant: by drinking bleach, taking a month's worth of birth control pills, or throwing themselves over the bumper of a truck.

The earthquake had faded into distant memory in an intensifying sequence of fires and floods in the Bitterroot Valley. The road by the Lee Metcalf National Wildlife Refuge was repaired, but Ruthie still felt herself to be on unsteady ground. She kept her few breakable belongings on the bottom shelf, and made sure Moses—so old and gray now that he hardly left his bed except to pee—didn't sleep under anything heavy.

Cheerleaders huddled together on the sidelines, their legs bare beneath flared yellow skirts. Red pom-poms clutched to their chests.

They looked into the crowd, on display, self-conscious and proud. The football players bumped into each other in bright red spandex, pads transforming their teenage shoulders into blocky battering rams. Michael Badger towered over his teammates. Only fourteen, he was already one of the largest. He looked dazed under the lights, his helmet hanging from his hand by the face mask. Ruthie tried to decide what to make of him, his innocence and size, his potential. They shared homeroom and since the start of high school he'd been a near-constant presence in her life, a looming shadow behind her in the halls. Homeschooled through eighth grade, he knew nothing of her father's beetle business nor the teal trailer where they lived, and from the joggled, awestruck look in his eye when he talked to her, she thought he might not care.

A whistle blew. The team circled, raised their white-gloved fists together, and brought them down with a shout. They ran onto the field under the lights; the announcer's voice crackled over the loudspeaker. The town's pageants sometimes made Ruthie overwhelmingly sad. She had twice won the girls under-twelve state trap-shooting competition. Rutherford kept the trophies atop the fridge, and she still caught him gazing at them before reaching inside for a beer, but for Ruthie the victories felt hollow. She was sure larger achievements existed in the outside world.

Pip leaned into her shoulder. "I only want the Indian boys."

"The coach hardly lets them play." Ruthie watched Badger line up beside the quarterback, who received the snap and deposited the ball into his arms. He plunged headfirst into the other bodies. Shedding one, two, before being pulled down in a mass of flailing limbs. Emerging with his shoulder pad askew, grass stuck in his helmet, grinning. Cheers ran through the crowd, followed by low chatter. Men drank from cans in paper bags. They spat chew into plastic soda cups. Rutherford sat beside Raymond Pompey down near the field. He wore his own varsity jacket from fifteen years before—when he'd been the smallest wide receiver on the team, awarded his position through sheer tenacity—and pointed toward Badger in the huddle.

"Are you going to sleep with him?" Pip asked.

Ruthie touched the silver stud in her newly pierced lip with her tongue. She liked Badger, but worried that enough touchdowns would make him arrogant or cruel. "I don't know."

"Scott Runningcrane took me to his cousin's cabin on the Lochsa. I told him if he wanted to do it he had to clean up all the mouse shit and make a fire. It smelled terrible."

"And?"

Pip shrugged. "There was no wood."

Ruthie laughed. "Maybe I'll tell Badger he has to bring me a magic slipper."

"He'd probably drive to the Wal-Mart in Missoula and ask."

"One of those special Bitterroot kids. They'd send him home with a Cinderella costume."

"But just think, if they win state, you could be prom queen."

"I think I'd kill myself," Ruthie said.

Seconds ticked by in gold on the tall digital scoreboard glowing before the dark mountains. Father Mike and his wife sat in the center of the bleachers in matching down coats. God and football. The priest's face was flushed with excitement. His voice rose above the others as Badger smashed forward, yard by yard, slamming his helmet into padded chests, his cleats gouging the grass. A holy chaos. Father Mike's wife looked embarrassed. Ruthie knew Badger by his size and the number thirty-three in gold on his red back. She watched the game as she'd watched the church services she'd attended as a girl: interested but apart. Pip fished the mouthwash bottle from her backpack. She drank and handed it to Ruthie. The blue liquid tasted like gasoline. Ruthie coughed, her throat burning. "Can't you ever steal anything decent?" She gave it back to Pip, who began picking at the label with her long, bony fingers.

"This is all a ritual," Pip said. "The game, the players, all of it. Like in the old days, when the Indians would pierce their chests with bone pegs and dance for hours."

"At least they had a reason. For the hunt or rain or whatever. Now we have to pretend like the score will make us better than Stevensville."

"I read that if the pegs didn't come out by sundown they'd start pulling and shoving each other to yank them out."

Ruthie tried to picture the men she knew, her father and his friends, Whipple and Father Mike, shirtless and pierced around the cottonwood pole. The hardest part was to imagine them dancing. Gesturing toward the game, Ruthie said, "Now they just slam into each other."

Pip smiled and nodded. "Until they fall down."

The referee blew his whistle and one of the coaches ran onto the field, furiously waving a clipboard. The team stood back. Ruthie still felt deeply her connection to the wild, but the world of parties and school and boys was pulling her in. She'd grown nearly as tall as her father, and despite her cropped hair and thrift-store clothes, she felt eyes on her in the grocery store. A new vibration when she moved. An awareness of her body as something that preceded her mind.

"Look who's here," Pip said, nudging Ruthie with her elbow.

Len Law stood at the bottom of the bleachers. He'd been absent for much of the summer, bringing his mother to the hospital in Missoula for diabetes checkups. He looked up at the crowd, his eyes searching until they came to rest on the two girls.

"God, he's disgusting," Ruthie said. "He's been watching me like that since I was five."

"He's scared of us," Pip said. "You know he has totems all around his scrapyard? To protect it."

"From what?"

Pip shrugged. "I don't know. Indians. Witches."

"He should be worried about pedophile hunters."

"I sometimes try to kill him with my eyes," Pip said. "Like this."

Ruthie smiled and the two girls trained their eyes on Len. Ruthie imagined beading the sight of her .22 exactly over his heart. He reddened and turned away.

"See, he's scared," Pip said.

Ruthie laughed.

The ball sailed through the air toward the end zone. The crowd held its breath, following the spiral path. It arced down toward outstretched hands. Touched fingertips, bounced off, fell to earth. The town sighed. Glory delayed, again. Ruthie took the bottle from Pip and drank deeply. She watched Badger jog off the field and wondered what any of them would prove to be.

10.

Rutherford stood in the bathroom in his underwear covering him-self with elk piss from a squeeze bottle. It was four-thirty a.m. and the darkness was just beginning to bleed from the sky outside the window.

"Jesus, Dad, you can put it on over your clothes," Ruthie said.

"No. They can tell," he answered. "It's got to mix with the sweat." His chest and belly were paper-white. His face, neck, and forearms were still darkly tanned from the work he'd done on the Stock Farm Club that summer. He'd been part of a landscaping crew adding another nine holes to the golf course. Rutherford had been forced to denude sagebrush hills where he'd once hunted lynx, while fat Californians sliced balls wildly on the fairways below. He'd hardly spoken to Ruthie in the evenings when he came home, drinking beer after beer on the porch and looking across the yard at the darkness of No-Medicine Canyon.

In the mirror, his body was a wiry sprig of muscle, barely five and a half feet tall. Slightly bowlegged, with a long chest, short legs, and a pregnant bump of belly. He was a stunted but surviving thing, like the high-altitude trees that live in the driest soil. The white briefs he wore were old and ragged, but his neon-orange socks were brand-new. He stared at himself, rubbing the piss into his pecs under the fluorescent light. Ruthie was relieved. Bowhunting season always lifted his spirits, at least temporarily.

"Where the hell did you find those?" she asked.

He glanced down at his feet. "Seventy-five percent off at Whipple's. Apparently they wouldn't sell."

"Can't imagine."

Rutherford shrugged. "I better not smell that bacon burning."

The bathroom and kitchen were practically on top of each other in the narrow trailer. Ruthie turned around and switched off the burner. Everyone else she knew put the scent on over their hunting gear, once they were out in the woods. Not straight onto the skin. She'd have to leave the windows open all morning to clear the air, and freeze her ass off. She scooped the bacon onto a paper towel. Then she opened the door behind her and dumped the grease from the pan off the steps onto the dead patch of lawn where they always dumped their bacon grease. Cold clean air rushed in. She could just make out the shape of her blind in the trees by the creek. Serviceberry bushes had grown up to cover the sides. It felt like another lifetime since she'd kept vigil inside, watching for the creature in the canyon.

"That Badger boy coming over?" Rutherford asked.

"He might."

Rutherford leaned out of the bathroom and peered at her. He'd put piss in his hair, too, slicking it back, and looked weirdly suave, like a banker in a movie. "Just stay out of my room. And if I come home and hear anything, I'll shoot him in the leg, and who knows but my aim might slip a little to the center."

Rutherford leaned back into the bathroom and began pulling on his jeans. "He's a big sack of shit, I'll give him that. Had a nice game last week."

Ruthie wondered if her father would be more disappointed if she didn't sleep with Badger. Rutherford claimed to have lost his virginity at eleven to a girl from Cut Bank who'd come down to Darby for Logger Days, so maybe fourteen was a given to him. As soon as he left, Ruthie planned to get back in bed and sleep away the Saturday morning, not worry once about homework or any other school bullshit, but she knew instead she'd spend it tossing and turning, prodding the silver stud in her lip with her tongue, waiting for Badger, and worrying over what she should do.

The first time she'd thought of sex, outside the framework of June and Reed Breed, was in seventh grade when a boy named Meadowlark Thompson said he was going to rape her. He was a fat, aggressive bully, two years younger, whom she'd taken to torturing at recess. She'd twist his arm, rub his face against the side of the slide, or chase him, as she'd been doing that day, until he wept from exhaustion and embarrassment. She socked him in the stomach and left him doubled over, but his words remained in her mind. A vague unease, the same one she felt every time she saw Len Law, suddenly became clear. Terry French was the only one of her father's friends he trusted enough to leave alone with her. None of the others, even those like Raymond Pompey who had daughters themselves. When Rutherford went to the Sawmill Bar at night, Ruthie was her own babysitter. He told her to use her .22 if any man besides him came to the door.

Ruthie felt drawn to violence. Badger had gotten in a fight for her at school the day before with a boy named Levi Jensen. The Jensens were known spotlighters, the lowest form of hunters, who drove dark roads at night, caught game in their headlights, and blasted them without even stepping out of their trucks. No sport, no skill to it, just pure slaughter. You could do it dead drunk or on amphetamines. It brought the veins out on her father's forehead, and he often threatened to lay nail strips across certain back roads to flip their deer-laden trucks coming home. Channeling her father, she'd told Levi that his family was trash, in the hall after school when she knew no teachers were around. He'd called her a cunt in response, and Badger, in his customary place behind her, hit him so hard in the face he fell back into the lockers clutching his eye. He hadn't been able to stand upright and had pulled himself away, fighting back tears. Badger looked scared then, rubbing his fist, and Ruthie had felt fear swell inside her own chest. She'd wanted Levi hurt, but she hadn't predicted the wobbled panic in his visible eye, so similar to the little boy she'd hit with the rock.

Rutherford's bow lay on the couch. His quiver with three arrows leaned by the door. "Why don't you take the Glock, too?" she said. The only method to get close enough to a bull elk to kill it with an arrow was to cover yourself in female piss and bugle like another male. It got them so confused and excited they'd practically trip over you. But lying in the middle of the forest bugling and stinking doesn't just attract elk; every couple years a bowhunter would get mauled by a grizzly. Ruthie preferred for her father to hunt with a gun. Recently, she'd found herself worrying about him in all sorts of ways: his loneliness, his debts, even his beetles. She dabbed the hot grease off the bacon with the paper towel and slid the pieces into a plastic bag.

Rutherford shook his head, buttoning up his shirt and coming into the kitchen. "Glock's too much weight." He had a crazed purity when it came to hunting. He liked to hamstring himself: carrying only three arrows, bringing no compass, and never having a radio or any way to call for help. The chance of getting eaten was part of the thrill. He stuffed the bag of bacon into his jeans pocket as Terry French's truck rumbled into the driveway. Ruthie knew that before they went into the woods they'd smear each other with green and black paint, a ritual startling in its intimacy, leaning in to each other's faces, rubbing long strokes down each other's necks, emerging transcribed and altered. It was in these moments that she understood their friendship: two beings united in the woods. Terry filled with the power of his ancestors and her father by dreams of the animal he wanted to be.

"If they ask me what to do with the bear that ate you, I'll tell them to let it go," she said.

Rutherford grinned by the door. He slung the bow over his shoulder and stooped to pat Moses, who barely lifted his gray head from his bed. "No, you won't," he said. "You'll avenge me. You'll come for my bones."

THE TRAILER HAD FIVE ROOMS. The living room on one end opening into the kitchen, then the bathroom and Ruthie's tiny room along a hallway leading to her father's larger bedroom on the other end. Already six feet tall, Badger didn't seem to fit anywhere. He nearly stepped on Moses, who growled half-heartedly. Badger's scraggly beard and bulging biceps made him look like a parody of both man and boy. He wore new clothes to fit in with his teammates. He didn't say anything about the shoddy furniture or cramped dimensions. Only how lucky she was that her father left her alone. His parents made him leave his door open whenever he had guests. Ruthie sat beside him on the living-room couch. He spread his legs against the coffee table and placed his hands on his knees. He filled the silence with pointless chatter about his coaches and how the whole offense had to run sectionals until they puked. Finally, to shut him up and because she'd noticed that the knuckles on his right hand were swollen from punching Levi, Ruthie leaned toward him. She felt his chest tremble with her fingertips, and poked her tongue against his lips. He made a choking sound and welcomed her with such enthusiasm that for a moment she was afraid he'd try to swallow her. Mercifully, he tasted like the peppermint he must've sucked on the drive over, with only a hint of Skoal underneath.

What are you doing? she asked herself.

Badger's excitement rattled the room. He pressed her back against the couch arm. His body felt much too large, crushing, but also exciting in its size. Warmth rushed through her pinned abdomen. His need was choking, overwhelming. She suddenly felt she couldn't breathe. She pushed him up, slid out from under him, and stepped quickly across the wolfskin rug to the bathroom. She paused to glance back at his bewildered face, then shut the door, turned the fan on, and sat on the toilet. She unzipped her pants but left them on. She looked down at her knees. She took deep breaths. She was on the verge of something, excited and afraid. Badger was still only a few feet away.

The single bulb over the mirror cast a sickly, greenish glow. Ruthie turned to see half her face in the mirror. Her short hair framed her sharp features. Her neck seemed too thin to hold her head. The yellow ring around her pupil had faded to pinpricks in the slate-gray iris, giving her eyes a wolfish ferocity. The red in her hair had darkened to nearly black. She pursed her lips so the new stud glinted. It made her look older than she was, which was why she'd gotten it. She hoped that when she came out, Badger would lift her up and press her against the wall.

Instead, he was sitting exactly where she'd left him, staring at her with dumb, childlike expectation. A little boy trapped in a man's body. "Let's go in there," she said, nodding to her father's room. "It's bigger."

Some of the color left Badger's wide face. "When'd you say he's coming back?"

"Even if they don't fill their tags they'll stop at the Sawmill on the way home, so who knows? Late."

Badger looked at her grimly. He had seventy pounds and six inches on her, but was correct in guessing that Rutherford could put him down. She'd seen her father choke out a wounded buck on the side of Red Sun Road when he didn't want to waste a bullet. She pushed open his thin door, making a note to return the mound of dirty clothes that had wedged it closed. After turning thirty, Rutherford had taken down all the posters except the one from Las Vegas. It was the only city he'd ever visited, and the memory was a source of pride. Ruthie knew only that her mother had been with him. The showgirl looked over his unmade bed with an expression both inviting and blank, as if nearing the end of her shift. The strip glittered behind her with its miraculous starlight. "I'm going there someday," Ruthie said. "My dad went when he graduated high school."

Badger tugged his belt, looking up at the poster. "My dad says that's where you go when you've given up on yourself."

"Well, he's a sheepherder."

Badger was stung. "What's wrong with that?"

"Nothing. He's just not the person to ask about Las Vegas. Ask him about Minnesota. Or Scotland. Someplace with sheep." Badger's parents had homeschooled him to protect him from the immorality of public school.

A skewed Glacier Bank clock—a giveaway for opening an account—was the only other decoration on the walls. An orange sleeping bag was kicked down to the corner of the bed along with a rumple of blue silk sheets. Two yellowed pillows showed signs of regular abuse, throttled over the course of Rutherford's wolf dreams. Different-caliber bullets were scattered across the top of the dresser along with a box of tissues, two small antlers, a rabbit's foot, scratched lotto tickets, and several knives. A samurai sword rested proudly on a stand. Ruthie was suddenly embarrassed—it was the room of a child, not a father—but Badger hadn't noticed. He was frozen in the doorway, staring at the bed. "Come on," she said, sitting on the edge and patting the mattress beside her.

The toes of Badger's boots were planted in the carpet. His thoughts were so plain on his face she could practically hear them.

"Or you can go home. I've got homework I should be doing."

Reluctantly, as though he were being pulled, Badger stepped forward.

Ruthie decided it was going to be a game of pretend. Of each pretending they knew what they were doing. Freshman year had only begun a few months before, but she could tell that most of high school would be made up. The girls she'd known in middle school were pretending to be someone else. The person Badger pretended to be with his teammates was different from the person he was when they were alone. Sometimes she felt like the only one who didn't pretend, which was why other girls called her a bitch and a slut.

Badger sat down next to her and put his hand on her knee. For all his size, she could feel his heart beating like something fragile trapped inside his chest. He was wearing the same belt buckle as the day they met: a cheap flaking horseshoe on a nickel-plated background. He'd won it at the county fair, and was proud of it. The smell of piss and bacon lingered in the air. Ruthie wondered where her father was at that moment. Lying in the underbrush beneath a lightning-struck tree, Terry bugling, while a bear crept down on them from the ridge above.

Taking each of her movements as approval for his own, Badger reached for her belt and they stayed this way for a moment, arms crossed, staring at each other. She wondered if anyone had ever lost their virginity at the exact same moment their father got mauled by a grizzly. Probably not. Rutherford had explained sex to her using a light socket and his electric razor's charger. He'd plugged it in, unplugged it, then plugged it in again, demonstrating how the little red light turned on each time. "See how it fits? See how the light goes on? That's all there is to it." Ruthie wanted to get it over with so she never had to talk to him about it again. She hoped the act would open up a new, adult world, like that of June Breed. She freed Badger's buckle. His eyes widened. She wrapped her arms around his broad shoulders and fell on top of him on the mattress, kicking the sleeping bag off the side of the bed.

His hands were everywhere then. Tugging up her shirt, pushing down her pants, squeezing her ass, her hips, desperately fighting with her bra. She'd expected the clasp to cause trouble, but not for him to literally not be able to undo it. He twisted and yanked and got such a furious, constipated expression that she rose and reached back herself.

When the bra fell down off her arms, he gasped. She couldn't believe her breasts could warrant such a reaction. He cupped his entire hands around them. His lips parted. No sound came out. Ruthie wondered what she was supposed to feel. If it was okay to laugh. Her face got hot. She felt squirmy. She pulled off his shirt. A line of wiry hair ran down his wide chest, through his belly button, to the waistband of his boxers. A smattering of pimples surrounded his nipples. The muscles in his shoulders stood out against the skin. Suddenly she felt like slapping him. She did, lightly. Badger's throat worked. "Ruthie," he managed. She slapped Badger again, harder. His cock strained against her stomach. She reached into his boxers and held it, then smacked him in the face. He sighed and went still.

Ruthie put her hand on his throat and rocked against him, wondering if the bear was coming down through the trees.

AFTERWARD, LYING WITH her head on his chest, feeling his breath slow and the lingering throb within her, Ruthie had visions of the earliest women in the valley, who'd borne children and then fallen into feverish spells. Wandering the woodlands conversing with spirits. Lost in a wilderness too vast to comprehend, grappling with the destruction they'd carried in their wombs. Seeing what the men could not: that the wild land would someday cast them off. She saw Pip on one of her forays, searching for the creature's tracks in the soft mud by Lost Horse Creek. She saw the bright red bear crashing out from the trees and the last wolf alone on the sagebrush hillside. She saw a mythology of un-birth, of rolling back the generations and watching the forests regrow.

Badger's heart beat against her ear like a drum.

WHEN HER FATHER GOT HOME, elkless and drunk but unmauled, Ruthie was in her room on her bed pretending to do math homework. All the numbers looked squiggly and meaningless. Ruthie's mind was a jumble. She didn't know if she should feel proud or ashamed. Whether she was harder or softer than she'd thought. If she was using Badger or falling in love with him. She stayed hidden behind her book. "Get one?" she asked.

Rutherford shook his head. "Near froze our asses off, and Terry forgot to gas up his truck, so Billy had to come roust us out. Dumbass Indians." He went into his room. Ruthie listened to him drop his coat and step around the bed. He put his bow in the closet and stopped. She listened for another sound. Nothing. Her heart quickened. She pictured him bending forward over the mattress. Sniffing. His nose acute after a day of tracking game. Examining his sheets, lifting up one corner of the rumpled sleeping bag. The silence drew on. Ruthie's stomach dropped. The only reason her father ever stayed quiet for long was if he was angry or sad.

She tried to duck farther behind her book when he came back into her room, but it was no use. He leaned over her and narrowed his pale eyes.

"You been in my room?"

Ruthie shook her head.

"What'd I tell you?"

Her cheeks were on fire. She was frozen, her heart pounding.

"I told you one thing." He hacked a wad of phlegm from his throat and held it in his mouth.

Ruthie stared up at him wordlessly. Terrified and embarrassed. He'd never laid a hand on her, but she never knew exactly what he might do.

He leaned forward and spat onto the sheet beside her. A huge green wad, the size of a silver dollar. It quivered there, flecked with black from his chew.

"How do you like it?" he asked. The fluorescent hall light flickered behind him and his shadow reared up the wall, double his size.

Ruthie sat perfectly still beside the misshapen orb, unable to speak. She wanted to throw up. The phlegm trembled with each of her shaking breaths. Her father turned and went out, slamming the door.

Men and fluids. That's all it was. Ruthie wished she could look down past the burning chandelier inside herself—the heat of her anger and desire—to something pure.

11.

That winter, the Happels moved away to a trailer in Hamilton after M. Happel got a job canning for the new organic brewery there. Their land was sold to a developer. Bulldozers razed the shack, cleared away the tires and car parts, and were swallowed up in the first snow. Leaving an empty property that Rutherford stared at through the frost-covered window, as if a dreadful city might suddenly spring forth. Snow fell throughout November, harkening the coldest winter of Ruthie's lifetime.

At the end of November, on her fifteenth birthday, when the nights were already dropping below zero, Rutherford gave her a .30-06. "There's nothing too big for you now," he said.

"What about the space elk?" she asked, trying to cheer him up with memories of their summer nights on the mattress in the yard. "The forty-pointers as big as school buses."

He smiled wanly, cupping his hand around the sputtering candle on her birthday cupcake. "I forgot about those," he said. "The biggest thing I ever shot was a bear on Stonehouse Trail by Rye Creek, when I was your age. He was almost seven hundred pounds. Now it's a five-hundred-dollar-a-night guest ranch, and they won't let me drive through."

In December, Ruthie moved a space heater into her closet room and slept in a sleeping bag in long underwear, socks, and a sweater while the wind rattled the sheet-metal siding and whined through the single-pane windows. Her father snored by the woodstove in the living room with the wolfskin rug draped over his shoulders. He was still passed out when she left for school, beer cans scattered at his feet. She stepped carefully around him onto the creaking porch and eased the door closed behind her.

Pip waited for her in the street. Ice coated the pavement but she still wore short pants and sneakers, her legs paler than the frost. Ruthie walked slowly beside her, dreading class. "What's happening to our valley?" she asked.

"It's filling up," Pip answered.

"Do you remember after the mill closed, how the newspapers said the town would die?"

Pip nodded. "They said everyone would have to move to Seattle or Denver to find a job." She paused. "Instead, everyone who doesn't need a job is moving here. I snuck into one of the mansions they're building up Trophy Road. I lost track when I tried to count the rooms."

"What do you think they put in all of them?"

Pip shrugged. "Books. Antiques. Junk."

"I'd take any house. I don't care how big. Our trailer is freezing."

"My uncle says winters were always like this when he was a kid. The whole river froze. You'd see deer walking across."

Ruthie nodded. "My dad, too. He talks about ice fishing."

They parted ways in front of the cafeteria. From the window of her homeroom, Ruthie saw Pip walking away from the school. She wondered where her friend was going, but Ruthie also liked to be alone.

On afternoons when her father was at work—laying Sheetrock or plowing mountain roads—and Badger was at practice, Ruthie would put on country music, turn up the electric heater, and make quesadillas in the frying pan. That evening, she found only a single tortilla next to the case of Busch Light in the fridge. Rutherford wasn't buying more groceries to accommodate all she was eating. She put on Wiley King and drank two of Rutherford's beers in retaliation, then shot a packet of hot sauce and defrosted one of the plastic-wrapped cuts of venison from the freezer. She cooked it sizzling in oil. She sang along while she waited. She secretly loved Wiley King's music, and knew most of his songs by heart. A small, sharp rebellion. She danced, too, kicking out her legs and spinning, making an S pattern out of the kitchen and around the coffee table in the living room, her toes curling on the wolfskin rug. Moses watched in confusion from his bed, occasionally mustering a *yap*, unsure whether to be excited or afraid.

"What?" she said, leaning down, holding his cheeks, and touching her nose to his. His small body was so frail she could feel the bones, but still his eyes sparkled and he licked her cheek.

She arranged her closet room so everything she owned was within reach at all times. Rutherford complained about her crap being everywhere, but she didn't like drawers. She liked to see her things. Her stereo CD player with the four-disc changer—her most prized possession, which Terry had given her from his pawnshop—sat by her twin bed. Her small armoire was crammed beside it, holding what little jewelry she had: a single cubic zirconium earring her mother had

left, a bear-claw pendant her father had made, and the small mala-
chite cross she'd saved up to buy after the earthquake and worn every
Sunday until she was eleven. Lip studs of different colors. Boxes of
bullets were stacked by the door where her new rifle leaned. She prac-
ticed every day, calibrating the scope through wind and snow, and
even in whiteout conditions it was not unusual for her repeated shots
to be invisible as they punched through the bull's-eye. She'd stopped
shooting competitively. Her only goal now was to be better than her
father.

After practicing, Ruthie would flop onto her bed, below the pictures of animals she'd cut from magazines, and her mind would leave
the trailer and travel along game trails over the Bitterroot Mountains
to Angel's Landing, where the rich lived in their castles around a
man-made lake. Where jacuzzi tubs were the size of her room. Where
her cook would make her anything she wanted. Where Moses, eternally young, held dominion between a queen's guard of two huge
Doberman pinschers. Other days, she visualized herself on the shore
of a remote glacier-cut lake with a wolf at her side, their reflections
mirrored in the glass-still water.

When she heard her father's truck in the drive, she closed her eyes
and pretended to be asleep, so she could stay in her imagination a
little longer. But she was always distracted by the sound of him sighing as he dropped his keys onto the table, shuffled over the linoleum,
took a beer from the fridge, and popped the tab with its familiar,
fizzing *snap*.

Loneliness lined his face. None of the women he'd been with
since Ruthie's mother had lasted. Only one, a stenographer from
Lolo with a pink streak in her hair, had taken the time to remember
Ruthie's name. The heads in his reserve freezer dwindled as winter
went on, and the beetle colony kept multiplying. Several hundred
thousand now, their post-quake shortage long forgotten. Most of
the valley's new residents sent their game to one of the fancy taxi-

dermists in Lolo. Rutherford mused about taking out an insurance policy on the colony and setting fire to the shed. Sometimes, when Ruthie came home late at night, she'd find him passed out on the couch clutching a pillow so tightly that the ligaments in his neck stood out, his lips working. Beer cans littering the carpet below him. His breath like a motor breaking down. She covered him with a blanket then, and, if her mood was right, laid her cool hand on his forehead and held it there until the tension and heat began to dissipate and he softened beneath her, his slack jaw falling open and the years falling away, until he looked no older than the boys she saw every day in school.

On his thirty-fifth birthday, just after the first thaw, Rutherford and Terry drove into the yard with a topper camper loaded onto the back of Terry's truck. Arguing the entire time, they mounted it on poles driven into stumps on a flattened spot at the wood line, past the burn pile and the dump truck, near Ruthie's old blind. It looked like a demented watchtower there, with the short ladder up to the door.

"Guest room," Terry said, shrugging as he passed Ruthie in the yard.

Inside was a loft bed, a stove, a small wood cabinet, and a padded bench. Nothing else. The side window looked out on Happel's former land. Rutherford kept it empty save for a shotgun, radio, and whatever hunting magazine he was reading at the time. He wanted it as clean as Ruthie was messy. It became his sanctuary, and he retreated into it whenever Badger came over, or he and Ruthie fought, or if he wanted to be alone. As the nights warmed, he took to sleeping in the loft bed. Carrying Moses out in the evenings and setting him atop the ladder, then climbing in after him. He said he liked the feeling of being in the woods, but Ruthie knew he was slightly afraid of her now that she was becoming a woman. His eyes avoided the changes in her body. He pretended not to see the tampons she put in their cart in the Super 1. They never spoke of what had happened in his bed, and he avoided Badger, always finding reasons to disappear when he came over.

This made her sad. Though she wanted the space, too.

The war against Wiley King had long ago been lost. A slew of lawsuits and electrified fences had left her father with nothing to do but mutter darkly about someday reclaiming his pond. Kent Willis's obsessions had shifted to the Rocky Mountain Labs, where rumors of experimental testing on live subjects had peaked with the story of Ebola-infected rabbits escaping and being eaten by mountain lions. These lions now supposedly roamed the foothills, crazed with disease. Willis reveled in it. He'd come over to the Fears', plant himself on the couch, and deliver a long lecture about what it meant to live near a biosafety level four lab, and the U.S. government's long history of testing chemical weapons on its own citizens. Ruthie could tell this held little interest for her father, who believed the federal government was evil but only in a massive way beyond his purview, like hurricanes or genocide. He nodded absently while Willis rambled, looking out the window at his topper in the trees.

He'd reached an aimless place in his mid-thirties. Ruthie saw it in the deflated, stoop-shouldered way he walked across the yard, a solitary figure on the dry grass, skirting patches of melting snow. He'd shot the last wolf, he'd had a daughter, otherwise this was all he'd ever be. She wished for him to have an enemy again. For that fire to give purpose to his life, even if it put him in danger.

"What about the condos they're building on the West Fork?" she asked. "That's near where you and Terry hunt, isn't it?"

He looked at her over his beer and nodded wearily. "It's all going. By the time you're my age, the whole valley will be a shopping mall."

The thought disturbed Ruthie. Missoula had already grown to fill its valley to the north, and was spilling over the hills into Lolo, with new box stores, strip malls, and developments. "Then I'll burn it down," she said.

"I hope you do." He sighed and clicked on the TV. "But they'll just arrest you and build it again."

MOSES DIED at the end of March, after arthritis made him unable to walk. Rutherford and Ruthie buried him in the woods between Ruthie's blind and the new topper. It only took a few shovelfuls each to make a hole big enough. He'd shrunk down to almost nothing at the end. But his eyes still looked to Ruthie the way they had when she was a girl, and they'd still lit up whenever she or her father walked in the door. Neither wanted to be the first to shovel dirt back over him. He'd been a part of the entirety of what Ruthie could remember of her life. They stood together in silence. Rutherford's eyes were wet. It was the first time Ruthie had seen him cry. She put her arms around him. He leaned against her and the tension left his body, as it did when she laid her hand on his forehead at night.

"Shit," he said.

After dark, when they'd smoothed the dirt over Moses's grave and made a cross of rocks, they sat side by side on the yellowed mattress. Rutherford wondered aloud if his old escaped beetles would find Moses under the ground. Ruthie looked up at the stars and imagined his little body twisting away through the black of space.

12.

In the following weeks, stirred up by Kent Willis and others, citizens of the Bitterroot Valley became so concerned over animal testing and the perceived lack of containment at the Rocky Mountain Labs that they organized a protest. Rutherford reluctantly agreed to attend with Ruthie. Moses's death had pushed him into a deep depression. Days passed when he hardly left the couch, watching TV with the volume so low she could barely hear it. His only sustenance Busch Light, cheese singles, and the occasional elk sausage. Work had begun in earnest on Happel's former land next door; the engines of earth movers rattled the trailer windows. Ruthie wanted Rutherford to get angry again.

The protest took place on a windy Saturday in late April, outside the labs' high spiked fence in Hamilton. A day when the layered clouds above the Sapphire Mountains contained the entire spectrum of gray, with the dark innermost threatening an evening thunderstorm. Looking up through the window of her father's truck as they drove north from Darby, Ruthie saw crows cutting across the sky. She felt a sense of portent, of forces gathering. Perhaps the Ebola-ridden lion queen herself would come down to reclaim her throne.

"Has anyone ever died on Trapper Peak?" she asked, looking up at its hooked finger.

Her father grunted at a bright yellow SUV in the oncoming lane. "I hope so."

Opposition to the labs was one of the few issues that united the valley's residents. The millionaires with mansions on Charles Schwab's Stock Farm Club didn't like it any more than Kent Willis and his neighbors in Whispering Pines Trailer Park. Nor did the hippies who'd opened a health food store in Stevensville and lived in increasing numbers in sustainable homes built of hay bales and corrugated steel along the East Side Highway. The polygamist Mormons in Pinesdale saw it as an unholy place—and bringer of unwanted federal attention—where man tinkered in the dominion of God. While for the Salish the labs were another blight on stolen land.

Ruthie had learned about the labs in science class. How their founding was the first act of the Montana Board of Health in 1910, to fight the spread of spotted fever that at that time killed four out of five settlers it infected. The initial cases of the disease had appeared on the west side of the Bitterroot River soon after Chief Charlo was driven from the valley. With each new death, the settlers' hatred of Charlo grew, as did the legend of his curse. Vigilante mobs attacked the few remaining bands of Salish at the foot of the mountains.

After successfully determining that the fever came from ticks and containing its spread, the labs' scope broadened. The biosafety level four facility, one of six in the United States, opened during the Cold War. It enabled the study of maximum-containment pathogens like smallpox, Marburg virus, and Ebola. Pathogens Kent Willis believed weren't merely being contained, but weaponized.

Ruthie was surprised by the size of the crowd in the parking lot beside the gate. Sheriff Kima looked surprised, too, leaning back against his cruiser with his hand on the butt of his gun. Usually the desire for privacy outweighed any civic unity in the valley. At least fifty protesters were huddled together in clumps against the wind, with their signs flapping and twisting above them. It was easy to tell liberals from rednecks by who was carrying a gun. Willis held his great-grandfather's musket at slope arms and had a SIG Sauer P320 at his waist. Terry French had an AK-47 strapped to his back and was being given a wide berth by white people nervous to see an Indian with so much firepower. Raymond Pompey's jacket was open to reveal his twin shoulder holsters and Three Percenter T-shirt. There also seemed to be some confusion between the two factions over what was being protested. The liberals carried signs about animal cruelty and stopping animal testing, with pictures of monkeys in cages and terrible scenes of operations, while the signs of the armed men were solely concerned with the dangers escaped carriers presented to humans and livestock. I SHOOT SICK CATS ON SIGHT read Willis's, with a crudely drawn, deranged-looking mountain lion in a gunsight. He struggled to keep the banner aloft in the wind with one hand while holding the heavy musket in the other.

Father Mike stood to the side in his vestments with a sign quoting Isaiah, FOR BEHOLD, THE LORD WILL COME IN FIRE. He had the same overexcited look in his eye that Ruthie had seen at the football game. Lines were etched deeply into his forehead and the hair at his temples was going gray. Rumors circulated through town— he'd become addicted to pills, he'd lost faith—as his sermons became increasingly apocalyptic. Ruthie wondered where his wife was. She wanted to tell him to go home to Boise. The valley seemed to be cracking him.

Rutherford hopped down from his truck, circled the bed, and leaned in to carefully remove the Banshee from its black leather case. A short-barreled rifle at .300 Blackout caliber with a Cerakote finish and radial delayed blowback, it looked like it belonged in a video game. He relished any opportunity to show it off. He held the barrel gently in his fingers, as if he were afraid to jar the pollen and spoil the bloom. It weighed only four pounds. Ruthie remembered lifting it alone in his room when she was a little girl.

The wind whipped her eyes. She turned away from her father. She always avoided him when he came in from shooting the Banshee, so postcoital was his expression. He'd told her to bring her .30-06 as well, but she'd been too embarrassed, not wanting to look like some crazed militia girl to anyone she might see from school. "You can't be ashamed of your gun," her father had said.

"I can do whatever the fuck I want," she'd answered. Which left him shrugging and secretly proud.

Security guards in tactical assault gear stood on either side of the entry gate, corralling the protesters in the parking lot. From time to time, a car exited the labs. While the driver hunched low over the steering wheel, the guards made a wall to let the vehicle pass, clamping their shoulders together and squaring the toes of their polished black boots. They looked nervous beneath their visors, unused to having their weaponry so openly matched. Ruthie wondered if the protest could turn into a firefight. Any stupid misunderstanding might start either side shooting. The animal rights protesters seemed to have the same idea, and were huddled in the far northwest corner of the lot, out of any lines of fire. Kent and Terry came over to meet her father, and Ruthie edged away through the crowd, smelling a peculiar blend of chewing tobacco and natural deodorant, until she was directly against the tall, black, spike-tipped iron fence.

She wanted to see the labs up close. She and her father had driven by dozens of times—it was only a few blocks from the lumberyard—

and she'd viewed it in the distance from the hills around Wiley King's ranch, but she'd never actually stopped to look around.

It was huge, faceless, bureaucratic, and disappointing. The complex seemed to have been designed to avoid any suggestion of menace. An American flag flew atop a flagpole. The new buildings were light gray, light yellow, and beige. In back were the old brick originals from the spotted fever days. Four stories tall and neatly kept with white trim and manicured lawns, they reminded Ruthie of the university buildings in Missoula. When the first townspeople learned scientists would be studying the infected ticks inside, they'd sued to have the labs closed. The judge threw out the lawsuit, but ordered a moat be built around it to protect the town, since ticks can't swim. Ruthie didn't see any moat. Maybe it had been filled in, or maybe history was more boring than people claimed. The labs had expanded when she was little, as its charter and funding grew, and she remembered huge semi trucks hauling in steel beams for the intricately vented and whirring warehouse. The newest addition was a glass L-shaped office suite folded around the back. All the windows were tinted. There was no sign of movement nor activity, save for a thin trickle of steam escaping from one of the vents. It was strangely silent and gave the protesters the feeling of performing solely for the security guards, who knew as little about what went on inside as they did.

Ruthie tried to imagine evil scientists torturing helpless rabbits with the deadliest diseases in history. Or worse, running experiments on drifters and Indians, placidly documenting their suffering, then dumping their bodies into a steam-vented incinerator or flushing them out into the river. But she felt her anger withering. Protesting the labs was like screaming at an office park. It was like banging the handle of a toilet. Here was another hateful aspect of the modern world she discovered: it was designed to make terrible things seem normal.

"I bet I could take out the head guy."

Ruthie turned, startled. She hadn't expected to see Badger. His parents were too reclusive for such events. He wore camo cargo pants, his horseshoe belt buckle, and a tucked-in American flag T-shirt tight across his wide chest. His brown eyes stared down at her from below his mussed brown hair. His forehead was growing above his temples. She realized he was already balding at fifteen. He held an antique Weatherby shotgun with a stag's head carved into the stock, and pointed the barrel up toward the top office window.

"Not with that," Ruthie answered. She calculated the distance and decided that—as long as she knew which window was his—with her rifle she could. Targeted shots along a low centerline would at least wound him.

"He's Dutch, the head scientist. Like from Holland. My dad saw him in the Super 1." Badger joggled the shotgun around in a way that, if it was loaded, was very dangerous. "Said he looked like a Nazi."

Ruthie hadn't known about the labs' director. Now that she did, she didn't care. Badger's dad thought everyone who wasn't from Idaho, Montana, Wyoming, or Utah was depraved. "What're you doing here?" she asked.

"My uncle," he said, nodding toward a tall man in a hunter's-orange baseball cap. "He thinks it's contaminating the groundwater on his farm. But this mountain lion stuff is crap. Even if they are infected, once one bites you, you won't live long enough to worry about getting sick. Remember that Cub Scout who got eaten a couple years ago? My coach was part of the rescue team. He said they found pieces of him up in the trees."

Ruthie kept her eye on the gun barrel. Badger was getting more strident by the week. He'd been named All-State for football, the first freshman to receive the honor in nearly a decade, and now a crowd of sycophant boys and cheerleader girls followed him through the halls. She imagined the lion in a frenzy over the Cub Scout, tearing and shaking the way Moses used to when he got a new chew toy. She'd only seen a lion once, deep in the wilderness past Twin Lakes, and even then it was barely a shadow. They were as elusive as they were powerful. The only animal her father was afraid to hunt with a bow. "You should be careful with that," Ruthie said.

"It's not loaded." Badger stuck the shotgun barrel under his chin and grinned. Ruthie imagined his oblong head exploding like a firework. She smiled back and his grin widened. The crowd jostled toward the fence as a car pulled out from the labs, and he was pushed into her. Smelling his spice cologne, their hands touching, she felt a familiar jolt of yearning: wanting him, being repulsed by him . . . was this what love was? He leaned close to whisper in her ear, "Maybe I'll come over later."

ON THE DRIVE HOME, Ruthie's mind wandered as her father bragged about the show of force they'd put on, how the government eggheads had stayed locked in their offices, and how they'd think twice before being so careless with their experiments next time. It made her happy to see him excited—his eyebrows bunched under the brim of his baseball cap, gesturing with his fist over the steering wheel—even though she knew the labs would continue tomorrow exactly as they had today. She wondered if he even believed what he was saying, or if men came to believe things by repeating them loudly, over and over.

The clouds were still massing above the mountains. Treetops swayed along the road. The trunks blurred together, seeming close enough to touch. Long evening light reached over the Bitterroots. It contracted the distances, throwing shadows from trees to cars. Ruthie felt like she could stretch out from the passenger window and run her hand through the alfalfa fields. She wanted to walk into the approaching storm and emerge anew. She imagined the Ebola lions running free through the valley while all the hunters were away protesting them. Their huge, muscled bodies leaping from mountainside to tree to roof, ecstatic with disease, devouring every chained dog, every loose cat, every caged bird, every baby from its crib, and the walker-bound crones in the nursing home. Upending trash cans and tearing down clotheslines, their jaws red with blood and their eyes yellow with ancient, crazed fire.

Yes yes yes.

She squinted up at the mountains, hoping to see a long thread of them padding home. Exhausted and full.

13.

Sheriff Don Kima pulled into the Fears' driveway in early July. The air was hot and stuffy inside the trailer. Badger was away at Bible camp and Ruthie had planned to watch TV all morning, target-shoot for a couple hours, then find Pip and drink with her in the woods. Her father only had time to grab his pistol as the cruiser's door slammed. "What'd you do?" Ruthie said, jumping off the couch in the cotton shorts and T-shirt she'd slept in.

"Nothing." His voice was tight. His eyes flashed around the trailer for anything that might be illegal.

"Please," she said, watching the sheriff make his slow way up the walk. "It's Don. Put the gun down."

He gritted his teeth and set it on the table by the door. "Wait outside."

"Don't start shooting in there," Sheriff Kima called. "I don't want any trouble."

Ruthie opened the door and stepped down from the cement porch into the heat of the day. The sheriff approached slowly. A tall, lanky, graying man in a wide Stetson, he had a deep hatred of drunk drivers, having lost his oldest daughter to one on the East Side Highway. Ever since, a permanent exhaustion had brought the bones out against his skin. Ruthie wanted to despise him, but his flinty dignity reminded her of western movies.

"What's his mood like in there?" he asked.

Ruthie stopped, looking into his tired eyes. "I wouldn't do anything sudden."

"Maybe you can help him understand: it'll be a lot worse if someone other than me has to come out here."

"You going to put him in jail again?"

A hawk drifted overhead. The sky was blue and clear. The sheriff wiped his hand on the front of his uniform and sighed. "I don't plan to, but it'll be up to him." He paused. "I know things aren't easy here." He held her gaze, then continued to the trailer steps. He stopped in front of the door, touched his hat, shook his head, then rapped his knuckles against the edge of the screen.

Trying to push down her fear, Ruthie went on around the trailer. As soon as she was out of sight, she broke into a run. She crossed the yard. Rocks jabbed her bare feet. She stopped, panting, in front of her father's shed. It was unlocked. The rotten beetle smell inside was as strong as ever. She looked at the bins, the little armored bodies of the adults and the wormlike, squirming larvae. She remembered watching her father put a fresh head inside, and started to panic. Was the sheriff going to take him away? What had Rutherford done? She didn't know where she'd go if her father was arrested. She couldn't stay with Terry forever. Moving quickly, she unlocked the gun safe. The heavy door swung open. Shotguns, rifles, semiautos, and fully automatics were clipped in place along the back wall. A dozen handguns were arranged neatly in front of them. It was the most organized part of her father's life. She reached in and took down the Mossberg 500—a tactical, pump-action shotgun. Her father had taught her that its short barrel and high velocity made it the most effective weapon at close range. "The best way to clear a room," he'd said.

Ruthie felt cold sweat on her neck. *It's just for protection*, she told herself. She wasn't going to shoot the sheriff. Just do what her father had taught her. She dropped an extra handful of cartridges into her shorts' pocket and ran back across the yard. The rusting dump truck and yellowed mattress looked like relics of another existence in the bright sun. A single cloud rested over Trapper Peak. A magpie flew off a fence post and landed on the gold payloader that sat dormant above one of the fresh-dug foundations on Happel's former land next door. Ruthie didn't see how her life could change on a day so calm.

A pair of cinder blocks were stacked against the trailer wall beneath the open kitchen window for a situation such as this. Her father had shown her all the best defensive positions on the property, and how to deal with intruders inside the trailer. She climbed onto the rough concrete blocks, hunched below the windowsill, and listened. The voices in the living room were clear. "I don't know what you're talking about," Rutherford said. "I ain't set foot there since Happel left."

"You haven't wondered why the work stopped all of a sudden?" Sheriff Kima said.

"Work stops all the time. When you stop getting paid. Ask anyone from the mill."

"It also stops when someone cuts the fuel lines in all the equipment. Salts the gas tanks. Rips out the starters. Slashes up the tires so bad they can't even tow them out. Six figures' worth of damage, they tell me."

"I don't know nothing about that."

Ruthie gripped the gun. She leaned against the sheet-metal siding and held her breath.

"That's criminal mischief. Four years minimum, and with your record, they won't send you to the county lockup in Hamilton like last time. You'll go to State, Deer Lodge. With the real criminals. What would happen to Ruthie if you got sent there?"

Rutherford's voice rose. "I told you I don't know a goddamn thing about it. You come into my home and threaten me? Threaten my daughter?"

"Dammit Rutherford, I've known you your whole life. I'm not threatening you. I'm telling you not to be a goddamn dumbass fool. This is right next door. Who else would have a reason to stop a development like that? Nobody gives a shit. I know you see this property and all the woods around it and most everything else in this valley as yours, but it's not. And when these big-money people come in, they don't take kindly to their investments getting fucked with. They'll call the state police and I don't know who else if it keeps up. There won't be anything I can do."

Rutherford was silent. Ruthie could feel the gears grinding in his head. When his voice came, it had the hysterical, cornered tone that she remembered from his arguments with the game warden when she was little. "What about Reed? Go bother him. Or another developer. They pull this shit all the time, for the insurance."

"Look, I came here as a friend," Kima said. "To try and help you. I'm taking no notice of the gun you've got pointed toward me there on the table, and whatever else you've got squirreled away on this property. But when the state police come, they'll blow your door down. Take you out flat and impound everything you own. I've seen it before."

Silence. Then movement as the sheriff stepped back outside. "Be smart. Do it for your daughter. If anything else happens next door, they're coming."

Rutherford didn't reply.

Ruthie waited, clutching the shotgun to her chest, until she heard the cruiser pull away. Then she exhaled in a shaking whoosh and slid down the siding to her knees.

"THEY DON'T HAVE ANY PROOF. They would've taken him in if they did," Pip said. She was standing at the edge of the clearing off Lost Horse Creek where she'd found the fertility icon years before. It was a place she and Ruthie often came to drink and be alone. Ruthie couldn't stand still. She paced beneath the ponderosas. Angrily, she rubbed the tears off her cheeks. Was this her fault? She'd wanted Rutherford to have an enemy again, but she hadn't thought he'd do something like this.

"The sheriff was just there to threaten him," Pip went on. "Probably the developer knows the governor, or gives a bunch of money to politicians. That's how it works with these big projects. My uncle talks about it all the time."

Ruthie pushed her hair—which she'd begun to grow out—back from her forehead. Her skin was damp with sweat. She'd run all the way from her yard. The sound of the creek mixed with the gnats whining around her ears. "I wanted him to quit moping around the trailer like he'd been doing since Moses died," she said. "I didn't think he'd go next door."

Pip glanced around at the trees. "Keep your voice down. As far as you know, he didn't do a damn thing."

"Six figures. You know how much money that is? That's enough to buy a house. That's more than everything we own. What am I going to do if they put him in jail?"

"They're not going to," Pip said. She came and stood before Ruthie. She put her hands on Ruthie's shoulders, then pulled her close and wrapped her arms around her. She spoke into Ruthie's hair.

Ruthie softened against her, smelling Pip's unusual mossy, treelike smell. "It's going to be okay. You could go into the woods if you had to. I think you could survive out there for years."

"For years?" Ruthie laughed.

Pip nodded seriously. "I'd help. I think about it all the time. First, you head up into the high country along the Idaho border, stay away from lakes, keep to the woods, don't light a fire. Move every couple nights. If you timed it right and had a shelter dug out by the first snow, you could make it. The Selway-Bitterroot is more than a million acres. They'd never find you."

"You sound like my dad."

"Well, maybe he's not all the way stupid," Pip said.

"Mostly he is."

RUTHERFORD WAS SITTING in a lawn chair behind the trailer with a beer on his knee when Ruthie returned. It was after dark and he'd built a fire. He was watching the sparks whirl up to the sky. His lips were pursed and she could see blood around his nails where he'd been chewing them. Ruthie fetched another chair and sat beside him. They were silent for a time. Then Rutherford looked up at her. "That son of a bitch." His pale eyes gleamed.

"He was trying to warn you," Ruthie said.

Rutherford shook his head. "He wasn't warning me, he was threatening me. Cops don't help people like us. Remember that. They're here to keep the rich people rich and the money in the banks—that's all they've ever done."

"Dad, it's not worth it. A few more fucking condos."

The moon lay fat and low over the mountains. Its brilliance obscured the stars, but the wing lights of planes shone white as they passed below. Traveling from city to city, light to light. Ruthie had never been on a plane and she wished briefly that she were among them, on a padded seat, sipping wine, instead of down here, broke and in danger. Rutherford rubbed the back of his hand across his eyes. Smoke wafted over his shoulder. He hunched forward and rested his elbows on his knees. "They keep taking things from me. My pond, my woods, my view. It's like they won't stop until there's nothing left."

"Dad," she said again. *I'm still here.*

His knuckles were white. He looked up at her, a small man with his back eternally against the wall. Part of the great body of men in the West. "I know," he said. "But it has to stop somewhere."

A FLATBED TRUCK arrived on Happel's property the next day. The damaged payloader and other equipment were loaded onto it and taken away. New machines replaced them, and by the end of August six foundations—rebar jutting from fresh-poured cement—had appeared at the foot of the mountain, only a stone's throw from the mouth of No-Medicine Canyon, and adjacent to the range where Ruthie shot every afternoon. Rutherford's face darkened when he walked by them. Ruthie wondered how the fancy new families would feel watching her shred the targets by their green lawns.

14.

When Terry French's brother Billy got foreclosed off land his family had used for four hundred years, he put out the word that anyone could hunt there. It was known elk country, fields the animals grazed every fall on their way down from the high country, and on the first day of open season trucks packed the shoulder, some squeezed in frontwise and leaning halfway into the gully by the road. A traffic jam off the West Fork, probably the first in history. Badger had to park a quarter mile away in front of Terry's place. Ruthie looked back at all the trucks.

"You sure about this?" Badger asked.

Her father had warned her not to come. "Bunch of jerkoffs with machine guns," he'd said. Terry had gone to visit Delilah in Arlee to avoid the melee, disappointed in his brother. Terry and Rutherford's idea of elk hunting involved covering yourself in elk piss, bushwhacking for miles before dawn, lying in wait all day risking your life, then just before dark shooting some massive bull with an arrow, chasing it until it died, butchering it in the dirt, and loading your pack so full of meat it was too heavy to lift. You had to lie down to put it on, then roll over onto all fours and pull yourself up against a tree, before hiking miles out in the dark. Ruthie had gone with them once and sworn never to again. Now Rutherford complained about having to share his meat.

Ruthie nodded and hopped down from the truck. Badger's baggy camo pants clashed with his red varsity jacket so jarringly that for a moment she wanted to shoot him. She still vacillated between affection and disgust, sometimes feeling overpowered by both. He claimed they were in love. They walked silently along the road in the frigid morning. The sun was rising over the Sapphires and Badger kept looking at it and squinting like he had something to say.

Lawn chairs were set up between the trucks, and the hunters had brought not only hunting rifles but military-grade AKs, bump-stocked AR-15s, and modified Desert Eagle sidearms. They were passing them back and forth, clicking the bolts, feeling the weight, and peering down into the barrels like they could detect the most microscopic miscalibrations. Ruthie had the .30-06 her father had given her. She'd used it to kill antelope and deer on her own but never something as big as an elk. She wanted to prove to him that she could.

Most of the hunters were strangers, weekenders in from Missoula and Salmon. Meadowlark Thompson and his father were the only two she recognized, sitting behind a camo pop-up blind in the back of their truck. The blind was completely unnecessary, ridiculous even, flanked by a half dozen other trucks on both sides, but they looked smug and content in its shade, drinking beers from an open cooler.

Meadowlark glared down at Ruthie as she passed. He was still fat but much taller now, with the same dull, mean cloddishness he'd always had. When Badger looked up, Meadowlark quickly looked away.

"What's that about?" Badger asked.

"Nothing," Ruthie said. "I knew him in middle school."

They set up in a gap between trucks. Badger laid down his pack and took out a Budweiser tallboy. He popped the tab and drank. Then he tipped the can toward Ruthie. She took it, her fingers going numb around the icy aluminum. The beer tasted metallic and nauseating but she was glad for the warmth that flooded through her. They unslung their guns from their shoulders and unzipped the soft shoulder cases.

Billy's land was on a rise in the foothills of the Sapphires, several hundred feet above the valley floor. A gentle incline stretched out underneath them all the way to Wiley King's electric fence and the distant shapes of the Rocky Mountain Labs on the Bitterroot River. Willow and ash shaded the bank of the West Fork at the far edge of Billy's property. Billy and Terry's father had farmed here but the brothers let it go to seed. Invasive knapweed grew among the old wheat, its thick spiky stems looking Jurassic. A million years from home.

The elk were crowded in the far corner of the field by the woods, slowly grazing their way toward the center. Ruthie counted twenty-six of them. A tacit agreement had been struck by the hunters to wait until they got to open ground, so everyone had a clear shot. Like the game at the fair where you shot down a parade of wooden ducks. Her father had been right: It was a bullshit way to hunt, but Ruthie couldn't turn back. She felt pressed forward by Badger and the other men.

Lacking chairs, she and Badger crossed the gully—their boots crunching through the trickle of half-frozen water at the bottom—and sat on the buckrail fence on the other side. He made a joke about

Indians and fences. A single elk calf had split off from the others and was making its way on gangly legs along the north edge of the forest. *Run*, Ruthie urged it with her mind. She checked the action on her rifle and loaded five rounds into the magazine. The cold metal hurt her fingers as she snapped them in. The crosshairs were sighted at a hundred yards with a slight rise against the grain. She figured the elk were closer to a hundred twenty-five away, but it was a clear, windless day and they were hardly moving. No trick to it. Just sight, breathe, and shoot, as she had ten thousand times on the range behind the trailer. Easy. One of the hunters had even brought a payloader to lift the dead animals into the trucks. Ruthie watched her breath twist up from her mouth. The cold air stung her cheeks. She set the gun across her thighs and swung her legs to keep warm. She felt her body small beneath her bundle of clothes. Was this any better than spotlighting? Ruthie banished the thought.

Early snow dusted the Bitterroot Mountains across the valley. They looked sharp in the clarified morning air, as if she could cut her hand running it across the serrated peaks. She wondered where exactly she'd hide if she had to escape to the high country, like Pip had said. Rock climbers had discovered the huge, split-crack faces in Blodgett Canyon, and their Sprinter vans were just beginning to leave the national forest campground for the season, pasted with NATURE BATS LAST bumper stickers and smelling of sweaty crash pads. Two had been killed in a fall that summer. Her father hoped, futilely, that the danger would keep more from coming. Ruthie knew what the Salish had learned two hundred years before: More always came. Like a new gold rush, adrenaline instead of minerals. She turned and looked at the line of trucks behind her. There was something festive about their arrangement, all nosed together and mis-angled along the road. A holiday feeling, flags flying from the hoods, the gathered hunters drinking and shouting back and forth. She was surprised not to see

Father Mike with a doomsday sign, pretending he was the kind of guy who killed all his own meat.

"Are we going to get shot?" she asked, realizing they were positioned twenty yards in front of the other hunters.

Badger smiled and squeezed her knee. "You're such a girl."

"Because I don't want to get shot?"

He ignored her. "When we play Stevensville next week, I think Conner Reeves is going to come after me. He took Derek out last season. Fractured his pelvis. He and Levi are friends."

Ruthie watched the elk continue their methodical journey out from the trees, heads bent to the grass. She didn't want to think about Levi—the wobbled look in his eye after Badger hit him. The lone bull, an eight-pointer with a shaggy beard and broad, tall haunches, stood imperiously among the females, not deigning to eat, raising his head to the first rays of sun knifing over the mountains. Ruthie lifted her rifle and squinted through the scope for a better look at his face.

"He's not as fast as he was," Badger went on. "But he's bigger. Derek thinks he puts metal plates under his shoulder pads."

In the wavering close-up of the scope, the bull looked back at Ruthie. His black snout and the heavy ridge of his brow formed a pointing arrow with the antlers spread overhead. The brown eyes were impassive, seeking only the warmth of the sun. Her irritation at Badger turned to sadness. She saw the bull dead in the grass, blood leaking from his thick neck. The men crowding around him for pictures, holding up his rack so his slack jaw and this same arrow of his consciousness faced the camera. The payloader rumbling in to scoop up his broken body and dump it into the bed of a truck.

You shouldn't be here, she thought.

But it was too late. Meadowlark started the hunt by blowing mightily into his bugle from behind the blind. Badger hopped down from the fence and lay on his stomach, sighting his rifle. Ruthie followed. She steadied the butt against her shoulder and felt the stock cool on her chin. She slid the bolt forward, pushing one of the rounds from the magazine into the chamber. Her legs stretched behind her. Her body and the rifle were one length, her eyes pointing where it would shoot. The men cheered. Every one of the animals looked up toward the road, and Ruthie understood why her father only hunted alone, or with Terry. There was a communion between hunter and prey, one that held either respect or mockery, and when it turned to mockery, the whole act was poison. She inhaled, trying not to think. Shots split open the morning and a fusillade of bullets shredded the air above her. Death in laughing flight. Badger's breath turned guttural as he squeezed the trigger.

Ruthie had sighted on a cow at the edge of the herd, a vacant-looking mature with no calves. But by the time she fired, in the cacophony of noise, she didn't know if her bullet hit it or someone else's. The cow pitched and staggered, shot through the gut. Keening wails rose from the herd, punctuated by bellows as the animals crashed into one another, trying to escape. Blood sprayed from hide to hide. Calves were trampled in their mothers' panic. Most of the bullets seemed not to have been targeted at all, as if the hunters cared nothing for their tags, or the regulations against killing mothers with calves. The spray ripped the animals apart in repeating waves.

Ruthie lowered the scope from her eye. She couldn't watch. The ground trembled as the herd scattered and collapsed. The calf she'd seen before was tangled in a section of barbed-wire fence, its leg broken. It lowed at its fallen mother. The sound made Ruthie sick. She slotted another round forward. She knew she should end the calf's suffering but she felt all her strength draining away. Her finger was lead over the trigger. She couldn't pull it. She laid the rifle down. She pressed her face into the dirt. She remembered how close she'd felt to animals when she was a little girl, as if she were a part of the natural world. More bullets whined overhead. Badger's breath beside her reminded her of the straining sound he made when his fists were planted in the sheets by her shoulders. She didn't think she could ever sleep with him again. She stared at the micro-world in front of her, the clumps of dirt and pebbles between the blades of grass. Bugs and worms and organisms too small to see wiggling through their kingdoms underneath.

When the shooting finally stopped, Ruthie lay perfectly still. Men shouted. Meadowlark complained loudly about ruined meat. "Better not break my fucking teeth on your townie fucking bullets." Triumph mixed with the rank smell of burnt flesh in the air.

A cloud passed in front of the sun. Its shadow darkened the sky. Slowly, Ruthie looked up.

Most of the elk were dead. Those still alive were down on their knees, dripping blood. Their eyes roamed helplessly. The mothers tried to find their calves, the calves tried to find their mothers. In this desperation, Ruthie saw the whole western movie, all three reels, from fifty million bison roaming the open plains to the first wagon train to the massacre that left the fields empty. The bull had tried to run for the woods. He'd made it farther than any of the others, but was toppled at the tree line, panting. The powerful bellows of his lungs shook his rib cage. Red foam dripped from his mouth. He stared into the trees, willing himself to their protection.

It was the worst thing Ruthie had ever seen, and she was a part of it. She had to close her eyes again. In the rushing darkness of her mind, she hated everyone. Herself most of all.

Badger touched her shoulder. "Come on," he said. "Before somebody gets yours."

15.

The red-and-gold HOMECOMING sign lay trampled and alcohol-reeking amid soda cups and a single translucent jelly sandal. Bright lights shone from inside the gym, where the dance had been. The cinder-block building looked small and tired beneath the mountains. Chaperones shouted into the bathrooms, clearing them out. Ruthie stood pressed against the grille of Dalton Pompey's F-150 in the parking lot. Dalton faced her. His beery lips shone with her lip gloss. He'd been kissing her and rubbing against her thigh, up and down, tirelessly, as if by generating enough friction he might ejaculate and suddenly become a man.

Ruthie tilted her head away from the smell of gin on his breath. She'd felt angry and lost ever since the hunt. It had left her unable to look at Badger without hearing the straining sound of his breath. He'd fractured Meadowlark's eye socket with a single punch after she told him she couldn't see him anymore, just as he'd hit Levi when they first met. Their relationship bookended by violence. Silver-edged clouds drifted over the moon. Police cars waited in the road. Blasts of diesel billowed from trucks. Headlights cut across the darkened lanes, briefly illuminating girls in pastel spaghetti-strap dresses frozen like deer in the sudden light. The diesel made Ruthie's eyes water. She was half drunk. She felt herself drifting up into the stars. Dalton grunted contentedly. She found Orion's belt and the Big Dipper nailed in place in the heavens. She almost laughed, remembering that it had been Dalton who first told her about black holes so many years before, one night when their fathers were drunk. Now she could feel the exact shape of his penis against her thigh.

A group of football players, including Badger, approached, looming over their cheerleader dates. The boys all had red-and-gold Darby Eagles varsity jackets on over their suits. Badger stopped in front of Ruthie and Dalton and spoke in the loud, ass-slapping voice of a huddle. "Courtney tripped over the speaker and when she tried to get up her tit fell out. Her whole tit."

"Even Mr. Holden saw it," Derek said.

The girls giggled. "She was so drunk." Slowly, reluctantly, Dalton withdrew himself and straightened, adjusting his belt to hide his erection. Ruthie smoothed the front of her dress.

"Surprised he didn't go in for a feel."

"It was real, too. I thought for sure she stuffed."

"I knew they were real," Badger said, glaring at Ruthie in the darkness.

"Bullshit," Dalton said. He looked diminished in his father's suit—fraying and a size too small—without one of the letterman's jackets over the top, though as a wrestler and an upperclassman he had one, too.

Badger's eyes flashed. Behind him, a massive rusted eagle guarded the entrance to the football stadium. Its eyes had been spray-painted red. The wings seemed to extend from Badger's shoulders, as if he might rise, infernally screeching, into the night. "Shut up, faggot," he said.

Dalton went white. "What'd you say?"

"I said to shut your mouth about what you don't know about."

Ruthie untucked the gum from beneath her tongue. She knew she should intervene. But she felt not quite herself in the tight, light blue dress. It was the most girlish thing she'd ever worn. Her father had looked away the first time she put it on. She felt lithe, dangerous, like her body could slip free and become part of the moonlight. Like she could walk into the highway and get in the back of the first truck that stopped. Badger had taken Tracy Trimble to the dance to hurt her, and Ruthie had taken Dalton for the same reason, but now she felt the night expanding around her.

"You never hooked up with Courtney," Dalton said.

"I sucked her tits and she blew me." Badger looked at Ruthie again.

"You liar," Dalton said. "Cut Bank is going to take your head off in the playoffs."

"At least I made the team, you fucking JV dropout."

Ruthie remembered the two of them slapping water back and forth in the community pool on Athlete Day the summer before. Practicing wrestling holds. Holding each other's heads against their breasts like oversized, grunting babies. She looked across at the swooping neck of Tracy's pink, coral-patterned dress, the way her breasts pushed eagerly against the glittery fringe.

"I have a job," Dalton said. "I can't play games and fuck sheep all summer like you do."

"I'm going to kill you," Badger said. His teammates laughed nervously.

Dalton shook himself like a bear cub, hustled loose his balls, and fell into a two-point stance. "Bring it, then, cocksucker."

They were both big and broad with creatine shoulders and veins popping from their forearms. Maxing out daily in the weight room, marking the results on the chalkboard, using their bodies like they wanted to burn them out. Ruthie sympathized with this desperate faith in slamming into things. Ever since the elk, she'd been searching for something so hard it wouldn't break when she hit it. As if by hammering away at herself she might finally expose the person she wanted to be. Badger started thrashing out of his suit jacket but Derek caught him by the shoulder. "Not here," he said, jerking his chin at Mr. Holden, standing with his arms crossed in the school's lit doorway, as the Spanish teacher dejectedly gathered up the discarded cups.

"I'll take you anywhere," Dalton said.

How romantic. Ruthie pictured them on the moon, wrestling naked in the lunar light, tossing each other into the air of its lesser gravity.

She smiled. She'd drunk more than she'd realized.

"Can we please just go?" Tracy said, touching Badger's elbow. He shrugged her off.

"Hooper's Landing," he said. "Right now."

"I'll be there." Dalton put his arm around Ruthie. He pivoted and hurried her toward the road. Fight, *fight*, the word crackled across the parking lot like electricity. Already she knew half the school would come. She stumbled to keep up, looking back at Badger, who stared after her in the moonlight with raging eyes and the eagle's wings stretched over his head.

"You can ride with us," Dalton said. He flagged down a lifted Forest Service Jeep full of his fellow wrestlers, blasting heavy metal music so loud the doors vibrated.

"No, I'll follow you." Ruthie scanned the rows for where she'd left her father's truck.

Dalton looked at her doubtfully.

"Then we can go straight back to your place, after you beat his ass." She smiled and blinked and felt the brush of air from the extended length of her eyelashes in mascara.

Dalton's face brightened. He hustled his balls again. "Good idea."

RUTHIE LOST THE JEEP in the scrum of traffic leaving the high school. She knew she should just go home, that her father would sleep better knowing she and his truck were back, but it felt too good to drive in the warm fall night. She'd gotten her license that summer and driving alone still hadn't lost its miraculousness. The smell of fallen leaves made the air papery and clean. The river, at its lowest point, seemed to speak over the rocks. Telling of ancient people who'd camped on its shore and lost beasts that drank from its water. Moths flitted up through the halogen lights over the football stadium. Their dreams sizzled away in the heat of the bulbs. Ruthie turned north onto Highway 93 and drove past the Lake Como turn and the golf course and the road up to Wiley King's mansion. She felt she could go on to Missoula, or farther still, up through the Flathead Reservation to the border. All the way to where roads ended in the Yukon.

Her foot was bare on the gas pedal. The high, pinching heels she'd worn were shed on the passenger seat beside her. She hardly glanced at Hooper's Landing. The wide dirt lot was filling with trucks. White moonlight illuminated the river; the bridge at Woodside Crossing was a distant shadow. She hoped Badger would know she'd gone home alone.

Lucky Lil's Casino and gas station in Corvallis was lit up pink and purple, casting wavering reflections on the hoods of the gun-racked hunters' trucks: in from the mountains to lose what money they'd made in meat. The sky was black and close, and each star held the promise of a world of icy perfection. Walking across the lot—junk-food-packed shelves visible in the brightly lit store, the warm air soft on her shoulders—Ruthie thought the stars might come raining down on her like shards of glass.

The clerk stared at her in her dress and bare feet as the door slid open. Two truckers also turned to stare, and Ruthie felt herself both shrink and enlarge. Prey. To be pinned, twisting, beneath their hairy bodies. But also able to wreck them with the lightest touch, the very tip of her finger. Desperate lonely old men. She could dance across their bones. She walked quickly over the linoleum, conscious of her body beneath the light fabric, wondering down which darkened road Badger planned to take Tracy, or if at that moment Dalton was punching his teeth in.

Maybe they'd make each other come. She smiled, glad to be alone.

Six flavors of Slushee filled the clear turning cylinders against the back wall: Blue Raspberry, Sour Apple, Hawaiian Punch . . . none of this world. She stared at the vivid ice and imagined the tropical fantasy country each came from. What sheer bathing suit she'd wear there. How she'd dive like an arrow into the waves. She wanted to escape the valley, and her memory of the elk. She was so engrossed that she didn't notice the masked thief enter the store behind her. Only when he raised the gun from his hooded sweatshirt did something (death) click into place in her mind.

Every nerve within her went electric, every hair raised. She stood perfectly still. She watched in her periphery as he crossed to the counter and shouted at the clerk. His voice was shrill and young, his command an impossible contradiction: "Get the fucking money out of the register and don't fucking move." He waved the gun. It was a Magnum. Big dumb cowboy gun, liable to blow up in his hand. Liable to shoot a yard wide of where he aimed. Reason enough for Ruthie to stay exactly where she was. To sink into the linoleum. To disappear. The clerk was frozen as well, until he sparked into motion, reaching for the cash register, the money.

And the night might have passed that way, a dream of her sixteenth year, were it not for the muzzle flashes that flamed out of the parking lot, followed by the roar of high-precision hunting rifles. Two holes were punched through the plate-glass window and Ruthie threw herself to the floor in time to see the thief spin wildly, scattering folded money as he fell back into a rack of motor oil by the door.

The shots continued in quick succession, *rat-tat-tat*, splitting her ears, splitting open the night, exploding the Slushee cases over her head and sending gouts of ice pouring down around her. A shelf of Coke cans crashed through the glass doors of the cooler. They landed at her feet, hissing like angry snakes. Time slowed to nothing, each neon millisecond endless. Her ears rang. A display of chips careened into the candy aisle before pitching over.

"Had enough in there?" a man shouted from across the lot.

Ruthie was curled up too tightly to answer, her arms protecting her neck and face. But the thief yelled back from some last well of helpless rage, "Fuck you!" and fired two useless rounds through the ceiling.

The whole store seemed to explode. A row of fluorescent lights on the twelve-foot ceiling disintegrated, the tube shards drifting like snow through the dust. Fragments of glass sprayed like grenade shrapnel, shredding whole shelves of canned goods and gum. Ruthie squeezed her eyes shut. She wondered where her mother was. If it was a place where things like this didn't happen. Where you could go into a gas station at night and not get caught in a firefight. The fire alarm began to wail. Who would tell her father if she died?

"Enough?" the voice shouted again.

"Enough!" Ruthie screamed, her voice raking out from her throat, and the clerk, also miraculously alive, echoed, "Enough! Enough!"

Rivers of cold beer rushed from the cooler and a punctured aerosol can wheezed in a slow circle. The alarm howled relentlessly. Blindly, Ruthie began to crawl through the carnage, desperate to escape the store, to get outside where she could breathe, unconscious of the broken glass causing blood to flow from her palms and knees, and the cold Slushee ice covering her arms.

Two hunters darted across the lot outside like infantrymen in a dream of combat, their long rifles held at ready.

They were already standing over the thief when Ruthie came upon him in the doorway. One kicked the Magnum away from his hand. The other nudged his shoulder with a heavy boot. It flopped limply back into place. They gazed around the ruined store in wonder, admiring their handiwork, their scoped rifles at port arms in front of their down vests.

"Got him," one of them said.

Unthinkingly, Ruthie reached out to the thief across her path. He appeared dead in the pool of blood and motor oil, but when she touched his hand his fingers grasped at hers.

"He's alive," she said. His fingers were warm, almost hot.

"Better not touch him," one of the hunters said.

"Time to get you out of here, girl," the other said, reaching down to pick her up.

"No," Ruthie answered. And perhaps it was something in her voice, or the blood running down the hand she raised against him, but both men stepped back. They mumbled to each other about waiting for the paramedics, the excitement turning to fear in their voices. Neither wanting to be responsible for damage to a young girl in a light blue dress.

A crowd formed in the parking lot behind them. The usual assortment of the shocked and curious and relieved. *Not me. Him, but not me.*

Ruthie pushed up the thief's black knit ski mask and a string of bubbly spit looped from his mouth. He was barely older than she was, with a long, acne-pocked face. His skin was mottled bronze and black hair spilled out behind. His brown eyes tried to catch hers but couldn't hold. One of his wounds was sucking air. Ruthie wondered which school he went to, if it was on the reservation, if they'd had a dance that night as well. His shirt was a mess of blood. The bullet must have wobbled after passing through the plate glass, because the exit wound was the size of a beer can below his shoulder. Life was pouring out of him. Ruthie looked up. The hunters stared down at her. Everyone else hung back.

No one was coming to help.

She bent over his face, half remembering the CPR certification she'd had to get before going backcountry hunting. She was afraid to move the boy out of the muck, or press down on his bloodied chest. She took his head in her hands, the closest she'd ever held a stranger. He stared up at her. His eyes finally caught hers. They shone with a hopeless intensity, as if he wanted to tell her everything at once. The story of his life up until that moment. The story of the valley. His lips moved. He struggled for air. A name, perhaps his mother's. Ruthie wiped the bloody spittle from around his mouth. She pinched his nostrils shut. She bent forward and pressed her lips to his.

A shock of energy greeted her so strong that she felt like her whole body was on fire. She pushed air from her lungs into his. Sometimes we can breathe for each other. He shuddered. His fingers clutched hers. Sirens approached in the distance. She tasted his blood on her lips, an intimacy she could hardly bear. She closed her eyes and saw the boy standing on a vast plain beyond the Bitterroots, a plain that stretched to the curve of the earth: lakes, rivers, and the steam plumes of sulfur hot springs. She breathed again. She saw his spirit rising. She saw herself in Angel's Landing, though this time not with her castle or Moses but alone, running down the airstrip, with nothing behind her or ahead save for the unmanned woods.

III

16.

"You're on gravel now, but if you get with God it's blacktop all the way," the old woman said, handing Ruthie a bottle of water from a cardboard pallet, on the hot bus to Las Vegas.

Ruthie rubbed her eyes. She emerged from the blurred half sleep that had carried her out of the Bitterroot Valley and down through Idaho. It was a trip she'd dreamt of her whole life, and then, in the exhaustion from packing and saying goodbye to her father, she slept through the whole thing. Her mouth was parched from the recycled air in the bus and the whiskey they'd drunk the night before. "Thank you," she said.

The old woman smiled. Her dark brown cheeks shone with sweat. Her gold tooth flashed when the sun broke through the clouds. She spoke of the Mayan calendar and its misplaced portents. "The world didn't end this time," she said. "But it will soon."

Happy birthday, Ruthie wanted to answer, drinking deeply of the cool water. *My fellow lonesome rider. May you one day escape the darkness and experience the light.* Lines she'd memorized from her favorite Wiley King song. She was twenty but felt much older. She'd stopped being young the moment the boy died in her arms.

Ruthie raised her eyes to the window, thinking of her child self and expecting to see a winged skeleton flying low over the bus, its shadow stretched out on either side. Or if not the skeleton, then the buckshot Rutherford had fired from his shotgun that day, bursting from the clouds to dent the roof after fifteen years of flight.

But she saw only the early summer sky of Utah, bleached to Technicolor and as wide as a dream. The sky of western movies, with the Wasatch Mountains marching jaggedly south beneath it. They passed silent Mormon towns and then they passed sprawling resort casinos and Ruthie wondered if the devout and the debauched lived close together so they might see their opposite reflections in the mirror, each secretly pining for the other.

Las Vegas appeared at dusk. Its red and gold lights called out from the desert in swirling, garish patterns. Desires etched against the outer dark: a circus tent, a pyramid, a golden tower. On a billboard, a man fed a woman a cherry, dangling the fruit just above her parted lips. Airplanes glided silently to earth. A shaft of white light shot from the pyramid and pierced the sky. Ruthie rested her cheek on the plexiglass. She thought of the thousand paths she could walk, the shapes her life could take. She had $300 in her bag, the most money she'd ever had at one time, saved from a winter of shifts at the Montana Café. Five cellophane-wrapped Bibles leaned against the waters beneath the old woman's seat. The old woman began to pray, her voice rising and falling, speaking for their entire fallen race.

Ruthie didn't believe the world would end. Even if human beings were banished from it, its molten heart would continue to beat for a billion more years until it was re-enveloped by the sun. And even then for a few moments more, as the dying goose's wing had continued to slap the ice. *My fellow lonesome rider.* Cars crowded in below the window. The bus slowed. Anxiety made Ruthie grip the arm of her seat. She'd never been on a road with more than four lanes before. She touched the stud in her lip with her tongue. She wanted to remain in the safety of the bus's artificial womb, breathing the circulating air and drinking water the old woman had brought. See the city through thick glass.

They exited the highway onto a street so jammed with traffic the bus couldn't fully merge. The long cabin remained wedged halfway in the intersection amid a storm of honking. Drunken tourists streamed around both sides, carrying shopping bags, cameras, souvenir cups, and beer bottles held by the neck like small, glinting clubs. One man stopped and pounded the luggage hold with his palm. He looked up at Ruthie and his loose, midwestern face was mottled with rage. He seemed ready to explode. With a wheeze, the bus pulled away and the man stood in the road gaping after it.

"The dark one is in him," the old woman said, craning her head around.

Ruthie wondered if for her Satan had an address in this very city, a bed they'd shared. She thought of Badger's angry, innocent face. The way violence had marked their time together. He'd gotten engaged soon after graduating, to a cheerleader at Stevensville High named Janine, and Ruthie felt herself to be a star freed from the planets that had held it in place.

The buildings were even bigger now that she was among them. They blocked out the sky. She had to tilt her head back to see the tops. Gamblers thronged casinos lit as if by daylight. They stared at the slot machines' flickering screens. Yanked the levers down. Watched the wheels spin. Lost, lost, lost, lost, won. The old woman reached down and touched the Bibles beneath her seat to reassure herself. The five she'd brought hardly seemed enough to compete with the men on street corners snapping escort cards in their own cracking prayer. A thin willowy branch held over the surging river of avarice. *Grab on.* Ruthie knew little of faith, but she expected madness, the crazed and ruthless wheel-turns of fate.

Lacy white scars covered her forearms from the glass on the gas station floor. Usually she hid them to avoid strangers' stares, but now she looked down at the landscape they formed. Ran her fingertip across the memory. She'd learned the boy's name in the paper the next day: Nathan Gardipe. Nineteen years old. His family lived on the Flathead Reservation, near Billy French. She'd gone with Terry and Billy to the memorial service in Arlee, where his three tall, defiant sisters had stood like sentinels around his crying mother.

Ruthie had remained in the back of the crowd, her arms bandaged, feeling like an interloper as the medicine man led the prayers.

The bus pulled to a stop at a wide intersection. Two liquor stores on one side, the Statue of Liberty shrunken to a profane replica on the other. The roller coaster that twisted above its tarnished head was like the path of its own imagination, constrained in the gathering night. Doomed to an endless, shrieking loop. *New York, New York.* Ruthie was amazed by its cheapness and majesty. She felt naked under so many lights, amid so much movement. The old woman ceased her prayers and pulled herself up by the seat back in front of her. She turned to Ruthie. "You remember, now, blacktop all the way."

Ruthie nodded.

The old woman smiled, humped her purse over her shoulder, and took up the waters and the Bibles. "If you see Satan, you spit in his eye."

The smell of sweat, smoke, and a sad, touching hint of strawberry perfume wafted from her skin as she squeezed past. Her wide frame moved down the aisle to the front. Angel of the Greyhound, patron saint of dehydrated travelers.

The doors hissed and clattered open as the old woman hobbled down the steps. Ruthie saw her again only briefly: stepping out from around the hood, then swallowed up in a mass of other bodies as the bus carried on. "Okay," Ruthie whispered to herself. "Here you are."

17.

On her first weekend in the city, Ruthie met a cowboy outside the cantina where she'd gone looking for a job. He drove her in his truck away from the Strip to a dusty rodeo ring on the edge of Henderson. The city's lights were like a mirage behind them. Ruthie was captivated by its size, its noise, the ceaseless churning of its unseen engine. She wore a thin yellow dress she never would've worn at home. She felt like running in it out across the desert, with the dusty wind reaching up to touch her skin. She felt like the dream of herself, as if whatever happened here she'd wake up and have it washed away.

All the cowboy told her about himself were his initials: RW. All she told him, besides her name, was that she came from Montana. They had yet to lie. They stood together in the long line and he took on a distant, enclosed expression below his hat, as if he didn't care if she stayed or went or disintegrated in a puff of smoke. She looked around, wondering how she could've ended up in a place so familiar. It looked just like the ring outside Darby where she'd shot skeet as a girl: ads for saddles and truck parts plastering the clapboard walls, trailers on dusty hillsides beyond, the distant glow of a truck stop. She tried to imagine the cowboy in a more appropriate time: crouched under a rock, a cheroot in his mouth, about to get tomahawked through the skull.

Around them, locals were distinguishable from tourists by the deep-worn dust in the creases of their jeans and the dark varnish on their belt buckles. She thought she glimpsed Kent Willis and his neighbor Danette by the cotton candy machine, and was surprised by the relief that flooded through her, but it was only a heavyset older couple with rhinestone buttons on their shirts. Children strained against their mothers' arms. Rock candy glittered crystalline on paper sticks, and the smell of fried sausages mixed with dust and horse manure and the diesel spitting from generators. The caller's buoyant cry crackled from inside the stadium: "That's August Hooper on 'Shine a Little Light on Me.'"

By the time Ruthie passed the checker, the stadium was full. She and the cowboy found a seat in the upper row and squeezed together beside a fat man with suspenders reefed down the center of his bulging breasts, neatly dividing each in two. He grinned at them from the midst of his crumpled face, revealing tobacco-stained teeth. "Here we go," he said, and turned back to the ring. He hunched forward, gripping a betting ticket and staring at the trodden dirt as if water might spring forth from the dust. Ruthie felt the tension roll off her cowboy in the way his knuckle brushed her thigh, and how his shoulders perked when a man walked by with a tall, sweating can of beer. She admired his simplicity: love of beer and hatred of lines. A slow, determined crawl across the ice, free of the dark, slipping desires that plagued her, and the ghosts that haunted her memory.

A small electrical storm crossed the Red Rock Canyon mountains. Its dark clouds were lit from within by a brimstone light, as if dragons might be waiting in the wings. Ruthie pictured these celestial leviathans diving between tridents of lightning. Impossibility always near, even as she approached twenty-one. She felt her dress sliding up from her knee in the heat. She felt her cowboy watching her. She wondered if they might spend years together without uttering another word. If they might never lie. She brought her eyes back down to the stadium, confused by the limits of weather and time: apocalyptic in one place, perfectly calm and warm here just across the valley, perhaps blizzarding at that very moment in the depths of No-Medicine Canyon, where her creature waited.

Three women on horseback held flags aloft as they galloped in a circuit around the ring. The rodeo clowns stood at ersatz attention in the center, their painted faces thrown back, bloated white-gloved hands over their hearts. The national anthem played tinnily from loudspeakers mounted all around. The cowboy tipped his bare head to hers. He was balding in the doleful shape of a horseshoe. "Might go and find us a beer," he whispered, and the spell was broken. He sounded like every other man.

Ruthie nodded, envying the shortness of his memory. One line braved, on to the next. She remembered how her father had held two beers at once along with the end of her ponytail as she tried to bolt off at the Ravalli County Fair when she was a little girl. He'd looked very small watching the bus pull away from the station in Missoula, amid a crowd of vagrants, junkies, parents, and lovers. She kept her hands palm-down on her legs to hide her scars.

The bull was holstered in the pen below the bleachers. After the cowboy had disappeared into the crowd atop the stadium steps, Ruthie watched its wide black shoulders ripple and bang against the boards. Confounded by the small space, verging with muscle, its hide taut, the entire body a pulsing, raging heart. The head was lowered forward, hooves dancing on the hot dust. The announcer spoke a name and the rider appeared on the rail. A young man, not much older than her. He paused for a moment, then lunged onto the bull's back. A tremor ran through the crowd as he settled himself, shifted the saddle, and gripped the horn with his gloved hand.

The bull stilled, knowing in some deep, half-remembered place that freedom was near. If only it let the rider sit, it'd soon be able to spray its sweat and violence in the wide-stamped ring while the crowd screamed its name. The rider coiled the lead rope around his palm: once, twice, three times, yanking it tight after each pull. Trying to battle and surrender to the bull at once. To become one with it, and tame it through this illusion. His shoulders jutted beneath his checkered shirt; his sharp, sparsely bearded chin poked from the shadow of his hat brim. Ruthie imagined his face to be shifty and cool, reptilian, with eyes that lingered a beat too long. The opposite of the wide blank docility of her cowboy's. She wondered if it was a womanly pleasure the rider found astride the beast, all that power between his thighs. If it manned and unmanned him both in his quivering depths.

He leaned back and nodded to the rodeo clown, then thrust his chest forward over the bull's shoulders.

The crowd went quiet. The rider tugged the lead rope and raised his left arm. He locked his eyes on a spot between the bull's shoulders. The gate banged open. They flooded out. The crowd roared, pure hell unleashed. Hot dusty breath caught in Ruthie's throat. The bull's pent-up fury was of such stomping, bucking proportion that the rider's grip lasted barely a second before he was discharged brutally headlong, and with a dancer's pirouetting grace, as if it had held this, too, in abeyance, the bull lowered its head and caught him on its horn, ramming the dulled point into his gut, then tossing him forward and off and leaping after to bludgeon him with dancing hooves. All before the clowns were off the rail.

His arcing flight and crashing fall astonished Ruthie. It seemed impossible the instant after it had occurred. Like peering through the fabric of what ought to be into the darkness of what is. She thought of her cowboy oblivious in the beer line, his head cocked, one knee skewed, fingering his belt buckle impatiently, longing for each tall, sweating can being carried by, wondering what calamity had sucked the sound from the night.

The bull was corralled but the fallen rider didn't move. The fat man beside Ruthie licked his lips and shook his head. He dropped his betting ticket to the pavement. His grin fell in on itself. "Hope that wasn't your first ride, missy," he said. "They don't all end like that."

Ruthie stood up. She climbed the stairs and was gone from the ring before her cowboy returned.

SHE WALKED OFF into the desert just as she'd imagined: alone with the dusty wind. Her bare feet carried her back toward the lights of the city, in the yellow dress with her boots in her hand. It never grew cold, even in the deepest hours of night. The temperature of the air and the temperature of her body seemed so perfectly aligned that she was no longer sure where her skin ended and the rest of the world began. The ground was dust and flat rocks, an unchanging expanse into which she dug her toes and felt herself sink, the slightest bit, with each step. Neither cacti nor thorns harried her way. Coyotes yipped in the distance and once she heard the hoot of an owl above the faded roar of the freeway.

The city lights before her vanquished all but the brightest stars. The sky pulsed with bluish ribbons, faint traces of atmosphere. Ruthie's thoughts were indistinct, her mind calm. She saw Nathan turning in slow motion as the bullets punched through the window. Badger glowering before the rusted eagle. The bull-rider floating eternally through the air. Suspended in amber before the fall. Every place the warm wind touched her skin awoke. She felt she was inhabiting her body in a new and secret way. She felt June Breed walking beside her, the June Breed of her youth, lips parted, back arched. Ruthie lifted her dress over her head and carried it also, trailing behind her in the dirt.

The Red Rock Canyon mountains stood to the west. Much smaller than the Bitterroots or the Sapphires, but not lacking in majesty for the way they erupted like fists from the flat plate of the desert floor, smashing upward as though through porcelain, and remained there crumbled but unbroken, calling out to the sky. Ruthie felt their power. She imagined the storm all around her, trident lightning and brimstone depths, dragon wings rushing overhead. She walked with her chest out like the prow of a ship. She felt she was meeting her spirit here, in the dry depths of the outer world, a thousand miles from home.

Grief ran through her. Nathan's face filled her mind. It had taken him several minutes to die. In the end, they'd been two helpless children. She stopped. Tears fell down her cheeks. She'd finished high school as though nothing had happened, and now she didn't know where to begin. She knelt in the dust. She placed her hands on the earth. She saw Dawn Gardipe, his mother, leaning against her daughters in the wind. She saw the teal trailer of her childhood and the creature lurching away into the darkness. Felt her father and the elk standing behind her. The city rose from the desert like a burning temple.

18.

The Bacchanal Buffet at Caesars Palace looked out on the Garden
of the Gods pool complex. Ruthie sat alone in a gold-trimmed
booth and watched women in white bikinis dive off the steps of the
Temple of Dionysus. The buffet itself was half the length of a football field. Piles of spare ribs, tri-tip, oysters, char-grilled T-bone,
and chilled crab legs turned to stations of tacos and sushi, dozens of
plates of watermelon salad, and a chocolate fountain drizzling over
lava cake. It was the most food Ruthie had ever seen. Diners shuffled dazedly past with mounded plates. Some were so fat they blocked
Ruthie's view entirely as they leaned forward to lance meat with long
chrome serving forks.

She'd come with her first paycheck from the cantina. Growing up hungry made her determined to try everything. She wanted to feel like Wiley King, or one of the residents of Angel's Landing—rich— but instead she felt overwhelmed. Slightly nauseated, and nervous to leave the booth. Whenever she went out in the city, she saw herself as a less-elegant version of the women streaming around her. Clicking on heels out of taxicabs, laughing and screaming in bachelorette par- ties, on the arms of clean-shaven, suit-wearing men. Even the mothers wielding children up the escalators of luxury hotels seemed more in control, more present in their own lives.

The waiter asked if she wanted all-you-can-drink wine. Ruthie shook her head, thinking of the many times she'd opened her refrig- erator to find it empty save for a case of Busch Light.

She washed her hands in the casino bathroom's marble sink. When she came out, she took one of each entrée, one of every salad, and one of every small plate, and arranged them to fill her entire table. She called the waiter back and told him she did want wine. White, with an ice cube. She'd made nearly $900 in two weeks, tripling her life sav- ings. She took one bite of everything in succession. Then she began to combine them: tri-tip sushi, oyster salad, taco topped with crab. She drank five glasses of chardonnay. She remained in the booth until the staff changed over between lunch and dinner. Then she stumbled out across the casino floor, feeling kinship with the tourists who'd squeezed their gigantic asses into rented mobility scooters and piloted them between slot machines, beeping furiously at anyone who stood in their way.

Outside, traffic blew by in waves, as if escaping some unseen disas- ter. There were no animals in the city. Not even rats. Only the white tigers seventy feet tall pawing across billboards, and the crows that constantly circled overhead, somehow unnoticed by tourists and locals alike. They seemed to be the only ones who understood. Scavengers waiting to feed. Ruthie's stomach hurt. She tried to walk off the discomfort, holding her midsection like she was pregnant. She pulled her hair up from her overheated neck and laughed at herself. The Strip felt endless. A parade of shouting men holding yard-long margaritas and women in crop tops with dangerously long lacquered nails.

At the MGM Grand, Ruthie followed signs to the lion habitat and stood in the glass tunnel looking up at a lioness sprawled on the ceiling, her tawny legs splayed behind her, a huge beef bone gripped between her front paws. The entire enclosure was walled in glass. The lioness stared across at a fake tree. She seemed to be fantasizing about prey—a plump antelope or zebra appearing in the branches. A waterfall poured over fake rocks into a pond. In Ruthie's bag was a small Desert Eagle handgun Rutherford had given her as a going-away present. She wanted to use it to shoot out the glass. Set the lions free to rampage over the blackjack tables, as she'd imagined Ebola lions rampaging through the valley years before.

A little girl with long black hair pressed her palms against the glass and stared in at the lone male. Much larger than the females, he stared back at her, ignoring the rest of the tourists. His mane was a shade darker than the fur on his body. His posture was a mix of laziness and menace; his tail flicked over the pond. His eyes glinted keenly. In two powerful bounds, he was at the glass above the girl. The muscles in his shoulders rippled. The girl looked up awestruck. Ruthie felt a sudden painful nostalgia for this bond between beast and child. The lion opened his mouth and gnawed the curved surface above the girl's head with his inch-long incisors, leaving a pale smear.

"What does he want?" the girl asked. Her mother was crouched behind her snapping pictures.

"He wants to eat you," Ruthie said.

The girl's eyes widened. The mother turned, glaring. Ruthie laughed, and left the casino the way she'd come, past slot machines, their players digging coins out of plastic cups with nicotine-stained talons. Back in the blast furnace of the desert sun, Ruthie walked below a bronze lion ten times larger than those inside, mounted atop a concrete pedestal. She ran her hand over its paw.

Blue glass edifices wavered in the heat around her. The streets were packed. The cars and people seemed to be orbiting some invisible eddy. Moving faster and faster as they spun into the darkness. Was this man-built chaos what would become of her valley? She pictured skyscrapers standing before the Bitterroot Mountains—Trapper Peak dwarfed in a series of shard-like roofs. The trailer on Red Sun Road lost between condos. Traffic jammed to a standstill. A dozen contrails slicing across the sky.

19.

The heat drew the strength from her and left her limp and exhausted in the bathtub of the run-down, off-Strip motel where she'd rented a room. The August sun seemed not to set but lurk just beyond the Red Rock Canyon mountains, exhaling its breath along the packed streets. Stifling, relentless, even at night. The air conditioner in her room panted weakly, hardly cooling the air above its vent. She knelt over it like a penitent. She lay naked on the bed. She showered three, four times a day, but the sweat never left her.

Small trucks pulled billboards for strip clubs along the street below her window. Men asked if they could take her picture. She assumed this was how you ended up on the escort cards filling the gutters. She only lasted three months at the cantina, too humiliated by the red miniskirt and black bodice uniform to stand another shift. Too tired of twisting away from groping hands. It was even worse than the Montana Café. She'd wanted to escape the men of the valley, but found their mirrors here even more abhorrent.

"Come home," Pip said, on the phone.

Ruthie didn't answer. She was embarrassed to return to the valley. Another Bitterroot girl who'd failed in the wider world. She didn't know what she'd tell her father or Terry or Badger. Pip described Badger's wedding. How Father Mike had managed to fit both the glory of Badger's football career and the rapid approach of Judgment Day into the vows. How the bridesmaids had dressed as cheerleaders and the groomsmen wore varsity jackets over their suits. "Len wasn't invited but he parked outside so he could watch all the girls in their dresses," Pip finished. "I can't believe you made me go on my own."

"Thank God I was a thousand miles away," Ruthie said, unable to hide the loneliness in her voice. "Remember when we tried to kill Len with our eyes?"

Pip laughed. "I'm still trying." She paused. "Your dad doesn't look so good. He's drinking too much and not eating enough. I hardly ever see him in the diner."

Sudden shame rushed through Ruthie. She'd meant to send money home. She felt a pull at her heart.

"I don't have anyone to talk to," Pip said. "Who am I supposed to tell about the idiot tourists who come into Whipple's looking for bear spray?"

Ruthie missed her friend. She missed her father. She missed the mountains, the trees, and the sound of the river. She even missed Badger and his helpless need. She wondered if Kent Willis had been right about every wild conspiracy. The leering drunks swinging wildly at one another in the street suggested that beneath the surface all men were crazed by greed and lust. Desperate pillagers in a land with little left to take.

The burger joints on the strip were full of tourists and the burger joints off the strip were full of people who frightened her. Emaciated in a different way than the junkies and drifters of Montana. Quieter, more snakelike. They ate slowly and watched her, as if sensing that her desperation would soon match theirs. In the overlit neon restaurants, she had moments of PTSD from the gas station. Expecting bullets to punch through the windows, the glass bottles above the bar to lacerate her as shrapnel. She began bringing convenience store food back to her motel room. Unwrapping the plastic from white-bread sandwiches, spreading mayonnaise from small squeeze-packets, pouring out little bags of chips. Eating off the air conditioner. Praying for snow. She struggled to recall the shocking, strong grip of the butterfly's feet.

Terry called and she learned that her father had been in a fight. "He doesn't pick up when I call," she said.

"Probably he's embarrassed," Terry said. "He was out cold in the street by the Sawmill when I found him. Doesn't even know who hit him."

"Is he all right?"

She could hear Terry shrugging through the phone.

Worry plagued her during job interviews in the backrooms of restaurants. The polo-shirted managers stared at her while she fumbled for words. "Your résumé," they'd say.

Dad, she'd think.

She sat in the yellow light of the motel bathroom and tried to reckon with her face. To make sure it hadn't changed. She pulled the skin down from her cheek. It seemed to have a greenish cast. She touched her jaw. She tugged her hair back from her forehead. She wished she'd brought the wolfskin rug, so at least she could sleep. She missed Moses.

Finally, Rutherford answered his phone. "It was just some god-damn tourist," he said.

"You can't do this, Dad," she said. "You're older now. You need to take care of yourself." Of the six light-blue condos that had been built next door on Red Sun Road, two sat empty, two belonged to scientists at the Rocky Mountain Labs, one to a manager at Lost Trail Ski Area, and one to a college student whose parents had bought it as an investment. Rutherford's anger burned at a low, steady flame.

He grunted. "It's bow season soon. Things will pick up. I'm expecting an order of bighorn skulls from the new guide outfit in Sula."

"I miss you."

Rutherford was silent. "You just do good out there. That's all I want."

Ruthie's money dwindled. Every day in the city it took so much to survive. She lost weight. She grew desperate and smiled at an older man in a casino bar. He bought her sweet pink martinis and told her about his work on an industrial dairy farm. How it was mostly just computers, but still someone, a real person, had to wean the calves from their mothers. Had to listen to them bellow. His thick forearm touched hers; a gold chain circled his wrist above a Navy tattoo gone muddy. He showed her his room key from one of the fancy hotels on the strip, but at the last minute insisted they go back to hers.

Ruthie led him. She wondered if her mother had dreamt of a place like this, and ended up in the same lonesome hallway.

The man's belly was taut as a melon beneath his shirt. He used it to push Ruthie through the door. She stumbled into the edge of the bed, and when she turned around he was grinning in the dim light as he shot the bolt in the lock. "You're a little wildcat, aren't you?" he said.

Two neon points from a sign outside reflected on the TV screen. In them, Ruthie saw the eyes of the wolf as her father had through the scope of his gun. Yellow-wild, frozen on a sagebrush hillside by a stand of juniper. Frightened and alone. They woke the animal inside Ruthie. The man stepped toward her. He unbuttoned his shirt. A gold crucifix hung between his hairless breasts.

"I can always tell." A gold cap shone on his left incisor. He gripped her hips roughly and shoved her forward onto the bed.

Listening to him unzip his pants behind her, Ruthie reached into her bag. She felt the cool metal grip of the Desert Eagle. She remembered her father's shooting lessons. How to breathe into the shot. She rolled over and pointed the gun at the man's throat. She held her finger over the trigger guard. She let him see the lacy scars all down the inside of her forearms, as wild as he could want.

His eyes widened. He made a choking sound. His expression flicked from confusion to terror. He stepped back and lifted his hands.

"Give me forty dollars," she said. "Or I'll kill you and take everything you have."

RUTHIE PACKED HER SUITCASE and dragged it to the bus station in the dawn. She used the man's forty dollars to buy a ticket. From the pay phone, she called Pip and told her she was coming home.

20.

Rutherford stood waiting for her on the dock. It had been three months since Ruthie had returned from Las Vegas, but he still waited for her outside whenever they met, as if he were afraid she might decide to leave again. Lake Como was empty, swept clean of the boats, tubes, and Jet Skis that littered its surface during the summer. A stinging wind gusted off the water—gray now, in late November. His hands were dug into the fleece-lined pockets of his jacket.

The sun sank into the snowy teeth of the Bitterroots. It lit the tree-tops and revealed a galaxy of silver minnows circling the pylon under the dock. "Sorry I'm late," Ruthie said. "The diner . . ."

Rutherford shook his head. "Happy birthday."

Ruthie was twenty-one. The milestone meant little to her. Rutherford raised his chin at the frozen sheets on the far, shaded shore.

At forty, there was resignation in his eyes, but below it the old ice-crawling stubbornness still lingered. "Might get real snow this year."

Marshall Mountain to the northeast had shuttered after a series of warming winters, and other ski areas nearby were close to doing the same.

"When I was a kid we'd skate across. The whole lake froze solid. We used to drill through and fish. Kent stuck his dick in the hole once. Only way he could get a bite." Rutherford smiled, half wolfish, half shy. "I reckon it's still shrunk."

Gray hairs flecked his beard. They made Ruthie want to hug him. "That's about the last thing I want to think about," she said.

"You get enough in tips to buy me a beer?"

"It's in the truck."

"How'd it feel to buy now that you're legal?"

"About the same."

He nodded, and together they walked up to the cabin. It was the A-frame they'd come to when she was a girl, after the earthquake. It belonged to a young lawyer from Seattle now. Rutherford's old boss at the mill had died. His children sold it off. The lawyer had hired Rutherford to make repairs and watch over it for the winter, giving him permission to stay when he wanted as part of the deal. Ruthie wondered if the lawyer knew her father was liable to move in. Even though it was run-down from years of neglect, it was about a thousand times nicer than his trailer.

The familiar deck still stood over the creek. Ruthie saw where she'd sat on the edge, her legs dangling, searching for otters in the rushing water. The deck's shadow slanted over the remains of a vegetable garden. The wire fence was rusted and bent; the beds crumbled. Ruthie carried the case of Busch Light and her overnight bag inside. Rutherford was waiting in the kitchen. All the appliances and fixtures had fallen into disrepair. They smelled of mildew and gas. He leaned on the yellow countertop. It was bubbled and peeling up at the edges. He chopped down one of the bubbles with the blade of his hand. "People sure used to like ugly shit," he said.

Ruthie handed him a beer. She remembered how pristine the cabin had seemed to her as a little girl. "They still do."

"Your mom, back when we were in high school, she wanted a house with shag carpet in every room. Lavender shag. She talked about it all the time. Even the bathroom, so her feet would never get cold. You believe that?"

Ruthie didn't know how to respond. Since her return, Rutherford had begun to speak about her mother. As if he were making space for her in his mind again, now that he was in his forties and unlikely to remarry. It was an intrusion to Ruthie, who felt her mother had no right to come back, even if it was only in her father's mind.

"What did *you* want?" Ruthie asked.

"Back then?" Rutherford looked at the strange little cuckoo clock hanging beside the fridge. A frightened-looking bird popped out when he banged the side. "I don't think I ever knew. Maybe that was part of the problem." He opened the beer and took a drink. "When I shot that wolf I thought I was going to be someone. I had your mom and you, and I don't know . . . I thought I'd be some kind of great hunter. Get on TV. Hunt things no one else could find. Catch the last this or that. But that isn't really a thing, is it?"

"No, not really."

He shrugged and stretched his fingers in front of his chest. They were bent and scarred from decades of missed hammer swings, saw nicks, pulling cartridges from hot barrels. Ruthie wondered what her mother had done with these years. If her nails were lavender, her cuticles perfectly trimmed. Her husband the kind of man who golfed in the evenings.

"I got you something," Rutherford said.

Ruthie hoped it wasn't another gun. There were already five in her studio apartment and two in her truck.

"It's out back."

She followed him to the rear door. A chain-saw-carved bear stood in the center of the barren yard. Nearly her height, painted black with a pale snout, it looked forlornly across to the creek, its paws hanging in front of the sharp-cut fur on its stomach. Raymond Pompey sold them at his nursery and she knew her father had gotten it at cost. Probably it had an extra claw. "What am I supposed to do with that?"

"Thought it'd look good in your new place," her father said.

She sighed, imagining it staring at her from across her small apartment, taking up an entire corner. "Thanks, Dad."

He nodded and took a drink.

Back in the kitchen, Rutherford returned to his station by the counter. "The guy who owns this place ain't much older than you. He has a Japanese car. Electric. Its clearance is about eight inches. Rich and stupid. I guess I should've gone to law school." He looked at the blue bird still sitting wide-eyed on the end of the clock's extended tongue. "I sure would've given it to them then."

THEY WALKED THE PATH by the water. It wound over tree roots and around boulders. To the south, the rocky public beach where Ruthie had thrown the rock at the boy curved along the shore to the dam. The two long docks reached out in front of the concrete embankment and spillway. She hadn't been to the lake since high school. She avoided it. The memory of the toddler made her question her own decency, and she preferred to spend her free time in the Selway-Bitterroot Wilderness with Pip, or wandering the foothills of the Sapphires. Away from other people.

"I hope she got her carpet house, and I hope the whole place stinks like cat piss," Rutherford said.

Ruthie was quiet. She was trying to enjoy herself. It was her birthday and her only night off. Moss was splashed over the boulders and up the sides of trees. It was a bright day, and somehow colder for its brightness. They followed clouds of their own breath. Rutherford's eyes skipped from tree to path to lake. He pointed out a bald eagle, nuts a squirrel had hidden for the winter, deer tracks.

A pileated woodpecker paused from hammering its red head against the side of a lodgepole pine. Ruthie looked into its black eye, wondering if the pecking would eventually damage its brain. The cold air tightened the skin on her face. She drew her lips back to stretch it out.

The trail climbed to the top of Left-Behind Point and then wandered through the woods. Pine needles muffled their footsteps. It was dim and the air smelled of sap. Ruthie caught herself breathing deeply. Taking pleasure in the sound of the wind in the branches. She wondered if this was part of getting older: learning how to listen. Cabin roofs were visible down by the water. One of the new ones was a multilayered expanse of green metal.

"Mormons," Rutherford said. "Tar sands money."

"Fucking Mormons," Ruthie said, half in jest, and half because they came into the diner, ordered hot water with lemon, and didn't tip. They were moving down from the oil shale fields in Alberta and buying up property all around. Building mansions that looked like they'd been dreamed up in the dollhouse section of Wal-Mart.

The trees thinned out, revealing the distant mountains. A quarter moon hung stubbornly in the blue western sky above Trapper Peak. The trail ended on a granite outcrop forty feet over the water. A chair was carved into the rock a few yards above and behind the outcrop, like a lifeguard's perch.

"Still there," Ruthie said.

Rutherford nodded. Len Law had carved it when Ruthie was a girl. It took him a whole summer. Out with his hammer and chisel every morning, pounding away. The hardest anyone had ever seen him work. No one knew what he was doing until he started sitting there and watching the young girls in bikinis jump off the cliff into the lake. Soon the fathers got together and chased him off. Now it remained like something prehistoric: a cave painting or midden ring, remnant of a lost civilization. Rutherford sat down between the rock arms and Ruthie went to look over the edge. The height rushed up at her, forty feet at least, pushing the air from her lungs. It was amazing to her that anyone ever jumped off, let alone children. The setting sun cast a thousand glittering pins across the water.

"Do it," Rutherford said.

"What?"

"Jump."

"Are you crazy?"

"It's the perfect time. Your birthday. Nobody around. No boats. No screaming kids."

Ruthie turned to him, sitting in the chair, drinking another beer, squinting at the water. His figure small in his stained canvas coat, enjoying the bitter cold. "You jump," she said.

"I'm too old."

"You're too scared."

He smiled. "We can't both jump. One of us has to be able to go for help."

The bald eagle swept off the branch across the lake and winged over the orange-streaked water, dipping its head at any sign of movement. It rose and fell like a leaf, its body outspread on currents of air. "I'd jump if I could fly like that," Ruthie said.

The eagle arced over the trees. Rutherford watched it go, squeezing the sides of his beer can. "There was a time you never saw them. You could go to jail for having a single feather. Now they're everywhere."

The great comeback. The bird everyone in America had joined together to save, so they could be loosed at halftime of the Super Bowl to soar around the stadium while Lee Greenwood sang. When Ruthie was a girl, she'd played with the shoebox full of eagle feathers in her father's shed. Taking them out and pretending to make headdresses and arrow fletchings. Who knew where he'd gotten them.

"There was a time you saw wolves, too," she said.

THEY MADE SALMON for dinner. Ruthie rubbed it in butter and salt, squeezed lemon on top, then wrapped it in tinfoil and gave it to her father to cook. The night was cold and they stood together in the kitchen. The closed grill smoked on the deck. Across the creek, the ponderosas loomed over the firepit. Not as tall as Ruthie remembered, but still seeming to tower. Light snow began to fall. Feathery flakes drifting down on the branches. The year's first. Sticking everywhere except the grill's warm hood. Bringing a quietude, muffling every hard edge, and filling Ruthie with calm.

Her father breathed raspily at her side. The sound brought back memories of all the years they'd spent squeezed together in the teal trailer. Ruthie was grateful for her own apartment. Never smelling elk piss, never hearing Rutherford curse at the TV, or finding him passed out on the couch. Scrubbing her plate and only her plate before putting it in the clean dish rack. Walking naked from the shower to the bed. Lying on her back on the comforter listening to Wiley King. The small pleasures of being an adult. She leaned into her father's shoulder.

"You hear about Wiley?" she asked. A health scare had forced him to decamp to a hospital in Seattle, and rumors about its severity filtered through the diner.

Rutherford nodded. "Something cardiac. They had to airlift him. Let's hope it's the big one."

THE FEARS ATE across from each other at the long wooden table in the dining room. Initials were scratched into the varnished top: LP and

LL and RB, who'd carved a little crossbones by his name—a pirate at supper. Rutherford refused the salad Ruthie had made, and instead poured potato chips onto the plate around his fish. He dug into the center of the salmon with his fork and peered at it, making sure it had been cooked to the rubbery, flavorless consistency he preferred.

"You know there are TV shows now where you can learn how to cook," Ruthie said.

"That right?"

"There are also ones where you can meet women." She figured maybe the way to get him to stop talking about her mother was to give him someone else to think about.

He raised his eyebrows and took a bite. "You think I should go on TV to meet a woman?"

Ruthie stifled a laugh, imagining her father among the tall, muscular, peroxide-toothed mannequins she and Pip watched on dating shows. "You shouldn't be alone, is all. Do you ever think about getting another dog?"

"I told you, I can't go through losing another one. Not after Moses."

"That was seven years ago. You kill animals all the time."

"Not ones I've lived with. Jesus, Ruthie, I watched them put the needle in. They wanted me there so he wouldn't be scared. Do you know what that's like? He was looking up at me . . . I'd never killed nothing that trusted me before. It wasn't fair."

"All right." Ruthie raised her hands. "Never mind."

"Not like you offered to come along, either. Said you had too much homework."

"I buried him," she said.

"*We* buried him. And I don't see you going on any dates."

Ruthie drank down the remaining third of her beer. She thought of the man in Las Vegas grinning as he locked the door. The carbonation squeezed back up her throat and made her eyes water. "I'm taking a break, is all."

"Me, too," Rutherford said. "I'm taking a good long goddamn break."

Snow blanketed the deck. An inch of it already, and still falling. Only the square of salmon skin and a few chips remained on Rutherford's plate. He patted his stomach. He grunted and pushed back his chair. He carried the plate to the trash, scraped the chips and skin off, dropped it in the sink, and left it there.

"Might use a little more salt next time," he said, squinting out at Ruthie's truck being buried in the driveway. She looked up at the loft. She imagined an otter staring down at them, curious to see how they'd changed, if they'd changed at all. Her father turned and followed her eyes to a dark brown stain in the ceiling's peak.

"Must be a leak," he said. "I'll probably have to stay another few weeks to fix it."

21.

When Father Mike said he was going to walk on water, even Ruthie and her father came to see, though neither of them had been to church in years.

The crowd filled the sand beach at Hooper's Landing—Kent Willis, Danette, the Laws, Pip—and kids were halfway up the willow trees, craning their necks like hungry birds. The Bitterroot River had fallen from its spring peak but still ran high and hard past the deep bend favored by out-of-state fishermen and alcoholics too lazy to find a less-trampled hole. All you'd catch here were sluggish, shit-fed trout from the hatchery upstream. Ruthie looked on disdainfully. The women in bonnets and Sunday whites made her feel like a little girl again: trapped. Terry French pulled his truck in across the lot. He slammed the door and leaned heavily against the cab. Three corrugated steel duplexes had been built next to his hogan on Billy's former land, nearly identical in size to the condos beside her father's.

Behind Ruthie, Rutherford clambered onto the bed of his truck, causing the axle to groan and people to look around. He'd worn his cleanest dirty jeans and slung a bolo around his neck to honor the solemnity of the occasion. He fished a can of beer from his cooler, popped it open, and drank. The chunk of turquoise in his bolo was the size of an elk turd. It hung at an angle over his work shirt. He shaded his eyes and looked over the assorted church people. Ruthie felt her cheeks flush. Embarrassed, but admiring him at the same time. Trailer trash of the most stubborn, ramshackle kind. The King of Ravalli County. The opposite of Deputy Badger, newly sworn in, who sat dejectedly in his cruiser at the edge of the lot, looking like he'd slept there, and ignoring the trucks haphazardly blocking each other in.

Deacons surrounded Father Mike on the shore. Their heads bowed, praying fervently as foamy water harried the robes around their feet. Two had worn galoshes in preparation. Another peeked down nervously at his suede loafers. Father Mike was already ankle-deep, oblivious to the cold, gazing above the crowd at the snowcapped mountains with a desperation on his face that Ruthie could tell had little to do with God. His brown hair was thinning and the youthful enthusiasm she remembered from after the quake had dissipated into a middle-aged disillusionment. His wife was nowhere to be seen. Ruthie felt it in the air then, the energy of a prizefight, not a Sunday service. Even the children hanging from the branches had a malevolence in their expression.

"Beer?" Rutherford asked. Several women turned their heads. Ruthie nodded. She wished she'd worn something other than her shapeless red Whipple's T-shirt and ripped jeans. She pulled herself up into the back of the truck and took the beer he handed her. She popped the tab. Her former classmates always stared at her. A few months in Vegas, a few scars, a few boyfriends, and they acted like she was Jezebel reincarnate. She didn't care what they thought, but she would have liked to have done herself up a little. Shown them what they could look like without their ratty kids and twelve-pack-a-day husbands. Father Mike caught her eyes from way out in the river; his torn expression made her look away.

Inadvertently, her gaze settled on Len Law, sharing a tattered blanket with his three scrawny children and his sister Eleanor in her wheelchair. Ruthie tried to shift her eyes away but it was too late. Len smirked. "Thought you'd left us for good. This little valley wasn't enough for you."

Ruthie didn't answer.

"Figured you'd be a star by now. Have your own show on the Strip." He winked at Eleanor. His youngest daughter was sucking a rock and tugging the spokes of the wheel of Eleanor's chair.

"I just missed the people here too much," Ruthie replied.

The conversations around them quieted. The deacons on the riverbank raised their arms. Her father nodded to the current and the priest. "He might best have waited a couple months."

Ruthie shrugged. "Maybe it's better to be fast if you're going to walk across."

"Dearly beloved," Father Mike began. "We are gathered here today to bear witness to God's love. To see His power over all things, and the mercy He has bestowed upon us." He lifted his trembling fist and Ruthie saw a blueness at his lips, the cold of the water already seeping up through his body. "I have fasted and I have prayed and now God has given me a vision. He has commanded me to show you the true power of His love." Ruthie scanned the upturned faces in the crowd. What were they expecting? A miracle? A humiliation? "For those of you who question His place in the modern world. Who look around at the violence and degradation and lies and ask, 'Where are you, Father? Why have you forsaken us?' Today I will show you how close He is. I will walk into the water and He will lift me up and guide me to the far and holy shore." The priest paused, seeming to lose strength, before regathering himself. "May His will be done."

"May His will be done!" the crowd answered, in a smattered attempt at unison.

The deacons began to lead the Lord's Prayer. Ruthie found herself mouthing along, "Our father, who art in heaven . . ."

Father Mike took a deep breath at the "Amen." The crowd's attention turned to him fully, all the devout and disbelieving and curious. "Watch me now, and bear witness to His power." He turned and waded deeper into the river, hesitating only a moment on an unsteady rock, his cassock twisting around him. Ruthie saw worry in the deacons' eyes. They glanced at each other as if one of them should intervene. But who would stand in the way of a miracle? Father Mike stumbled against the current and pushed farther. The crowd shouted after him. He stopped with the water swirling around his midsection. Only his head and torso were visible, like a disembodied creature. Ruthie couldn't imagine the strength it took to remain there. She'd been knocked over by water at her knees this time of year. She felt a stab of fear. She remembered the crazed look in his eye at the football game. When would he rise? Would no one help him? But all were frozen: watching, waiting. Veins rose on his bluish forehead. His lips twisted into a strangled grin, straining against the great forces beneath. "Hallelujah!" he shouted.

"Hallelujah!" a sole woman answered.

No one else spoke. Father Mike lifted his arms. The crowd gasped, as if he might suddenly stride onto the churning surface, but instead he succumbed, and the river bowled him headlong into the current.

For a moment, no one moved. Then with a shout the entire crowd began to run along the riverbank, Badger among them, plunging out of his cruiser, suddenly wide awake, stumbling and hitching up his gun belt. Kent Willis beside him, moving faster than Ruthie had thought him able. The crowd trampled the reeds, tripping and smashing through the underbrush, children leaping from the trees, as the priest was borne into the rapids. His body sailed below the bridge at Woodside Crossing and was dashed against the rocks on the other side, before being lost again, twisted and sluiced in a cacophony of white spray.

Ruthie found herself alone with her father and Terry in the parking lot, save for a lost, weeping child and a knot of teenagers so dazed they'd forgotten the lit cigarettes in their fists. She touched the stud in her lip with her tongue. Rutherford muttered what sounded like a Hail Mary. He shook his head. Ruthie slumped back against the wheel well. She remembered the priest in his collar and vestments shopping in the Super 1, or filling up his truck at the Sinclair. Something reassuring in his uniform: a link to ancient order, rituals fighting against the dark.

Terry walked slowly over to them. "I didn't need to see that," he said.

DRIVING BACK TO DARBY, Ruthie passed Sheriff Kima standing on the bridge, looking down wearily at the fire team all roped together below him on the river's rocky shore, dragging Father Mike's body from the current. The priest's cassock had been torn off and he had nothing left on but his shoes. Ruthie saw the frail blueness of his flesh, and wondered who could bear the weight of a godless world. Cruelty without reason. Suffering without reward. It was what she'd felt when Nathan died in her arms: an emptiness opening inside her. Kima shook his head, seeming ready to toss his gun and badge into the water and walk away.

A new hotel was being built by the river. Three stories of steel balconies girded by pine railings. Constructed in the same alpine-ski-lodge style as the organic brewery in Hamilton. Sunlight reflected blindingly off the plastic-covered windows. Rebar littered the rocky dirt. Ruthie turned to the spring's snow-white peaks. She saw the strings holding the valley together, as thin and taut as fishing wire.

•

THE RUMOR SPREAD like a pox through the Montana Café. From old man to old man, then from Pip Pascal to all others, that a week earlier Father Mike had discovered his wife in bed with another man. A much younger man, a ranch hand, hardly more than a teenager. A boy, the old men surmised. In her work apron, pouring coffee, Ruthie watched them chew this vision in their minds as they would a tender piece of meat, their mouths going dry. The pastor's pretty wife, of the broad forgiving hips and honeysuckle hair, astride a hairless teenager. Pinning him down, rocking over him with her flushed body. One of them sighed and Ruthie slipped and poured hot coffee on his gnarled hand. He yelped and jerked the hand away and looked up at her, stunned tears springing to his eyes.

"Sorry," she said, dabbing his hand with the hem of her apron. Of all her customers, she hated the gossiping, pinching, leering old men most, but now, in grief, she felt consumed by a benevolence so overpowering that she wanted to crumple up every check and kiss every wrinkled forehead. "I don't know what's the matter with me."

The old man looked up at her, gratitude and suspicion clawing at his worn face.

She smiled at him, but the pain in his hand was already forgotten.

"He wanted us to see," the old man said. "He wanted us to *see*."

Looking around at the faces in the diner, Ruthie felt kinship with each one. The couple holding hands across the table, the couple refusing to look at each other, the father and son sharing a plate of pancakes, even Len arguing with his wife at the darkened table in the corner. She realized she was already three years older than her father had been when she was born. Pip was flushed with sorrow on her customary stool at the counter, drinking coffee and talking rapidly to a pair of truckers. Ruthie touched her arm as she refilled her cup. "Don't forget to eat something today."

"It doesn't matter," Pip was saying. "Anybody should have the right." She'd been a staunch supporter of suicides ever since finding her father. The young woman version of Pip was much like the girl had been: speaking whatever crossed her mind, scrapping to get by, always in short pants with her backpack full of supplies. She was often gone for days, and then she'd reappear at Ruthie's door with strange objects she'd found in the wilderness. Ruthie knew she still hunted for the headless creature, though they never spoke of it.

The front door jingled as Terry and Billy French entered. They sat at the small table by the window. Terry carried a heaviness in his body and Billy was similarly weighted down. The loss of his land had hardened Billy, and Nathan Gardipe's death—whose mother he knew well—had hardened him further still. Wider and shorter than his brother, with the same long black braid, he was in conflict with the world. Fighting against it, drinking against it, falling down against it. Married and divorced, struggling to support his daughter Delilah, who was now in nursing school in Spokane. Ruthie sighed. She turned and looked at Cook through the service window. An escaped Mormon from Utah, his ponytail was tight and unscathed beneath its hairnet as he baptized a basket of french fries in hot oil.

"You ever hear of a priest killing himself?" she asked.

He shook his head. "I thought they were the ones who were supposed to keep the rest of us from doing it."

"The fewer priests, the better," Billy said loudly, leaning back in his chair. "My people learned that a long time ago."

The diner went silent. Len stopped eating to stare.

"All right, brother," Terry said quietly.

The sound of Cook's knife on the cutting board could be heard in the kitchen. Even Pip stopped talking. Ruthie crossed the linoleum to Billy's table. She leaned over and filled his coffee cup. "Maybe not today," she whispered. He watched her closely. After Nathan was killed, the county judge had ruled that the Gardipes were cul-

pable for the damage to the convenience store, rather than the hunters. A decision the majority of the valley agreed with, but which
Ruthie and the Frenches found despicable. The Gardipes had to sell
their house to cover the cost. Nathan's mother now lived in a rented
trailer in Ronan.

Always ready to make things worse, Len broke in. "It'll probably
bring some more tourists to town," Len said. "You know they still go
taking pictures of the spot where that Cub Scout got eaten."

"Now, there's an idea," Billy said, keeping his voice loud enough
for the whole diner to hear. "Ruthie, you and me could go in on
something together: a tour of the valley for all these new people.
Show them where Father Mike went under, the sites of all the hit-
and-runs, the graves of Charlo's people, and where Nathan got shot
down at Lil's. There has to be at least one white sheriff who got killed
in Hamilton. He'll be Custer, the big draw. A new Wild West show.
You be the pretty white girl, I'll be the solemn Indian. We can charge
ten bucks a head."

Len snorted. "You both know that boy got what he deserved."

The coffeepot was suddenly heavy in Ruthie's hand.

"You go in someplace and try to rob it, you're liable to get shot.
Doesn't have anything to do with being an Indian."

Billy clenched his fist on his knee. "Oh no? Same as when your
grandpa hung those four on the courthouse lawn?"

Len paused. "That was a case of sabotage. Everybody knew they
made my little sister sick."

"He lost his badge over that. He should've been shot."

"I can't listen to this nonsense. After all my family has done for this
valley. We brought law to a heathen swamp."

"And you took the name. Biggest joke I ever heard. We'll be sure
to have your junkyard on the tour. Show them all the totems you have
to protect yourself since you're so proud of what your family's done—
your grandpa who killed himself and your daddy who ran off."

Len huffed and turned to his eggs. He glared at his wife. "Don't need to debate with no damn Indian," he muttered.

Ruthie set the coffeepot down on the Frenches' table. To hell with the rest of the customers. It had been a bad day and it was only getting worse. She dug her fingernail into the edge of the laminate, remembering Father Mike's blue flesh. She spoke to Billy. "Do you think it was better here, before all this?"

Billy was quiet for a long moment, glowering at Len. Then he looked around. His eyes paused on his brother. Their paths had diverged when Billy married and moved to the reservation, and they'd had many differences over the years, but they remained as close as any two people Ruthie knew. The heat began to go out of him. He shrugged. "There were fewer of us," he said. "Maybe that's as better as it gets."

22

Ruthie sat on her apartment building's front porch in the warm evening light. The setting sun smoldered the horizon in a gradient of violet, pink, and orange, so beautiful she found it hard to look at. Two raccoons emerged to sniff a rabbit rug on the highway and were chased off by approaching headlights. She imagined the rabbit hopping down the yellow lines, wanting to escape the valley, amazed by the clearness of the territory, the expanse of pavement shooting toward the mountains, then blinding light and the engine's roar.

Once, at the Sawmill Bar, a man had squeezed blood from his palm into a shot of whiskey and offered twenty dollars to anyone who'd drink it. Standing in the dim light, with all the male eyes searching up and down her body, Ruthie had taken it, so disappointed in their flimsy, craven bravery that she nearly wept.

Yet still she was trapped among them.

A semi rattled past and she watched its taillights move through town and disappear, then reappear as it slowly wound up the highway to Lost Trail Pass. She imagined the animals there shedding their winter coats on the snowless ski runs and leaving sign for one another in the excitement of spring. She felt this same need: to move, find new people, new territory. She drank absinthe out of a plastic cup. An intern at the Rocky Mountain Labs—a summer fling—had left it behind when he went back to school in Bozeman. He'd been testing adjuvants at the labs. He'd explained how the lipids from soap bark cell walls were used in vaccines. No Ebola or anthrax or monkey testing. Just quality control for purity, day after day. Killing her with boredom. The bitter licorice taste reminded her how he'd bounded up her steps, reaching under her shirt before they were even inside. For some men, the whole world is a playground. The new moon was a single slivered horseshoe trodden in black dirt.

It came as no surprise when the cruiser made its slow way up the street. Even though Badger was married now, he still dropped in whenever he had reason, real or imagined. Ruthie allowed him this if her mood was right, but today had been no good for either of them.

"Can't find his wife," Badger said of Father Mike. He shuffled slump-shouldered up the walk. A three-day beard hid his cheeks. Full-grown, he was six-foot-three, with flesh beginning to sag around the muscled blocks of his arms and chest. "No one wants the body." His voice held a note of accusation, as if tonight Ruthie stood for all women.

"Should've left it in the river, then," she said. "Where he put it."

Badger paused, swaying in the moonlight. She realized he'd been drinking. "Oh, you're a hard one, Ruthie Fear."

"I'm tired. Don't come here drunk."

Badger leaned against the porch railing. He looked up at her. She couldn't tell anymore if he wanted her back or if he just didn't want anyone else to have her. "We found the boy she was fucking, though. He's our age. He started crying when he heard." Badger paused. "Thought we were going to put him in jail." He hooked his thumb through his belt. The silver bison buckle was of higher quality than the one from the county fair he'd worn when they met, but not so different in size or shape.

"It's still not illegal for a wife to cheat?"

The apartment building behind Ruthie was empty. Only two of the other units were occupied, by Cook and Pip, and they were both out. She wanted to lock her door and finish the bottle alone in her apartment. Not think about the ranch boy, or Father Mike, or the Laws, or any of it.

"Do you remember Levi?" Badger asked.

Ruthie shook her head. "What do you want?"

"He died in a car crash last year, when you were gone. I had to tell his mother. She had four sons. Levi and his three brothers. You know what she asked me when she saw me on her porch?"

Ruthie waited.

"'Which one was it?'"

"I remember the elk," Ruthie said. "That's what I remember. And Nathan. Why don't you arrest those hunters?"

Badger climbed ponderously up the stairs to stand over her. The silver bison shone into her eyes. His whiskey smell made her nauseated. "A man has a right to defend himself."

Ruthie scooted back the plastic chair. She stood in the fading light. "Is that what it was?"

He shrugged.

"Where's Janine?" she asked. "Shouldn't you be home helping with her homework?"

"Where are your boyfriends?" He raised his fingers as if he were counting one through five. "At least one of them must be free."

"Go do your job. Find his wife. I don't want you here."

Badger winced, shifting his weight. His uniform strained to contain his gut. Already he was getting heavy without two-a-days, summer tryouts, nightly practice. No more use for running, no more linemen to pop. Nothing to slam into. Only Indians and drunks to harass. A steady slide of weeks and months, a buildup of sadness and disappointment that could, in a heartbeat, turn to anger. Being a cop was liable to make anyone worse, but Badger especially. All that imagined power to wrap around a smallness inside. The little boy caught in the man's body. "I thought I'd ask you where you'd go," he said. "Like the cops do on TV. Become a killer to catch a killer. Become a whore to catch a whore."

"Check the river," Ruthie said. "Right out in the middle."

Badger steadied himself against the railing. "Sometimes you make me want to set myself on fire." His head was framed by the sun's irradiant farewell. Stars began to appear over the Sapphires. One at a time in the advancing night. "I love you."

"Don't menace me again. Ever," Ruthie said.

"Let me come inside."

"No."

Hurt and anger played in Badger's eyes. She thought for a moment that he might reach for her but instead he stepped back down the stairs. He paused on the front walk and looked back. "You know I've always only done what you told me to."

RUTHIE TOOK THE BOTTLE INSIDE, bolted the door, sat on her bed, and watched dark clouds pile up around the peaks through her window. Badger's cruiser turned onto Miles Avenue and rolled away past Whipple's store. She felt a nameless guilt. She wished she'd done something more for Nathan's mother after his death. Ruthie's walls were bare save for a painting of herself surrounded by wild horses.

Her hair swirled along with their manes in a reckless cacophony of brushstrokes. A boy had painted it for her. *Wild Woman with Tame Horses*, he called it.

Moths beat the shit out of themselves against the screen door of the lit porch across the alley. They looked like smoke. Ruthie refilled her cup, saw her face above the sink, and wondered why it appeared different in every mirror she passed. She took a long, throat-stinging drink.

Trees swayed gently around the high school. Beyond it, the crucifix atop the church steeple was silhouetted against the foothills. Ruthie could see most of Darby from her window, including the diner where she spent her days, and the turn for Red Sun Road where she'd spent her childhood. It seemed terribly small.

23.

Ruthie sat between Terry and Billy French in Terry's old pickup. Terry drove out of the valley, through Missoula, and over Evaro Hill onto the Flathead Reservation. Turns jostled Ruthie into the brothers' shoulders. There were no seat belts on the bucket seat. The tobacco-and-sage smell in the cab was a comfort.

Nothing changed when they crossed the line onto the reservation. The few homes along dirt back roads were the same. The Bucksnort Saloon in Evaro looked like any other bar. Trees and mountains and fields were all brilliant green in the early summer. Only the highway signs revealed the difference, now in Salish as well as English. The Salish names were much longer, and Ruthie had never seen most of the characters. The Flathead Allotment Act had given much of the land back to white homesteaders at the turn of the twentieth century, so these signs were late and pitiful reparations.

Billy and Terry argued about whether Darby High's basketball coach should be fired after another losing season, as the truck climbed through the hills of the National Bison Range. Ruthie searched the flowing grasslands for the herd. Settled on a single, distant shaggy head. The Mission Mountains appeared suddenly to the north. Snow-white against the blue sky. They were thicker than the Bitterroots, without the menace of hooked, craggy peaks, but somehow more demanding. As if in their breadth they required fealty from all who passed below.

A waterfall split the cliff face above St. Ignatius. The white adobe steeple of the mission rose above the smaller buildings. The highway dropped onto a long, swampy wetland, too marshy to farm—the reason the Salish had been forced to move to this land in the first place. The Bitterroot Valley had the longest growing season of anywhere in Montana. Egrets stood motionless between the reeds. Swallows darted overhead. An abandoned trading post marked a crossroads. FOUR WINDS read the sun-bleached sign.

The outskirts of Ronan reminded Ruthie of the little towns in the Bitterroot before wealthy people started moving in. Pawnshops, bars, a drive-in, Harvest Foods, and a motel. All faded and crumbling at the edges but well kept. Bright blue flower boxes were fixed beneath each of the motel's windows. A ten-foot-tall plastic brave stood on the drive-in roof. Terry turned down one of the small side streets. It quickly became gravel. Dogs barked. Toys were scattered around dirt-and-grass yards. Hastily made additions sprang from the sides of houses, evidence of generations spreading outward. A rusted gate was wedged permanently open at the entrance of Big Springs Trailer Court. Graffiti covered the slumped remnant of a clubhouse. The trailers were crammed a dozen to a row. The little wooden porches nearly touched. Ruthie felt claustrophobic.

"The Gardipes' old place was out on Timberlane Road. Had three acres and a view of the mountains," Billy said. The truck bounced to a stop before the second-to-last trailer in the row. The lower half was flaking brown paint, the upper half was white. Small attempts had been made to spruce up the exterior: white shutters, a flowerpot on the porch. "Dawn raised all her children there." He paused. "I'd hang that judge upside down in the sun."

Nervousness dampened Ruthie's palms. *Dawn.* She wondered if Nathan had always caused his mother worry. If he'd had a wildness in him from the beginning, or if he'd been a happy child, laughing when he fell down. She wondered if it frightened Billy to think of his own daughter in a city to the west. Ruthie had asked for this meeting, but she was suddenly so anxious she wanted to tell Terry to turn the truck around and gun the engine back home.

DAWN GARDIPE OPENED the door in jeans and a white blouse. She was younger than Ruthie had expected, not yet fifty. She'd looked older at the funeral. A beaded clip held her hair in place. It was the only jewelry she wore. She was nearly as tall as the brothers, with broad shoulders and blunt, rounded features. Her feet, in old cowboy boots, were planted solidly on the entry mat. She seemed determined not to be blown over. She looked at Ruthie with hard brown eyes.

"Come in," she said.

She spoke to Billy over her shoulder as she led them through the dim, carpeted living room to the kitchen. "Ronnie Twofeather is looking for you. Says he has more tools to sell."

Billy looked at his brother. "Need any more broken saws?"

Terry shook his head. "Christ, no."

"Lemonade?" Dawn asked, turning around to face them in front of the sink.

"Thank you," Ruthie said softly. It took her an effort to find her voice. She felt cowed in the presence of this woman, a stranger whose suffering had occupied so much of her mind. Old photos covered the front of the refrigerator, including one of Nathan in a basketball jersey, holding the ball tightly in front of his chest. He was grinning at the camera and Ruthie tried to connect this expression with the face she'd held in her lap.

"Maybe a beer," Billy said, winking.

Dawn shot him a look. "You know I don't keep those here." She gestured for Ruthie to sit at the small kitchen table, then set a glass of lemonade down in front of her. "How's Delilah?"

"Real good," Billy said. "She's studying medicine."

"Maybe someday she'll be able to tell us where she got her brains." Terry ribbed his brother and together they drifted out to the porch. When Ruthie looked up again, they were gone.

Dawn leaned back against the sink and studied Ruthie. Her belt was snugged tightly across the top of her hips, and her blouse was buttoned to the collar, as if each morning she made sure her clothing held her together.

"I've never been here before," Ruthie said, feeling her cheeks redden. "And I've lived an hour away my whole life."

"That's how it goes," Dawn said. "Unless you're passing through on the way to Glacier."

"I've never been there, either." Ruthie touched the cool side of her lemonade. A hand-carved wolf stood on a small shelf by the sink. She wondered if Nathan had made it. "I'm sorry I didn't come sooner," she said. "I didn't want to make your life harder."

Dawn looked away through the window.

"But I thought you should know." Ruthie stopped, trying to think of what to say, even though she'd rehearsed it many times the night before. "I was with him. At the end. He said your name. It was the last thing he said. He was in my arms and he said your name."

Tendons rose briefly on Dawn's neck. Some of the color left her face. "How long was it?" she asked.

"What?"

"Before he died."

"Not long. A minute or two." But Ruthie wasn't sure. It had felt like forever.

"You held him?"

Ruthie nodded. "I tried mouth-to-mouth, but I was scared to put pressure—" She gestured at her chest. Warmth rushed up to her eyes. "I didn't know what to do."

Dawn pushed herself off the sink. A steely pride held her shoulders erect. Her eyes were dry. "You did what you could."

"I'd only learned CPR that summer. I don't know if I did it right."

"That's enough."

"It doesn't feel like it." Ruthie looked back at her. She was suddenly desperate, as if this conversation were her only hope of understanding what Nathan's death had been for. "I saw him when he died, like a vision. He was standing alone on a plain with mountains and trees all around, like the last person on earth."

In the pictures surrounding the one of Nathan on the fridge, his sisters held babies of their own. Swaddled in their arms, gazing back at the camera. Dawn brushed something invisible from her shirt. She sighed. "He would've hated that. He never wanted to be alone in the woods, or hike or fish. Just play basketball and go to the mall with his friends. He was always with his friends. That's why he did it, you know. He wanted new sneakers. I couldn't afford them." She pulled back a chair and sat down heavily.

"Maybe I said it wrong," Ruthie said. "It wasn't bad. He wasn't alone. There just weren't any other people."

"Isn't that what alone is?" Dawn smiled wearily. "You white people love to think about the end of the world. I just want to go home, to my house, with all my children."

Sunlight divided the tabletop before them. The refrigerator began to hum. Ruthie hadn't meant to burden Dawn with her own pain. She'd worn long sleeves to hide her scars. Now she realized she was asking for something instead of giving it. "I see his face all the time," she said. "In the store, on the street. I have dreams about it."

"I see him, too," Dawn said. "Sometimes I'm sure he'll walk through the door. He'll just reappear. That it was a mistake somehow." She paused. "When they told me he was dead, I wanted to die, too. Now I get dressed every morning. I make breakfast. I go visit my grandchildren. I know what I want is impossible, but I keep doing things anyway." She knit her hands together. "All the stories I grew up with tell me he's in the trees, the rocks, the animals—that his spirit is still here with us, along with all our ancestors. And maybe he is. But I have to keep going on my own."

Out the window, an old Buick bumped past and turned at the end of the row. Dawn's voice went soft.

"I have to remind myself to notice things: The way my grandchildren smell, the feel of them in my arms. The children I have left." Her shoulders softened and she looked down at her hands. "I sometimes feel like a blind woman in a light-filled room."

Ruthie felt time slow in the air around her. She turned from Dawn's face to the carved fur of the wolf. She thought of how her mind had flown above the mountains when she was a little girl. How she'd looked down over the valley and seen all the way back to the People of the Flood. "I've felt that, too."

Dawn cleared her throat. She straightened, emerging from her reverie, and unclasped her hands. She looked sharply at Ruthie. "How many guns do you own?"

Ruthie was too startled to answer.

"I've heard about your dad, I know you have at least one."

"Seven," she said, reluctantly.

Dawn nodded. "Seven." She laid her hands flat on the table. "Do you think those hunters are still out there, killing things they don't have to see?"

Ruthie was silent. She knew they were. She'd seen one of them in the parking lot of Super 1, carrying groceries to his truck. His hunting rifle racked in the cab behind him as he drove away.

"Get rid of your guns. All of them," Dawn said. "It might save your life."

IV

24.

When Wiley King died, it set everyone in the valley on edge until they learned that an ex-NFL star was buying his property. Before the player's identity was known, rumors swirled: Joe Montana, Brett Favre, Terry Bradshaw . . . all the white heroes of days gone by. Howie Long had a place on Flathead Lake and people were sure this name would be even bigger. Rutherford was more excited than most, convinced that a football player, with his sporting disposition, would be reasonable when it came to the hunting rights to his pond—from which he'd been banned for almost twenty years.

"We've got to lay a *groundwork*," he said to Ruthie over beers in the Sawmill Bar. "Can't leave it to chance like last time." He finished three Busch Lights laying out a number of scenarios on how to win over the big man, whoever he was. Most of which involved her delivering a large quantity of fresh meat to his door as the first salvo.

"Are you trying to get me to seduce him?"

"What? No, Ruthie." Her father huffed and looked at her intently. With the gray hairs in his beard, his lips firmly closed, and his pale eyes set even deeper into his face, he'd gained a certain gravitas in his mid-forties, like the hermit who comes stumbling back into town after many years. "That pond is the best I've ever found for goose. The very best. It's your birthright."

She smiled. "I remember."

RUTHIE HAD BOUGHT HERSELF an old truck when she turned twenty-five, and thrown a used mattress from the thrift store in the back. On summer nights, she drove into the mountains and slept under the stars. She found peace in the woods, rarely thinking of Nathan or the encroaching development in the valley. Her favorite spot was the Lost Horse Lookout, beyond the Camas Lake Trailhead. The rocky precipice looked west up Lost Horse Canyon to Twin Lakes in the heart of the Bitterroot Mountains. Ruthie would lie on the mattress beneath the vault of stars—one occasionally shooting across in an unfathomable display of speed and light—and let her mind wander as it had when she was a child. She imagined living in a fire lookout on one of the distant peaks, her view sweeping into Idaho. A new Moses yapping as he greeted her at the door. Wood stacked to the ceiling to warm her through the winter. She observed blood moons and harvest moons and a full lunar eclipse, which sent a heat down her soul so deep that she didn't sleep for the entire night, as if she, too, might flame through the firmament.

Terry had told her that the human soul grew more restless as it aged. Preparing for eternity when it would range over the earth in constant motion, with ocean tides, atmospheric currents, and the migrations of birds and animals. Never resting, never sleeping.

In the mornings, Ruthie built a fire in the blackened firepit and sat on a stump beside it, watching the stars disappear one by one. From this vantage in the first misty light, the wilderness looked endless. It was easy to envision herself alive a thousand years before. Camped with nothing but her satchel of tools—flint knives, spearheads, home-made traps—preparing for another day outside history. Surrounded by bear, elk, and wolf. Small before the outstretched hand of the universe. What did infinity mean to a speck of dust? Even the satellites passing overhead, blinking red, didn't disturb her, for she was sure there had always been strange sights in the sky, and knew her ancestors had not neglected to look up and wonder.

ELEANOR LAW HAD DIED ALSO, and Ruthie moved into her old house. Renting it from Whipple Jr., who gave her the same discounted rate Eleanor had paid. It was a small prefab unit with a huge handicap-accessible shower and walls all her own. She loved the space. The only problem was the neighbors: Kent Willis in the Whispering Pines Trailer Park across the street and the rest of the Laws a half mile down the road. Len was a constant presence, lurking around her yard, telling her what needed fixing, asking if she needed help with weeds (though his own yard was entirely overgrown), and peering in through the windows. Luckily, he was wary of Pip and kept his distance when she came over in the evenings.

The two old friends sat on the porch drinking wine. "I hiked through Wiley's ranch," Pip said. "Not much has changed. The slough looks about the same as when we were little. The water's all silted, though, since no one uses it for irrigation anymore."

"The fence is off?" Ruthie asked.

Pip nodded. "No one's paying the power."

"I touched it once, just to see. It knocked me on my ass."

"Ten thousand volts. I heard Lonny Jensen grabbed it on a dare and his brother had to hit him with a two-by-four to get him free."

"Guess kids are going to have to think of another way to try and kill themselves."

"They can still drink and drive." Pip paused. Her eyes traveled up over the Sapphires. She wore a bulky sweatshirt over her short pants, and sat with her bare legs tucked underneath her. "It's the strangest thing: I've been having dreams where I'm pregnant."

Ruthie looked at her friend to make sure she was serious. The bottle of wine between them was half empty. Ice cubes melted in their glasses. She'd thought they stood apart from the other residents of the valley, who dreamt of marriage and children. "I still have nightmares about forgetting to have an abortion."

Pip smiled. "I used to have those, too. I'd drive all the way to Hamilton for a morning-after pill. But now something's changed. I don't know, I wake up and it's like a warmth inside me."

Ruthie remembered her visions of the first women settlers in the valley. Going mad after bearing children in the face of the wild. "The last thing this valley needs is more people."

Pip nodded absently. "That's true."

"I met a woman in the Super 1 yesterday who moved here from Boston. Since when have they heard of Darby in Boston?"

"From a magazine, most likely. The next one of these 'best small town in America' reporters who comes through, you're going to have to shoot." Pip picked up her glass and tipped an ice cube into her mouth. She crunched it with her molars. "These new people won't even know Wiley King ever lived here. It's strange—with him gone, there's nobody for everyone to hate anymore. Just the labs."

Ruthie leaned close to her friend and whispered, "I *love* his music."

Pip laughed out loud.

"'My Fellow Lonesome Rider,' oh my God, I listened to it all the time when we were in high school."

"You never told me!" Pip threw her head back and sang, "*May you one day escape the darkness and experience the light.*"

"Shhh," Ruthie hissed. "My dad will disown me."

"I liked Wiley, too. Other rich people were way worse than he was. The summer I worked cleaning houses, there was one family that dumped chlorine in their stretch of Rye Creek because they wanted the water clear. It killed everything. At least Wiley was trying to protect the fish in the slough."

"Seriously, don't let my dad hear you. I can't remember anything making him as happy as finding out Wiley was dead."

Pip grinned. One of her new jobs was helping Rutherford keep the books for his beetle business. Bitterroot Beetle Works had grown dramatically after being featured in an article on "genuine Montana" in a popular hunting magazine. Now skulls arrived from as far away as Louisiana, and Rutherford was making payments on a new truck. Ruthie could hardly believe it when she found a white leather couch in the living room of his trailer. He'd seen one on a Florida cop show and ordered it the next day.

The two women laughed. Down the street, a shadowy figure moved between a pair of trash bins. Nearly as short and decrepit as the bins themselves, the man quickly ducked behind one.

Pip squinted into the darkness. "Old fucker. I expect he's hoping to see us cast a spell."

"Or make love in the grass." Len was hidden now, but Ruthie knew he was still there. "You think anyone would mind if I ran him over with my truck?"

THE NFL PLAYER who bought Wiley King's land was Jon Sitka. He was unlike anything the valley had expected. A quarterback for twelve seasons, winner of five division titles and a conference championship, veteran of nearly ten thousand snaps and two Pro Bowl appearances. They'd imagined him to be a grinning colossus who would arrive by private jet, like those of Angel's Landing and the Stock Farm Club, to retire with his feet up on oaken outdoor furniture, loudly telling tales of last-second touchdown drives and willing cheerleaders. Instead, he was the picture of great, fumbling helplessness. A creature lost and in awe of the world, knocked back to innocence by repeated blows to the head. A bear without fur, yet so fragile as to leap aside at the sight of a squirrel.

Ruthie had planned to despise him, due to her father and everyone else's insistence that she do the opposite, but when he walked into the diner for the first time, her determination fell away. Here was a man at war with his own nature, a feeling she knew well. She saw it before she even heard him speak, simply in how he hung in the doorway, filling it awkwardly, letting in the cold, the screen door banging against his back, as if he needed to be invited to step all the way in.

When she told him he could sit anywhere he liked, he stared around the diner. Taking in each table, Pip smiling at the counter, Cook in his hairnet through the order window, the old pictures of Fort Owen on the walls, the faded portrait of Father Ravalli, the flowers Ruthie had set out by the register, and her behind them. His head was shaved and he seemed entirely devoid of hair save for the blond threads on his arms. His neck reddened in embarrassment. He shuffled over to the smallest table by the window, where she knew instinctively he would sit every time he came in from then on.

All the other diners stopped to watch him. One old man even let the beans slip from his spoon, so great was his distraction. Sitka was the biggest man any of them had ever seen. His dimensions seemed not quite real, as if the diner would need to be torn down and rebuilt to accommodate him. His hand covered the entire back of the chair when he pulled it out, and the silverware and place setting looked like a doll's. He sat with a creak that threatened the floor. The chair back barely reached the middle of his spine. His thighs pressed against the tabletop. Sighing, he turned to the window and gazed out over the roof of the high school.

Ruthie found herself walking toward him with the coffeepot in her hand.

He turned from the window when she filled his cup. She remembered her father's plans, the bounteous deliveries of meat, but from the look in Sitka's wide eyes, she figured a person could hunt his pond whenever they liked, without him even knowing. He gestured out at the snowcapped mountains. "I can't believe it," he said. "It's so beautiful." Awe brought out the web of pain-wrinkles around his eyes.

It had been a long time since Ruthie was amazed by the beauty of the valley. The feeling returned her to girlhood. "You should see them in a couple months when the larches are turning. They look like they're on fire."

"I might have to close my eyes."

Ruthie smiled. She found herself lingering by his table, staring up at the peaks, wanting to tell him about the winged skeleton shattering across the sky, or the anchor tree like Sasquatch alone on the mountainside. The grip of a butterfly's feet on her fingertip, otters speaking to her in the night.

25.

Some things aren't meant to be seen. Ruthie Fear froze. She stared at the juniper tree in the shade of the rock outcropping on the ridge. A white foot poked out from its shadow. A paw. A right hind-paw. She didn't want it to be, but it was.

The antlers went heavy in her arms. Her heart began to pound.

Jon Sitka approached behind her, and she felt the weight of him, his dimension and smell, the pain held in his battered body. The way he leaned toward her, his shoulder centimeters from hers but never quite touching. His pond lay sparkling below them; for Ruthie, its memory was so powerful that every time she saw it she heard the sound of cracking ice and saw her father plunging into the dark water. She and Sitka were shed-hunting on Sitka's ranch in the early spring, walking the faint game trails over the hills looking for fallen antlers in the last slushy snow. She had an armful and he'd found only one: a buck's first, with two small tines no longer than his pinkie. He held it tenderly as if it might break. It had been in an eagle's nest on the rocks and Ruthie had felt a pang of fear watching his big, damaged body clamber up to it. Both his knees were rebuilt, he had slipped discs in his back, countless concussions. Any new exertion made him wince. He carried bottles of painkillers in his pockets.

The paw was snow-white and skewed out in a wrong, painful way. Ruthie didn't want to see the rest of the animal, but she knew she had to. She reached out, as if to drop the antlers and grab Sitka, turn him around, and walk him home, but instead she stepped forward.

The coyote had chosen to die beneath the tree. She could tell as soon as she saw the rest of its body. It had come there for that purpose, had used the last of its strength to find the safety of the only shade on the wide sagebrush hillside. Perhaps it was a place it had been before, where it had slept on cold nights, or where its mother had taken it for shelter as a pup. The way its body lay was peaceful. The gray and white and ocher fur along its back curved slightly to its head, which rested across its thin front legs. But the skewed hind leg spoke to the suffering of its final moments, a last desperate clawing, striking out at death.

"Oh no," Sitka said quietly. Ruthie knelt beside the animal. For a moment she was afraid to touch it. She set the antlers down and pulled the glove from her right hand. She looked up at Sitka. His orange hunting cap—which she'd bought him so he wouldn't get shot as he lumbered around his now-open land during hunting season—was pushed back on his forehead, and his hairless face was awestruck: at the coyote, at death, at the wildness the valley kept hidden past the roads, and at her, the woman who'd led him here. He hunched over and his lips parted in a familiar expression of confused wonder, as if something extraordinary were about to happen.

Ruthie laid her palm across the coyote's spine. She was surprised by the warmth of its fur. It had just died. She worked her fingers deeper as though they might still find a spark. She felt the sharp knots of its vertebrae and the muscles of its back.

"What happened?" Sitka asked, his faith in her piercing. He knelt, took off his glove, and laid his hand beside hers. They looked like father and child's: one large, one small.

Ruthie shook her head. "I don't know."

But she did. It was young, barely more than a pup, with no sign of any wound. There were plenty of ranchers among Sitka's neighbors who left poisoned meat on their fence posts for this very purpose. Coyotes, wolves, mountain lions, Indians—they'd staked claims against them all. Ruthie strove to keep Sitka's vision of the valley pure. She wanted him to see it untarnished, and she craved moments when she saw it this way, too: old forest hiding the clear-cuts. She looked down at the willow trees around the pond, where her father could now be found every weekend morning, happily blasting geese. Sitka's mansion was below it, with a view of the Rocky Mountain Labs amid the low, strip-mall skyline of Hamilton at the base of the mountains.

Mountains and strip malls, pond and labs, hillside and poisoned coyote. The dichotomies were sometimes so jarring they made Ruthie dizzy.

Blood pulsed in Sitka's hand. The threads of hair on Ruthie's pinkie rose toward his thumb. His smell had become as familiar to her as that of the sage. He'd been a regular in the diner throughout the winter, and now at the beginning of spring they'd begun to walk together every evening after her shift. One night, they'd seen the aurora bore-alis dance green across the northern heavens from this very hill. But they'd never held hands, never kissed. She didn't know if he was frightened, or in love with someone else. She didn't ask because she didn't want to spoil what they had. When they walked, she could feel her heart swing in her chest. It was a happiness like none she remembered.

"Look." He nodded west to where the sunset had begun to turn the sky from blue to a purple and crackling orange. The colors were so vivid they seemed unnatural, as if the scientists in the labs were altering the very composition of the atmosphere. "It's like fireworks," he said. "Like halftime."

He looked down at his hand resting on the coyote's back. It was so large he could easily have picked the animal up and held it in his palm, as Ruthie would a rabbit. "That was stupid. It's not like halftime at all." He shook his head.

"Maybe it is," Ruthie said. Feeling a pause in the air around them.

DESCENDING ALONG the two-strand barbed-wire fence that separated Sitka's land from the ranch beside his, Ruthie saw something white clenched around the lower wire. Talons. Disembodied from the rest of the bird. She knelt, letting Sitka go ahead in his slow, limping walk. They were owl talons, their grip so tight they remained even though the rest of the bird was ripped clean away. Its gray, white, and brown feathers were strewn across the ground. Its body was gone. Eaten or plundered. She touched the right talon. She gripped the ankle where it had been ripped asunder and tried to pull it loose. The talons held; they were so tight she'd need a saw. Every ounce of the bird's strength had riveted it in place, fighting whatever had caught it. And what was that? What was loose on this hillside? What ate owls?

Sitka's wide back grew smaller below her. From a distance, he seemed half man, half bear. He moved gingerly but with a power that cowed even Badger. His presence turned men into boys, searching wide-eyed through their pockets for scraps of paper for him to sign, in perpetual awe of the professional athlete. The gladiator sailing home across the sea. Sitka had gone through the fire and come out softer than before. A miracle, Ruthie felt. She looked at the labs. The ugly, winking face of the modern world.

If a monster did come, she saw her body curled beneath Sitka's as the coyote's was beneath the tree. Safe for all time.

26.

The hot springs at Jerry Johnson were closed due to *E. coli*, so Ruthie and Jon Sitka laid a trapline going to each bar on the way back to Darby. She piloted his huge, gleaming Yukon while he lay fully reclined in the passenger seat. It was painful for him to sit upright, and Ruthie wouldn't let him drive when he was on painkillers. He'd eventually get a look in his eye where she could tell it hurt enough that he wouldn't mind going over the guardrail.

Highway 12 twisted along the Lochsa River. Kayaks tumbled on the high, foaming water. The kayakers seemed suicidal to Ruthie. She expected to see them flipped and dashed on the rocks around each turn. It would serve them right. All the rock climbers and mountain bikers and kayakers were ruining the wild just as surely as the miners and loggers had. Even in the deepest wilderness, you couldn't go anywhere without seeing chalk marks, treads, and carabiners. Little reminders that they'd been there first, and had their *experience*. Cedar groves towered to the left, and the windward side of the Bitterroots, more densely forested due to precipitation from the coast, rose to the right. They felt unfamiliar to Ruthie, though they were the same mountains, the same wilderness, where she'd spent her life. She sighed and focused on the road. She'd picked Sitka up that morning wanting only to get as far away from Len as possible, and thinking the hot springs would settle her mind. It was a long stretch before the next bar, the Lumberjack, on Graves Creek. Clear over Lolo Pass.

They were nearly to the top when Sitka spoke hoarsely, "Pull over. Here."

"What?" Ruthie turned.

"Please." His face was pale. "I gotta get out."

The Yukon took a moment to slow, and the tires skidded when she pulled onto the shoulder. They jerked to a stop. A runaway truck ramp rose steeply above them. She pictured careening up it and shooting off the top like Evel Knievel, soaring over the peaks and bouncing to a stop in front of the Sawmill Bar. Sitka shoved open his door and pitched onto the gravel. He squirmed over and lay flat on his back. His huge chest heaved. He was so large that in some positions he looked mythical, like a giant. "The pills," he said. "By your feet."

Ruthie reached into the compartment at the bottom of the door. Felt several bottles and drew out the fullest one: oxycodone, forty milligrams. A horse dose. Enough to put her in a coma. She got out, staying close to the hood as a semi downshifted past, and handed the bottle to Sitka. Half the people in the valley were on pills of some kind. You could see them sitting dead-eyed in lawn chairs while their children played with rusty car parts. The blood was gone from Sitka's lips. His eyes reminded her of a dog's: goodness in there but also a profound lack of comprehension. *World, why do you hurt me so?* Ruthie thought of bending over to kiss him gently on the lips as he swallowed two pills dry, his huge throat working. She thought of unbuckling her jeans and squatting over his face. Rocking against his tongue. Sweet broken football boy. Forever child.

"Shit," Sitka said. "Sometimes it just comes up on me." He paused. "They always talk about brain damage. Brain damage is the easy part."

Ruthie knew he was lying. She'd watched his old games. Flying tacklers spearing his helmet. Four-hundred-pound linemen crashing down on him. The hits that bent him backward in half. Football had never mattered much to her, beyond being the site of Badger's adolescent heroics, but now she saw it for what it was: an operatic snuff film played out in slow motion, in which the bodies and minds of young men were destroyed for the viewing pleasure of millions of drunk imbeciles. The camera zoomed in pornographically on the hits, then backed away in mock respect for the motionless bodies on the field, never showing the way their limbs twitched in the fencing reflex, or the blank, wobbled searching in their eyes. Sitka claimed he didn't remember the second half of the NFC Championship Game he'd played in. Just blurs of red.

Seeing his head battered this way and that, Ruthie was amazed he'd survived at all.

"You were good at something. Most people can never say that," she said.

Color began to return to his face. The oxycodone silencing his nerves. It was a wonder none of the junkies in the valley had broken into his mansion. Probably they were too scared of him, even though he was the only man Ruthie knew who didn't own a gun. She'd tried to give him one but he wouldn't allow it in his house. Ruthie had pawned three of hers after her conversation with Dawn, but had kept one for protection, and three to hunt. Sitka smiled weakly. He patted the ground beside him. Ruthie sat down. Gravel bits poked her butt through her jeans. "When I got drafted I thought I'd won the lottery. Not ruined my life."

"What about halftime?"

He shook his head. "Even halftime was awful. All that yelling."

"Sounds like you need another drink."

"I need about a hundred."

"There aren't that many bars between here and there."

"You think any of them have a hot tub?"

"You have a hot tub."

He shrugged wearily. "I was looking forward to something new. Who knew *E. coli* was a real thing?"

His blunt features were somehow featureless; his shaved skull like an oversized thumb. Only the wrinkles at the corners of his eyes revealed his kindness. Men in bars often tried to fight him for his size, so he rarely went out at night. Instead spending his evenings in the vibrating orthopedic chair in his basement—made special for him by doctors in Seattle—watching the fishing channel.

Ruthie often joined him. Sometimes she dreamt of moving into the mansion with him and becoming a fable of the valley: the poor trailer trash girl from Red Sun Road who married the football star from far away. She'd walk out of the diner wearing diamonds. Buy a mountain and put her name on it, like the M on Mount Sentinel in Missoula. Set Rutherford up in an outbuilding in a distant corner of the ranch, with satellite TV, a fully stocked bar, all the geese of his dreams, and whatever idiotic, oversized trucks he wanted.

But here she was, by the side of the highway. "This is new," she said, looking at the gravel and the mountainside plunging off beyond the guardrail. Patches of dirty snow still clung to shadowed places below the guardrail. Blood smeared one of them. The broken remains of a doe on the other side of it.

Sitka shook his head. "Not for me. I've laid by a thousand different roads." A hatchback full of college students with kayaks strapped to the roof zoomed past toward Missoula. Sitka stared straight up at the clouds, like patches of snow themselves on the blue sky. Sometimes, when the pain in his back caused him to squirm on the buzzing cushions of his gigantic chair, he seemed to glow, as if his suffering were elevating him to a higher plane. He'd told her he had no family left. His parents had stolen money from him, his sister lived in Thailand.

"At least you're not paralyzed," Ruthie said.

He grunted. "Would you roll me over and stand on my back? It helps sometimes."

She got her hands under him like a side of beef but she never would've been able to move him if he hadn't helped, propping himself up on his elbow and flinging over so he thudded onto his chest. He groaned, his mouth in the dirt, his dusty ass raised. Any remnants of sexual thoughts Ruthie had disappeared. She stood and surveyed the broad plain of his back. "Should I take off my shoes?"

"Doesn't matter." His voice was muffled by the dirt.

She stepped her boot onto his spine and pressed down lightly, then lifted her other foot. He sighed at her full weight. She walked back and forth on his soft, muscled width. He felt like a wrestling mat, and she thought of Dalton Pompey, married now with three children and three fewer fingers, who'd tried to have sex with her one day after practice. She'd pushed him off, afraid that Badger would walk into the gym. Maybe she should've done it. Given herself a memory. She pressed down harder. Had her life really changed? Or had she only graduated to a better football player? She felt the huge bunches of muscle below Sitka's shoulders, like the whorled knots in a cedar trunk. No, this one was kind. All that maimed power turned in on itself. She had yet to hear him say a cruel word about another human being, and though he watched fishing shows for hundreds of hours, he winced every time the angler withdrew the hook from a fish's lip. His forehead creased in amazement when she spoke of her childhood, the hunting and fights, as if her life had been a frontier fairy tale. She knelt between his shoulder blades and gripped the back of his neck. Her hand wasn't big enough to get around it, so she just squeezed, feeling the sharp stubble of his hair, squeezing and releasing, as tightly as she could. He softened beneath her, melting into the gravel. She realized she could lie down on top of him and curl up like a cat.

"Mmmm," he said. "Just leave me here."

"They'd need a crane to get you out."

"It'd be a sky burial. Like the Vajrayanas in Tibet."

She wondered how he knew about that. Sometimes he'd get so glazed and confused he couldn't answer the simplest question, then he'd mention a culture she'd never heard of.

"An act of generosity," he went on. "For the vultures and the crows."

Ruthie pursed her lips and looked up the road. "You do have a lot of meat."

"WHAT ARE WE DOING OUT HERE?" Sitka asked, when they were across from each other in the largest wood booth in the back corner of the Lumberjack Bar on Graves Creek. There were no windows but they could hear the current through the open door. He was wedged in sideways with his left leg straight out in a way that would be painful for a normal person but seemed to give him relief. Ruthie's fingers were cold as she picked at the label on her beer bottle. "I mean, why did you get me this morning?"

"Len Law," she said finally. "He's my neighbor. He's got all the sheep and junked-up trailers at the end of Thornton Loop. I . . . I told him I was going to rape his mother and kill his dog."

Sitka raised his eyebrows. Ruthie had yet to see him truly surprised. Maybe being blindsided so many times during games had knocked the ability out of him. "Why'd you do that?"

"I don't know, it just came out. He's been haunting my property ever since I moved in. Watching me. He's been watching me since I was a girl. He's a seventy-five-year-old racist and he sniffs around like a teenager." She took a drink. "Whenever I come outside he tries to tell me what needs fixing, and I know he's looking through the windows at night. I can't change clothes in my own room without checking the blinds. Early this morning, he was at the end of my walk." She put the bottle down and pulled the last silvered strip off the glass. "Just standing there staring, as if he doesn't mind everybody knowing what he's doing. And I lost it. I don't know why it makes me so mad, but it feels like . . . like he wants to have me and then curse me."

Sitka nodded slowly.

"Like he wants to fuck me and then burn me like a witch."

"Jesus Christ." Sitka set the beer down. "Don't think like that. Don't let those things in your head."

"I know it's probably not that bad, but you don't know what he's like. I've known some men . . . and he's the worst in the valley."

"I know men," Sitka said. "And I know curses. The Cowboys, when I played for them, they had a Haitian guy who'd come in with little bones and feathers and put a hex on whoever we were up against that week. Saying so-and-so was going to get his arm broke or his knee blown out or concussed. Usually it came true, too. When I got traded, I got this." He lifted his shirt to show her a small coiled rune tattooed on his massive rib cage. "For when I had to play against them. It's a shield."

"Does it work?"

Sitka shrugged. "I can still walk sometimes. And I didn't have to kill anyone's dog."

Ruthie smiled. Little crumpled balls from the beer label littered the tabletop. "It was just the worst thing I could think of," she said. "I don't know where it came from. His mom's about a hundred, she hasn't left her trailer in years. She might already be dead in there. Sometimes a meanness just comes through me. It's like it's coming from somewhere deep in the earth and I can't help myself. The first time was when I was seven, I threw a rock at a little boy for no reason." She lifted the bare bottle but didn't drink. "In high school, I had my boyfriend punch a kid whose family I didn't like. Another time I told my dad I could see why my mom left. It was the same. The worst thing I could think of."

"I'd say trying to scare off the old pervert next door is different from the things we say to people we love when we're mad at them." Sitka rested his palm on the edge of the table. "You want me to talk to him?"

"No." Ruthie shook her head slowly. "I can handle it. I've been handling it my whole life."

"It might be easy. Men around here seem to love me."

"Oh, some of them hate you, too. They hate anyone with a house and a fence like yours. Even if you let the hunters back in."

Sitka pondered this. He looked down at his hands. It seemed hard for him to fathom that anyone could not like him. It was a problem Ruthie had found in other men as well. They imagined that if they acted with magnanimity in their station, everyone in the whole world would love them. Women knew better. They learned early on that envy and meanness come from nothing and nowhere and would always remain.

Only one other couple was in the room: a pair of leathery bikers leaning against the bar rail. They were sniping at each other about the shake-a-day—if the payout warranted another try—causing their neck waddles to twitch over their beers. They were the kinds Ruthie saw in the early afternoon in every bar she'd ever been to. Man and woman worn down to wrinkled twins. Oscillating between love and hate. Gone back to their holes before the night crowd came in.

"This place used to be famous," Ruthie said. "You can't tell now, but when my dad was a kid they had shuttles from Hamilton and Mis-soula. They'd pick you up on the street and bring you back the next morning. Big-time bands played and they never stopped serving. People came from all over and slept in the field. My dad says he kissed a famous country music star here once, but he wouldn't tell me which one." She stopped, touched by her father's lies.

"I didn't have a beer until I was twenty-two. My dad said it would make me soft."

Ruthie tried to picture Sitka's father. She saw a hulking shadow in a recliner, a fist like a cinder block gripping a protein shake on its arm. Dead fish eyes glittering. Who steals money from their own child? She tipped the neck of her bottle toward Sitka. "Well, cheers, we're catching up."

A wedge of sunlight slanted in through the door. Sitka's eyes followed the lazy pattern it made on the floorboards, the motes of dust rising through the golden air. "That meanness was all I had as a kid," he said. "I'd have killed someone on the football field if I could've, and been proud of it. Harder, meaner, stronger. That's all he wanted from me. It's not in the ground, it's in here." He tapped his chest. "Waiting, all the time, and some people let it take over."

27.

The early summer heat had gathered by the time Ruthie and Sitka left the bar. Ruthie turned on the air conditioner, an automotive luxury neither she nor her dad had ever been able to maintain, and drove east along Lolo Creek past an old schoolhouse and a ranch that had burned in one of the fires of Ruthie's youth. Only the hearth and chimney remained of the main house. The white fence had also been spared. The wrought-iron gate looked tragic guarding the burned-out waste. A two-story townhouse had been hastily erected in the far corner with the insurance money, but all the grandeur of the former ranch was lost.

At the 93 junction, they turned south into the Bitterroot Valley. The Second Nature Taxidermy lot was full of trucks. A pile of antlers lay bleaching in the sun. A naked plaster woman kicked her feet from the steel tub above the awning of the Hayloft Saloon. Ruthie saw shimmering figures atop tractors in distant fields. WIFE LEFT. GONE TO EUROPE. EVERYTHING MUST GO, was spray-painted across three huge sheets of plywood in front of Happel's used car lot. Ruthie squeezed her eyes shut and opened them, wanting to laugh. Happel's wife in Europe? With her sallow face and dumpy legs? She remembered when they were too poor to rebuild their shack after the earthquake. How long and strange life was. After another mile, Terry French's pawnshop came into view. The hand-lettered marquee read the same as it had for her entire life: FRENCH PAWN, and then below: GUNS: AN INVESTMENT THAT SHOOTS. Ruthie imagined turning off the highway and smashing through the Old-West-style plank building. Artillery, Indian jewelry, and belt buckles scattering in her wake. Hauling Terry into the backseat and taking him with them over Skalkaho Pass to Philipsburg.

A disjointed arrow of ducks flew overhead. *Bang, bang, bang.*

Sitka rolled his head toward her. "I heard ducks have a corkscrew penis," he said.

"Who told you that?" Ruthie was fairly certain she knew more about ducks than he did. They passed Hooper's Landing and the Lake Como turn. The outskirts of Darby came into view: a tire shop and Whipple's, with the bulk of the high school beyond. Whipple had retired and his sons now ran the store, fighting to stay in business with the new Wal-Mart in Hamilton. Ruthie tried to picture a mallard's undercarriage. Saw a literal corkscrew, steely and sharp, creeping out from beneath the feathers.

"The females developed corkscrew vaginas as a protection because there's so much duck rape," Sitka went on. "So the males got corkscrew cocks."

"Do you know anything useful?" Ruthie asked, slowing in front of the diner, and thinking for the thousandth time that she'd spent too much of her life there. "Like how to change a tire or cheat the IRS?"

"Nah." He shook his head. "Just how to throw the old buttonhook."

DEPUTY BADGER WAS WAITING on Ruthie's porch, leaning against the railing in his uniform. Another figure lurked in the shadows, but it wasn't until she parked that she realized it was Len Law. Shrunken and pale like a decrepit goblin against the siding of her house, his last wisps of gray hair pushed back crazily from his skull.

"You've got company," Sitka said, rising up on his elbows from the reclined seat.

Ruthie nodded. She shut the engine off and handed him the keys.

"Want me to stay?"

"Better if you don't." She could feel Badger's eyes boring through the tinted windows. They'd hardly spoken in the past two years. He'd studiously avoided her, even in the diner and Super 1 checkout line. She could feel the strain in him when he did, like he was telling himself a story he didn't believe, but it was a relief to her. This was the first time he'd been to her new house. She hoped it didn't herald more visits. Ruthie got out and rounded the hood, feeling Sitka's steady, fragile bulk as he came to take her place in the driver's seat. He stopped awkwardly to hug her goodbye. She stood up on her tiptoes, took his cheeks in her hands, and pressed her lips to his.

Sitka turned bright red. His lips slowly parted. He touched her hips. She held him, warmth filling her chest, for as long as she could.

"I've been wanting to do that for months," Ruthie said, leaning back and looking into his blue eyes.

Sitka turned even redder. "Me, too." He smiled, gulped down a breath, and stepped away. He raised his hand to Badger.

Badger raised his back, clearly against his will.

"I'll come by the diner in the morning, and . . . and see you then,"

Sitka stammered. Aglow, he pulled himself into the Yukon and started the engine. He waved to Ruthie. Her heart thudded. She waited for him to pull away, then turned back to her yard. The edges of her lawn were overgrown at the chain-link fence, but she'd cleared the vegetable bed, and a row of tomato starts were growing up the wood stakes. She'd taken out the handicap ramp and painted the house's trim marigold. The chain-saw bear her father had given her wore an old pair of aviator sunglasses by the porch. Ruthie felt she glimpsed a brighter future.

"Where you been?" Badger asked.

"Tried for the hot springs but it was closed," she said, coming up the front walk.

"I could've told you that. Been shut down all week. Maybe let me know next time you're going." Jealousy gave his voice a hard edge. He turned to Len, his palm on the butt of his gun. "Len here says you're planning to rape his mom and kill his dog."

Ruthie felt the eyes of her neighbors on her back. "Why don't we talk inside?"

"You said you were going to," Len said. "Don't try to squeeze out of it. I been in this neighborhood sixty years. I won't be made to feel unsafe. And what're you doing with that football boy?"

Ruthie unlocked the door. "Inside."

Len narrowed his eyes and looked at the deputy. "She make the rules now?"

"Oh, get in there," Badger said.

"I told them not to send you. Still all wrapped up—" Len stopped, seeing the look in Badger's eye. He sucked his teeth and reluctantly stepped into the small living room. He peered around his sister's former house at the mismatched furniture and the TV. Ruthie had little interest in decorating, picking up objects that caught her eye in the thrift store and setting them down on her shelves at random. Wolf and bear figurines, dream catchers, old Forest Service posters, rocks and teeth and antlers that she'd found. Seeing it now, she was suddenly worried that she'd replicated the childishness of her father's room.

"Eleanor used to have it real nice in here," Len said, wrinkling his nose. He turned to Badger. "I want it on the official record in case something happens to me. So everyone knows who done it."

Badger closed the door behind him. They all three stood in the semidarkness. Badger scuffed his boots on the welcome mat. A strangely large ruby glinted on his wedding ring. Clearly his wife had picked it out. His belly sagged over his belt. He and Janine had been married for six years and still had no children. Rumors of his impotence swirled around the valley; people smirked at him in the grocery store. He turned to Len. "How's she going to rape your mom, anyway? No one's seen her in years."

The two men stared at each other. "That's not fair to ask," Len said finally. "To make me picture it."

"Well, you're going to have to if you want to press charges. Gonna need a full statement. Diagrams." Badger grinned bloodlessly. He balled his fist and set it on the back of Ruthie's recliner. She'd stopped in the entrance to her kitchen. He looked at her like she'd owe him after this. She wanted to climb out her window. She should've kept driving with Sitka. Gone home to his mansion and never left. These were the last two men she wanted in her living room. Len kept glancing at her bedroom door, as if hoping it would swing open so he could fill in the spaces in his fantasies. See where she slept. All her lacy underthings.

"Used to be families on this block," Len said. "Nothing like this ever would've happened."

"You need to stay the hell away from my property," Ruthie said. "And stop watching me. I ought to press charges on you."

Len huffed. "Watching you? I've been looking out for you your whole life. You and your daddy both. Who do you think gave you a patch for your roof when your trailer was fit to blow away? Or made sure you and Pip didn't get kidnapped, always out playing alone in the woods?"

Ruthie was too stunned to speak. He thought he'd been *helping* her?

"I've kept an eye on this neighborhood longer than you've been alive," Len went on. "We came to this valley when it was savage. Couldn't fetch water without facing a bear or Indian, and both were worse. My grandpa knew what it took to keep it safe. You come in here, ungrateful, hanging around with the Frenches, sleeping with a new man every night—"

"Watch your mouth," Badger said.

"The Frenches?" Ruthie said.

"And you." Len turned to Badger, his indignation making him wild-brave. "Out there doing whatever she says, panting like a whipped dog. You got no pride. What's your wife think?"

Ruthie's mouth went dry. She felt a ringing in her ears. "You racist old shit," she said. She saw on Badger's face the same expression he'd had after the homecoming dance, faced off with Dalton Pompey in front of Dalton's truck. Tiny helpless rage, like a much smaller man trapped inside his body, screaming to be let out. And worse now, compounded by the years of thinking it would change, that something would finally be understood.

"You might have crossed the line," Badger said quietly, shifting his bulk to block the door. "Nobody in this town likes you much." He paused. "You know why Kelly from dispatch sent me, even though you told her not to? Because she's married to Guzman, who works at the nursery. And how many times have you called the cops on Guzman just for walking to his truck at night?"

Len blinked and took a step back. "Just a second, now."

"Who're you going to call?" Badger tracked him slowly, his big body suddenly nimble, the old athlete still in the balls of his feet. Moving with a controlled rage, as if he'd been waiting for this moment since he saw Ruthie kiss Sitka in the street. He pinned Len in the corner. "The police?"

"I don't have to take this," Len said. "My granddaddy was ten times the lawman you are."

Daylight slanted through the blinds. Ruthie looked at the window as if she might will herself through it. Outside, birds were chirping, insects buzzing. Sitka would just be getting home. Badger knotted his hands through the old man's shirt. Len drew into himself, his entire frail body flinching as Badger lifted him off the floor and threw him onto the carpet. He made a choking sound when he hit. He cursed and mumbled, holding his arm, his eyes wildly roaming the room.

"I've heard about you when you were young," Badger said, standing over him. "How you'd jerk off in that chair you carved over Lake Como. How they had to run you off. You remember that?" He grabbed the wisp of gray hair on Len's skull and jerked his face up.

Len's lips worked silently, spittle bubbling out the sides.

"You and your kin have been plaguing this town for long enough," Badger said. "If there's a curse in this valley, it's you."

He tightened his grip and yanked the gray head from side to side.

"Stop it," Ruthie said. "That's enough."

Badger looked up, and she saw in his eyes all the years of not being the person he wanted, of trying so hard and failing a bit more each day. He wetted his lips and dropped the hair. "All right, Ruthie," he said. Then he kicked Len hard and clean in the stomach.

Len curled into a ball on the carpet. He clutched his ribs, fighting for air. Tears filled the lines on his cheeks.

"You let me know when you want to press charges," Badger said.

28.

As soon as the snow melted in the high country and the road became passable, Ruthie drove Jon Sitka to the Lost Horse Lookout. They sat shoulder to shoulder looking up the canyon with their legs dangling off the rocky edge. "I want to live there," Ruthie said, nodding to the far peak where her fire lookout would be. Fifty miles from any road, with a panoramic view of the wilderness.

Sitka took her hand. "All right," he said.

THE FIRST TIME Sitka blacked out, Ruthie thought it was a game. In the months since they'd begun sleeping together, he'd never pressed her face hard into the mattress. But she didn't mind. Usually she wished he was more forceful; too often he treated her like she might break. Then his fingers tightened around her throat. She found she couldn't breathe. She struggled. She was drowning, suffocating. Her excitement turned to fear. She saw flashes of white light on a growing black plain.

The blackness had nearly overpowered her when she heard a strangled moan from above, and as suddenly as he'd begun, Sitka toppled off and she was free, gasping in a tangle of sheets on the mattress.

It took her several seconds to catch her breath, and for the flares of light to leave her eyes. When they did, she heard Sitka crying. "I'm sorry," he said, over and over, from the edge of the bed. He was slumped naked off the side with his back to her, elbows planted on his knees, and his huge head folded over in his hands. Carefully, Ruthie touched her throat. It was bruised, tender. She was dazed. She didn't know what had happened. She found that she wanted to comfort Sitka, and was briefly revolted.

"What was that?" she asked, when she could speak.

"I blacked out," he said. "It happens sometimes from exertion. When my testosterone or adrenaline go up. The doctors say it's from CTE, but they don't know why, or when it's going to happen, or if there's any way to stop it. They don't know anything." He shook his head, then gripped his forehead, his fingertips going white. Ruthie stared at his pale, hulking form on the edge of the bed. So here it was: the thing that had popped loose in his brain. She'd been waiting for it. Their time together had been too good, too easy. She'd expected the ground to start to shake.

"It's why I waited so long and never kissed you," he said. "I was scared I'd ruin everything."

The bedroom walls were bare and the massive gray bed was the only piece of furniture. Ruthie felt she was on a ship drifting away from shore.

"Exertion," she said.

He raised his tear-streaked face to hers. "I could have killed you."

She shook her head. "No man is going to kill me." Her mind was a jumble. She feared the pull she felt toward violence. Badger and Sitka seemed to have separated the two halves that men carried inside, and distilled them down to their pure essence. Brutality and calm. Dark and light. "Does it happen other times?" she asked.

He looked away. "It can. When I get angry or . . ."

"Or what?"

"Or it just can." He looked at her helplessly. "I can't control it. Usually I just hurt myself. Punching walls. I broke my leg kicking through a shower door. Severed an artery. That's why I moved here. They've tried all sorts of things. The doctors . . . tests. They're afraid I'm going to kill myself. I thought if I just lived alone, quietly, in the mountains for the rest of my life, I wouldn't hurt anyone and I might come to understand what it all was for. Then I met you." He stopped.

"You should have told me."

His neck glistened with sweat. Sadness shone in his eyes. "I know. I was afraid you'd leave me. And I felt better with you than I ever have in my life. Seeing the world the way you do, all the beauty, the mountains and forests, the animals. Being a part of your life here in this valley is the best thing that ever happened to me. I felt like I was becoming whole. I thought I could control it."

Ruthie smelled herself and Sitka mingled in the air. Two animals, dashed together.

"I thought my life could be different."

"It can." The old stubbornness gathered within Ruthie. She saw his broad back moving away on the hillside, owl feathers scattered in the sage. She refused to let him go. "I know it can."

He shook his head. "It wasn't worth it. It wasn't worth this."

She saw how his entire being had been pushed one way, and he was now fighting to go another. The shape of his life. She hated the games old men forced young men to play in pursuit of their lost dreams. Wars and conquest and football. "I've changed," she said. "I'm not the same girl I was. I'm not my father. You can be different, too."

29.

The valley was shrouded in smoke. Ruthie, Billy, and Terry French sat on lawn chairs on the riverbank at Hooper's Landing. Ruthie didn't usually deign to fish here—the shit-fed hatchery trout tasted pre-frozen—but it was the closest spot to Darby and the air by the water was easier to breathe. She watched the fire planes curve over the mountain peaks to discharge plumes of red retardant on the burning trees below. People hardly remarked on the fire season anymore, except to say whether it was early or late. This year it was late. September was nearly over and the fires continued to burn. Ruthie imagined her bright red bear burrowing into his den, hungry and frustrated.

"Father Mike's not the only crazy white man to kill himself in this river," Billy said, tying a hook on to the line of his spinning rod and threading on a grasshopper from the perforated beer can at his feet. Ruthie had caught the hoppers that morning in the field behind her father's trailer, when they were still sluggish in the dew. "Old Hark Law came down here during the coldest January I can remember, back when we were kids and winters got cold like they're supposed to. The river was in overflow, frozen solid on the banks with the water underneath getting pushed up and freezing again. He lay down on it and went to sleep. Was a solid block by the time he was found. Whipple Sr. had to come down with a blowtorch to thaw his body out."

"He killed himself," Terry said. "That's all. And it was better than he deserved." He shook a hopper from the can and held it up. Its front walking legs waved wildly. "I'll be glad when all the Laws are gone from this valley."

Billy shrugged, smiling, and cast up the current. He looked fresh out of bed in sweatpants and a rumpled T-shirt, his straw hat pushed back from his forehead, his black hair hanging loose down his back. Terry wore cowboy boots, stained jeans, and a red collared shirt. The brothers looked more alike as they aged. The flesh on their cheeks tightening to the bones beneath. Wrinkles working across their foreheads. Terry stooping slightly to match his brother's height. Billy standing straighter as his self-consciousness faded away. He and Dawn had moved in together in a double-wide on a small plot of land outside Lolo. They were planning to get married in the spring.

Ruthie wanted distraction from her life, and her love of Sitka. She was happy for Billy and Dawn but envious also. Somehow a dead son seemed easier to manage than a damaged brain. "Tell me about the winter bear," she said. "That was always my favorite when I was a girl."

"Oh, the winter bear," Terry said solemnly. "You don't see those anymore."

Billy shook his head. He twitched his fishing pole contemplatively. The split shot twisted in an eddy but the line remained tight. "Not in a long time. Used to be one just about every year. A big old male, who'd given up on denning to roam his frozen range. Knowing he didn't have many years left."

Terry nodded. "Not wanting to waste them asleep."

"Out wandering the snow, sooner or later he'd find a patch of open water on the frozen river."

"He'd refresh himself, like bears do."

"And get his fur all wet. Then he'd roll in the snow and a thick plate of ice would form over his fur."

"Armor, hard as steel. Arrows would break against it."

"Heavy enough to stop a bullet."

"Nothing you could do if the winter bear came for you."

The brothers stopped, pleased with each other, having remembered all the old lines. They'd told the story countless times to Ruthie and Delilah in the autumns of their youth. Ruthie held her pole between her knees and clapped.

"Did you ever see one?" she asked.

"Of course not," Billy said. "We wouldn't be alive if we had."

The smoky air hung low over their heads. Occasionally a breeze pushed aside the haze and revealed the flames running down the flanks of the Bitterroots. The fire had nearly reached the foothills and many of the farms west of Stevensville had been evacuated. Firemen shuffled through the diner with soot-stained faces, the steel toes of their boots burned black.

"Do you think it's more good than bad? Life, I mean," Ruthie asked, thinking of Sitka.

"Fifty-fifty," Terry said.

"No, come on, brother. She wants a big, Indian answer." Billy cleared his throat and cocked his hat farther back on his forehead. He eyed his bobber and nudged the cooler of beers at his feet, settling himself. "Like this: Coyote was sent down by the Old-Man-in-the-Sky to rid the world of evil. He tricked the Elk-Monster into a hole and buried it alive but its hoof remained uncovered, which is why we still have greed and anger. And why that mesa you see to the east is called Evil Hoof." He nodded to Ruthie.

Terry raised his beer to his brother in salute. "You should've been a medicine man."

Billy shook his head. "Too many curses." He popped open a can. "I would've made the whole valley sick." Gnats hovered over the surface of the rushing water. Cottonwood fluff swirled in the shallows. Ruthie looked across at the spot where Father Mike's cassock had tangled on the rocks.

"Were the Laws always the worst?" she asked.

"They set things off," Billy said. "But everyone else followed. All the settlers wanted the Indians gone so they could have the valley for themselves. Now it's filled up and they want each other gone. Rich people want the poor people gone. Poor people want the rich people gone. I might laugh if they weren't burning the whole place down."

A piece of ash floated down on Ruthie's leg, as if to emphasize his point. Ruthie thought of Dawn alone in her and Billy's trailer, doing each thing carefully, moving blindly in the light.

"I think we're going to get it back," Terry said.

Billy shook his head. "The vultures will get it back. The coyote and the crows."

Ruthie tried to picture this. An empty place. Vines growing to cover Whipple's store. The labs being washed away. Coyote padding through the aisles of Super 1. She felt the valley's long memory in the dirt beneath her feet. All the people it had seen come and go. "You know they're tearing down Lil's?" she said. "Putting in some health-food place."

Billy's line jerked momentarily, then went still. A reed. Some phantom fish—or Father Mike's lonesome spirit. "Of course I know," he said. "Dawn has to drive by every day on her way to work." He shook his head. "What happened will still be there, though. No matter what they build over it."

"Like everything else," Terry said.

30.

Each time Ruthie entered the mansion she felt like a trespasser, even though she had her own key. Walking down the long hall past Charlie Russell prints to the main room with its thirty-foot ceiling and panoramic view of the Bitterroot River. A few miles and a million years from where she'd grown up on Red Sun Road. Some of Wiley King's belongings had been left behind, including two gold records hanging over the stone fireplace. On the left was "My Fellow Lonesome Rider"—Ruthie's favorite. She was sure they were replicas but she liked to look at them, as if she now ruled the empire of her father's vanquished enemy.

One of Sitka's former teammates' wives—an interior decorator—had chosen all the furniture and art. It looked like the fantasy of someone who'd seen western movies but never actually been to Montana.

Wagon wheels, Navajo blankets, plump leather furniture. A saddle on a mesquite stand. Horseshoes. Coils of rope. Cast bronze stallions stampeded across the dining room table. A massive antler chandelier hung over the fireplace. Ruthie had asked Sitka where his belongings were, his pictures and mementos and trophies. "I wanted to leave all that behind," he said. It worried Ruthie, who felt at times that his real life existed elsewhere, apart from her.

She lingered upstairs before descending to the basement where Sitka spent most of his time, near his giant TV and private gym, in rooms he kept at seventy-five degrees. She wondered if she could ever make the house feel like a home. The only other visitors were the maid and Hector, the property's caretaker who delivered Sitka's meals.

THE FISHING CHANNEL played softly in the background. Ruthie wished Sitka would turn it off. She didn't want to come while hearing how to properly draw a hooked bass along an eddy current. The room was warm, almost hot. She was sitting in the giant vibrating ortho-pedic chair with Sitka on his knees before her. Her bare legs dangled around his head. His tongue moved in quick circles, then long strokes lengthwise, causing Ruthie's stomach to involuntarily tremble. His eyes flicked up to hers for approval.

This was their sex life now. Sitka didn't allow her to reciprocate for fear that the stimulation would trigger another blackout. She squeezed his ears with her thighs. The image of his face between them had made her come almost instantly at first, but it held less of a charge now. She closed her eyes and let her head roll back. Her mind drifted along with the thrumming of the chair's motor. The fishing announcer spoke of belly reels, pencil-length sinkers, and a great angler he'd known who kept his bait warm inside his lip. Ruthie imagined how she and Sitka would look to someone peering in through the basement's egress windows. A giant hairless man prone before a small vibrating woman.

She thought of the other deviants she knew in the Bitterroot Valley: the Breeds; Whipple Jr. and his wife, who chained each other to trees in their yard; Len Law lurking outside her window.

She'd expected to understand the world as she neared thirty, but she felt more dumbstruck than ever.

"HECTOR SAW SOMETHING on my land today," Sitka said, walking shirtless to the fridge and taking out a labeled Tupperware container. "He told me when he dropped dinner off. It scared him. He couldn't get back to his truck fast enough." A scar ran down Sitka's side from where he'd had kidney surgery after a late hit in a preseason game. He had a number of other scars, and tattoos besides the rune, including one at his waistline of a bear roaring on its hind legs. Ruthie held her arm up to compare its topography to his.

"What was it?"

"Some kind of animal. He only saw it from a distance and couldn't describe it, even in Spanish. He just said it didn't look right."

"A deer with mange, maybe," Ruthie said. "They get bald and look like fucking demons." Sitka shrugged. He opened the container and smelled whatever was inside. The back of Ruthie's neck suddenly went cold. She realized she had echoed her father from twenty years before. A presence pushed against the edges of her mind, one she still felt every time she looked into No-Medicine Canyon. "Did he say if it had a head?" she asked.

"I think it's quinoa." Sitka stopped. "What? No. Why wouldn't it have a head?"

"I saw a creature once without a head." Ruthie paused. "When I was a girl. It was in the canyon behind my trailer."

Sitka considered this for several seconds. His expression didn't change. Still impossible to surprise. He set the Tupperware down. "You're sure it was real?"

Ruthie shook her head. "No. But I was then. It was shaped like a kidney, with insect feet on two long, double-jointed legs. Taller than you, taller than some of the trees. Its body was covered in gray feathers and it lurched when it walked, as if it were just learning. Pip and I looked for it for years. I think she still does."

Pale afternoon sunlight reflected off the snowy hills through the windows. Ruthie watched Sitka lower his bald head. She wondered when he'd last been outside.

"Were you scared?" Sitka asked.

She nodded. "I hated it. It reminded me of pollution and all the horrible things I was learning about. How whales were choking to death on plastic bags, baby pelicans getting trapped in oil spills, the clearcuts." She remembered wanting to crush the creature like a mosquito against a rock.

"Back East, everything is paved over," Sitka said. "I never thought much about animals when I was little. Just sports and TV and schoolwork." He'd grown up in New Jersey, a place she equated with a crowded parking lot. He paused. "I didn't even know there was a natural world."

"I felt that in Las Vegas. I ended up almost shooting someone."

"When I first got here, it was like I'd come to another planet," he said.

The sound of the front door opening upstairs interrupted them.

"Hello?" The voice echoed off the high ceilings. Ruthie looked at Sitka in bewilderment. It was her father.

"What's he doing here?"

Sitka laughed. "He drops off a goose just about every week."

"Oh, Christ." Like a tithe. "Do you ever eat them?"

"Not really. I give them to Hector or else they just pile up in the freezer."

Her father's footsteps approached overhead. "Ruthie? You here? I saw your truck outside and the door was open."

She knew she hadn't left the door open. She looked down at her nakedness, then across at Sitka. She swore to herself. "I'll deal with him," she said. "Then let's find out what Hector saw."

Sitka smiled. "You're lucky, you know. Does he always follow you around?"

"He just wants to hunt your pond." Ruthie pulled on her jeans and sweatshirt. She patted down the sides of her hair and looked in the mirror to make sure she was presentable. Then she jogged up the carpeted stairs.

Rutherford looked tiny in the massive living room, half cocky, half afraid. He was dressed the same as always—thrift store jeans, a black T-shirt, and canvas coat—even though he could afford new clothes now. He grinned at her, showing the gap of his missing incisor.

"Christ, this place is big," he said. "Look at that chandelier."

"Just because my truck is parked someplace doesn't mean you can waltz inside."

"Been wanting to come in here for years. You know I built the roof?" His eyes darted around the room as he spoke. "That was a shit job. Three straight months in the sun. The fucking roof never ended. And look at the thanks I got." He set the bloody butcher-paper package of goose on the table. He wiped his hands on his jeans. "That's for Jon." He caught sight of Wiley King's gold records over the fireplace and went toward them, squinting. "The son of a bitch. I never met one person who actually likes his music."

Ruthie didn't respond.

Rutherford turned back to her and his face lit up like a boy's. "Think if he saw us now. Right here in his living room, with his fancy records." He raised his arms.

"All right, Dad." Ruthie couldn't keep from smiling.

"He'd roll over in his grave."

"I imagine he's rolling as we speak. You know you don't have to keep bringing Jon geese. He likes you. You're not going to get kicked off your pond."

"I want to." Her father shuffled over to the fireplace and stooped to peer up the chimney. "Have you seen the size of him? He needs all the meat he can get." He picked up the fire poker and tested its weight, as if its mass would determine the quality of the entire mansion. "Where is he anyway?"

"Downstairs."

"Should I fry her up?" Rutherford said, pointing the poker at the goose. "We could all have dinner."

"Time for you to go," Ruthie said. "I'll walk you out."

He squinted at the ceiling. "Fine, fine. I'm supposed to meet Terry anyway. We'll do dinner another time. I just wanted a peek." He set the poker down. He took a deep breath, inhaling the whole room, and stuck out his chest. "Old Wiley would shit himself if he saw me here, that's for sure."

AFTER WATCHING her father's truck drive away, Ruthie walked around the side of the mansion and looked up at the hills of Sitka's ranch. In the twilight, they formed a rolling white plain that rose steadily in a seamless incline to the Sapphire Mountains, which stood as great white mounds themselves. Holy and silent in their stillness. Sitka owned nearly a thousand acres. Wiley King's old bait feeders were knocked down and decaying along the slough. The owl talons, Ruthie was sure, still clung to the fence. The headless creature suddenly felt real to her again after talking about it with Sitka. For many years it had been a specter in her mind, lingering at the edges. She wondered what was loose here and what was loose in Sitka's brain, if the two were somehow conjoined. If by killing whatever was on his land she might also fix the break inside him. She pulled her hat over her ears. It was a stupid thought. One her father would have.

A stinging wind gusted down the hillside. She scanned the white distance. The valley was changing rapidly. A Thai restaurant had opened in Hamilton, two blocks from the labs, and they were putting a bike path along the Bitterroot River all the way to Missoula. Soon it would be lined with condos and breweries and coffee shops. Traffic lights blinking over standstill roads. Car dealership balloons dancing in the wind. Ruthie loved the winter for all the people it kept inside. The tourists it swept away and the houses and towns it covered over. An erasure, a hint of what the valley once was. When she could have struck out alone over the roadless mountains, following game trails through the pines. The sound of wolves howling in the distance. Her tracks vanishing behind her in the snow.

31.

Sitka disappeared that spring. At first, when Ruthie came to the mansion looking for him, she thought he'd been robbed. The dining room table was upended and a bronze horse had been used to smash the huge mirror over the stairs. Drops of blood spattered the wood floor. Her heart jumped in her chest. "Jon," she called, running down the stairs.

The basement was trashed. The glass wall of the gym lay in shards. An elliptical had been thrown into the TV. More blood stained the walls. Water pooled around the overturned refrigerator. Bloody footprints crossed the white carpet. He was gone. She felt it suddenly, an emptiness inside her as much as in the room.

He hadn't left a note, but she pieced together what had happened from the destruction around her. Sitka had been working out. Perhaps feeling the strain of their last conversation—another argument in which she'd urged him to let himself be more intimate with her—he pushed himself harder. Adding more weight to the bench press, lifting against the tension, the final snap. He'd been on the bench when he blacked out. He'd thrown the barbell clean through the glass wall. Then followed, cutting his feet when he lifted the elliptical. Attacking the fridge, the TV. Mindless in his rage.

His bloody tracks led upstairs to the dining room table and the mirror. Ruthie assumed he'd come back into himself when he'd seen his face in its shattered surface. She imagined him gripping his head as he had on the edge of his bed. Trying to root out the broken place. Leaving bloody fingerprints. Then bandaging his feet, looking around the mansion—which held nothing he needed to take—and walking out.

V

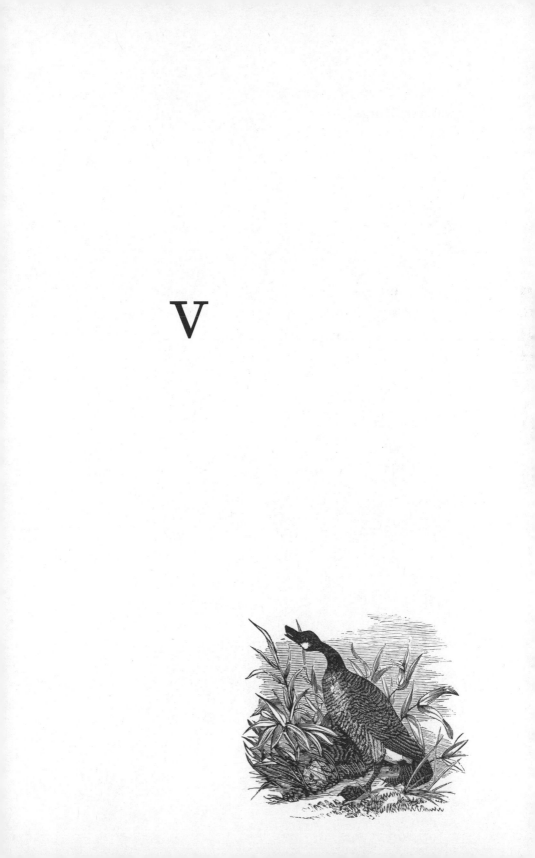

32.

The fall when Ruthie Fear turned thirty, a flock of more than two thousand Canada geese died after landing on the waste pond behind the Rocky Mountain Labs. Everyone in the diner talked about it for several days, wondering what would happen if there was a flood or if the water leached into the ground, but soon conversations turned back to zoning disputes and grazing rights and new developments, and the labs once again became the domain of Kent Willis and his few acolytes, who still muttered about Ebola lions and an earthquake that most people were too young or new to the valley to remember. The labs' director assured the city council that the waste met all federal standards, and alarm sensors had been installed to scare away any other birds. Rutherford bemoaned the loss of the geese as a hunter, but knew the smarter, fatter fowl preferred his beloved pond anyway, where he continued to hunt almost every weekend below Jon Sitka's deserted mansion. Ruthie figured there should be a sign at both ends of the valley warning all animals away. If they didn't get shot or run over, they'd die when they tried to take a swim.

From the following April to October, mountain bikers zoomed back and forth from Missoula along the freshly paved path by the Bitterroot River. Neon in their spandex, helmets gleaming in the sun, happily pumping past the place where Father Mike's body had riddled up on the rocks. They stopped in front of the diner to hydrate. Ruthie watched them through the open door. They held water bottles several inches from their mouths, squirted the water into their throats, and let it splash down their chins in a way she found grotesquely sexual. Then they eyed the little town appraisingly, clearly wondering if they could live out here. How quaint and quiet that life would be.

Ruthie watched with growing anger. The valley was being paved over. Alone, there was nothing she could do. She couldn't stand going into the Wal-Mart in Hamilton because it made her too sad to see the people she'd known all her life looking so tiny and overwhelmed amid the endless fluorescent aisles.

THE ICE MACHINE, firewood, and a community bulletin board lined the wall behind the four checkout lanes in Super 1. The store was tiny compared to the big chains, and still rented DVDs. It was only a matter of time before it was gone. Like the buffalo. Like the passenger train. Shopping after her shift, Ruthie was surprised to discover that she was capable of being nostalgic for things she despised.

Waiting shoppers clogged the aisles: a barge-like woman carefully inspecting the items in her packed cart before setting them on the conveyor, three teenage girls holding identical baskets of Diet Coke and Twizzlers, a buff guy in a tank top joggling on his toes. Ruthie didn't recognize anyone except for Kiley Pompey, Dalton's niece, manning the second register. The valley's population had doubled in Ruthie's lifetime. The new people were outdoorsy types. They could work remotely. She remembered the newspaper's prediction that Darby would die after the mill closed. Now corrugated steel bungalows with solar-panel roofs lined Lost Horse Creek, parking lots sprawled across former pastures, and only the newspaper was gone.

Early winter darkness pressed in on the windows. Bitter cold, yet with no snow. Ruthie weighed her options. The far-left line was the shortest but the barge woman had already set aside several items in anticipation of price checks or a battle over expired coupons. She looked like the type who rarely went out in public and needed conflict when she did, to justify her lonesome life. The buff guy was joggling even more rapidly. He looked like he wanted to lift something heavy, starting with the gray-haired old lady tottering in front of him.

Just go. Ruthie maneuvered the cart on its rickety wheel into the lane behind the teenage girls. All three wore matching volleyball warm-ups. "His parents were upstairs," one of them said. "Like ten steps away." Ruthie thought of herself at that age: the afternoons she'd spent with Badger in the trailer, the feeling that each moment was of vital importance. She wondered, if she had a daughter, would she turn out this way. She imagined the girls at practice. Eyes wide, chins upturned, their young arms outspread like wings as they watched the ball sail over the net, holy with anticipation.

"He was out cold," the girl went on. "We weren't even sure if he was still alive."

"Madison had to pepper spray him to wake him up. *Pepper spray.*" They laughed.

Ruthie squeezed the cart's handle. Brightly boxed frozen meals mocked her from the cart. The girls were watching the shaggy-haired checker mumble to himself as he ran items across the scanner.

They hadn't even glanced back to note that Ruthie was there. She was becoming invisible as she aged.

The only news of Sitka she'd received was a letter from a neurology center in Houston, thanking her for supporting her loved one while he participated in a CTE study in former professional football players. That letter had come more than a year ago. Ruthie still spent many nights in the mansion, sleeping crosswise in the king-sized bed. The maid and Hector had been let go, so the property's upkeep fell to her. She'd cleaned up the glass and blood, and righted the dining-room table, but left the broken TV on the wall. It was the only thing that had truly belonged to Sitka. She thought of selling the bronze horses but never did. She set up a target range in the field behind his deck and resumed her practice of shooting every evening, as she had when she was a girl. Occasionally she broke a figurine or one of the southwestern vases on the shelves, to distract herself from her sadness. The emptier the mansion became, the more like him it seemed. A great quiet space to hear her thoughts.

Ruthie marveled at the strength it had taken her father to care for her in the years after her mother left. Suddenly understanding the way a heart breaks over and over again, at something new each day.

Some evenings she walked up to the pond and pictured herself crawling across the ice. A lone, determined figure on the creaking white void, precariously suspended above frigid depths.

THE SLIDING GLASS DOORS past the firewood hissed open and a short, dirty man wearing green fatigues and a tattered brown sweatshirt stumbled into the store. He stopped in the bright light and looked up, as if surprised to find people in a place he'd expected to be abandoned. His face was so wrinkled and leathery it took Ruthie a moment to find the features: sunken puckered lips, bent nose, and bright blue, twitching eyes. He looked like all the other vagrants who gathered around the bus stop, or on the shoulder of the highway trying to hitch a ride over the pass into Idaho.

"Hey," the man said. His voice rose to address the store. "Hey!" He took three more steps and stopped in front of a table of discount cupcakes. He squinted at the red Christmas frosting, then turned to face the waiting customers. "You better watch out."

He sucked in a raspy breath, gathering his strength, and Ruthie felt a jab of fear. Was this a shooter? She remembered the fluorescent lights exploding in Lucky Lil's, glass raining down around her. Just that morning she'd read about three children shot in an Oklahoma elementary school. Not to mention Parkland, Sandy Hook, Umpqua. But she'd never heard of a massacre in a grocery store. Was this a new breed? Would the pathetic image of her body pitched forward over a cart full of frozen broccoli fettuccine and chicken parmesan come to represent the next step in American decline? She cursed herself for leaving her pistol in the truck.

"It's coming," the man said. "I've seen it. Aisle five, the reaper. Do you even know? I'm from here." He stamped his foot. "Right here. And all you . . . you . . ." He paused, his lips twisting as he reached for the word. "*Tourists*. Fucks. You come here and it's coming. I've seen it. I've *heard* it."

A blue-vested manager appeared from Produce. Brown-haired, pale, and over-young, she approached slowly between the potatoes and the onions, clearly hoping the man would disappear.

"Sir," she said.

"This used to be a lake!" the man went on. "You don't even know. A lake of water, and then a lake of fire!"

Ruthie found herself forgetting her fear as his words rang in her head.

"Excuse me, sir," the manager said again, and reached out to touch the man's shoulder. As soon as her fingers were an inch from his sweatshirt, an internal sensor tripped in his head and he swung around and smacked her arm away. The manager shrieked and the man stumbled back as though stung, a stream of unintelligible invectives issuing from his mouth. Ruthie and the other customers watched in stunned, motionless silence.

Then the muscular man sprang into action: tossing his basket onto the conveyor, sprinting across the linoleum, and grabbing the back of the man's sweatshirt with both fists. The man screamed, trying to twist free, and the muscular man swung him roughly to the floor. He planted his fists into the man's dirty shoulder blades, pivoted neatly, and drove his knee into the small of his back, pinning him. Then he looked up, sweaty and proud, like a golden retriever with a squirrel in its jaws and no idea what to do with it.

The checkers stared at him with shocked eyes.

The homeless man flailed and shouted, then went still.

A hush fell over the Super 1. Ruthie heard the hum of the ice machine, the distant hiss of produce misters. The teenage girls leaned together, their eyes wide. The bright frozen tableau of the prostrate man, the muscular jogger, the stunned manager, and the huddled girls struck Ruthie briefly as beautiful: a portrait of humanity awash in the modern world. She thought of a line she'd read in a photography magazine years before. "It's just light reflecting off surfaces."

Just light. . . . The thought drifted through Ruthie's mind.

The manager broke the reverie by profusely thanking the muscular man, fumbling through her pocket for her cell phone, and calling the police. The shoppers began to talk quietly among themselves—Ruthie even joining in to offer that, yes, this valley had been a lake fifteen thousand years before, one of the biggest in the world—and then came a strange interval when the giddy relief dissipated and they were simply waiting: for the police to arrive, the man to be taken away, and the store to revert to the beep and chatter of normalcy.

On the ground, the man's face was turned away. A frail ankle showed between the cuff of his pants and the top of a filthy sneaker. He remained still save for an occasional shuddering twitch.

"Is he crying?" one of the volleyball girls asked. As soon as she said it, Ruthie realized it was true, and a fog settled over the aisles of chips and juice and canned soup. The buff guy looked up at the ceiling. The body beneath him shook. Ruthie wanted to go and shove him off, but who knew, maybe he'd been right. Maybe the man was dangerous, unhinged. A shooter, as she'd thought only minutes before. But the sight of him pressed into the linoleum shuddering in his rags was like a portal opening in the ground through which the most terrible darkness streamed forth, and Ruthie had to look away.

ANGER. IT GREW IN RUTHIE'S CHEST as the police—two deputies nearly as young as Badger had been when he started—handcuffed the homeless man and yanked him to his feet. It grew as she watched them lead him from the store, gripping his arm above the elbow, forcing him to march quickly, his head down, the fluorescent light glinting off his tear-stained cheeks.

Ruthie wanted to apologize. Offer bail money, a place to stay. She could give him her entire house. He could sleep below *Wild Woman with Tame Horses*, clean himself in her shower, wear her old clothes, take over her job at the Montana Café. Flirt with the other old men and complain about the tourists to Cook. All while she slept in the mansion.

No longer the hero, the buff guy got back in line, sheepish but also defiant, his chest out, his recently activated muscles taut against his tan skin. If anyone had said anything he would've shouted back. But no one did. The three teenage girls stared at him with a mixture of attraction and revulsion.

Ruthie began to unload her cart, smacking each cold box onto the black conveyor. She had convinced herself Sitka was protecting her—

that he'd only left so he wouldn't hurt her—but she was starting to wonder whether any of it had been real. She was afraid he'd come to occupy the same part of her mind as the winged skeleton and the headless creature: fleeting visions that grew less trustworthy over time. She crammed more boxes on, dislodging the bar that separated her items from the girls'.

The checker glanced back disapprovingly. Beneath the shaggy hair, he was the kind of tall, skinny, twenty-year-old boy who always appears drowsy, as if he wouldn't fully wake up for several more years. For some males, the emergence from the womb wasn't complete until late in the third decade. Ruthie thought of several cutting things to say but they all involved residing in one's parents' basement, which was hardly even embarrassing anymore. Reluctantly, she pulled back the offending items, arranged them into rows, and waited for more conveyor real estate before adding the rest.

A poinsettia drooped atop the register. It reminded Ruthie not of Christmas but of her own loneliness. She pictured seizing the plant and hurling it at the table of cupcakes. The girls were huddled around the credit card reader, gazing at the checker as he rang up their soda and candy. He was ignoring them, instead casting glances at Kiley in the next lane. She had petite features, dark bags under her eyes, dyed maroon hair, and a lip ring. Ruthie touched the old hole in her lip with her tongue. At least kids were still doing the same stupid things: chasing each other around, getting piercings. She saw a gob of green spit on white sheets and wanted to laugh.

"I saw that guy here last week," the checker said to Kiley, handing across the final girl's receipt and continuing to ignore her as she hip-swayed out the door. "On the curb in front. I know it was him. He had a dog, though."

Kiley nodded. "I saw him, too. He was there all afternoon. Bert even brought him some day-olds since it was so cold. There's more and more of them."

"It was big, like a pit bull. He had it tied to the bike rack with a piece of cardboard to sit on."

"They probably bused him here from Bozeman. My dad says that's what they do with all the crazies there."

"No way. You can't get a dog like that on a bus. Besides, he said he was from here."

Kiley looked miffed at this rebuttal. "He said a lot of things."

Ruthie listened with rising disbelief. She rapped her knuckles on the credit card reader. "Excuse me. I'm waiting here."

"Hi, Ruthie," Kiley said, and turned back to her next customer.

SECONDHAND LIGHT from the store weakly illuminated the sidewalk. A group of ragged men stood shivering and smoking in the shadowed corner by the street. Hunched together in tattered coats, they looked identical to the one who'd been taken away. A chain of carts pointed toward them below Super 1's ad-plastered windows. No dog, at least not that Ruthie could see. Maybe the cops had taken it. It would do Badger some good. He still hadn't been able to impregnate Janine, and people whispered that she was ready to leave him. He looked more slumped and dispirited than ever. Ruthie carried her bags into the darkness of the lot.

The air was freezing with the faint, crisp smell of distant snow. In her peripheral vision, Ruthie saw one of the men toss his cigarette onto the pavement and break away from the group. The moon shone overhead like a pale commandment. Instinctively, Ruthie sped up. She scanned the shadowed edges of the lot for the shape of a dog. She remembered Moses running down the hill from Happel's after the earthquake. Multiple dog generations ago. An entire testament. Her truck was two rows over and a half dozen back amid an unbroken line of cars.

People, people everywhere.

Spindly, new-planted maples ringed the lot and lined the dirt divider in the center. All the new construction seemed rushed and shoddy, as if the developers were racing against a crash. The man moved between the saplings without seeming to move at all. A gliding shadow, visible yet spectral. He was making for the woods behind the store—not following her—but still she felt her palms grow clammy holding the grocery bags. What if all the homeless men were rising up? They had every right. Ruthie couldn't remember ever helping one of them.

The Bitterroot Mountains were cut black from the western sky. The clouds drifting around their peaks had a vaporous, ethereal cast, as if they were seeping from a cosmic swamp. She stopped at the door of her truck. She thought of the kindness around Sitka's eyes, and how he'd set his palm on her cheek when she was upset. Sometimes when she woke up in his bed in the mansion she still felt him there, the weight of his arm across her chest. She clung to these precious seconds in the dark. She set the bags down and dug through her pocket for her keys, glancing to the side to see the man passing out of the lot. She felt a presence behind her and knew it wasn't Sitka but imagined it was, his figure hulking over the pavement, his tree-trunk arms reaching out to her.

Slowly, she turned around.

The pit bull looked up cautiously. His head was lowered and his hindquarters were raised, asking if his presence in Darby, Montana, Planet Earth, was acceptable. A small scar marked the white fur beneath his left eye. The right was surrounded by the short brown fur that covered the rest of his body. Ribs showed on his sides. His stump tail wagged.

Without thinking, Ruthie fell into a crouch and held out her arms. "Here, boy," she said. The dog raised his head happily and stepped forward. His mouth fell open, his pink tongue fell out. "Who are you?"

He slapped her cheek with his tongue's wetness. It was the first smile she'd registered in months.

33.

That spring, mountain goats came down to lick salt from the highway in Darby. They stopped traffic all the way to the Lake Como turn. The old men gathered to squint and hock in the morning sun, as if summoned. Ruthie watched in her apron from inside the Montana Café. She'd only ever seen the goats in the high country. They were more handsome than the men. White shaggy heads bent, winter coats falling out, patchy, near-ragged, determined pink tongues. A great patience for licking. Strange, cracked-agate eyes hunting out the particles amid the viscous shimmer of gasoline.

Trapped behind the counter, with her pad, pen, and a familiar dryness in her throat, Ruthie wished she were home with Pharaoh. She'd brought him to the police station the day after she found him, but the homeless man was gone and hadn't said anything about a dog, so she'd adopted him and named him in tribute to Moses. He'd taken over Sitka's mansion completely: bounding down the long hallways, scratching the wood floor, nudging all the throw pillows into a nest on the couch, covering everything in fine brown hairs. Filling the long, quiet evenings with rambunctious sound.

Customers chattered back and forth about why the goats were here. The usual, everyday apocalypses. Her father claimed there was a time when no traffic of any kind passed through Darby. Ruthie longed for it. She longed to walk among the goats. Speak goat. Spread salt by the fistful. Lead them like a shepherd back up into the mountains.

"Wouldn't catch me licking no road," Pip said, from the counter. She'd appeared along with the goats that morning, after a weeklong absence. Ruthie tried to picture it. Pip's bony rump skyward, her tongue extending. Finding its tender place among the gravel. Tasting salt, pavement, and Indian bones. Diners shifted. Pip's eyes flicked around. Ruthie wondered where she'd been. It was unlike her friend to leave town for so long without telling her where she was going. The old men stared on, sucking their teeth, belt buckles glinting, eyes screwed with suspicion. On the other side of the order window, Cook observed his daily prayer to the deep fryer. Only Terry and Billy French, leaning together at the table by the window, seemed to find humor in the situation. They grinned back and forth over their scrambled eggs.

"Too much traffic to get to work," Terry said, when Ruthie refilled his coffee.

"They followed me through town on my way here," Billy said. "Like I was some kind of salt lick. Kept bumping my ass." He clinked his wedding ring against the edge of the table, a proud habit ever since his marriage to Dawn.

In the road, Sheriff Badger arrived. Recently elected, rumored impotent—his popularity tied to people feeling sorry for him. Don

Kima had retired to his cabin in the Absarokas. Badger clambered heavily from his angled cruiser and surveyed the goats. Slump-shouldered, planless. He took off his hat and waved it. Stamped his boots. Shooing the goats as if they were flies. Sunlight a tragic burst on his bald spot. His heavy frame paltry before the line of cars. Ruthie was surprised to find a soft place for him again, after all the years. The shiny patch on his head, his desperate consternation. She saw the boy on the threshold of her father's room with his fists clenched at his sides. He flapped his arms. Shouted. Finally, a large female goat spooked and the rest of the herd bolted after her. To the gap in the high school fence. They funneled through, stopped on the baseball diamond, and clustered around the kids, looking back wistfully at a fine meal lost.

Badger replaced his hat, turned in a circle, caught Ruthie's eye, and looked quickly away. The old men in the street hitched their belts and spat, unimpressed. Why hadn't one of them done the shooing? They'd aged into pure judgment. Remembering their own fathers, who could knock a duck out of the air with a whiskey bottle. Cars began to move. A lone honk. Tourists craned from passenger seats, cell phones held aloft. Children screamed from the backseat, "*Let me see, let me see.*" The last time Darby had standstill traffic was two years before, when Happel's cow trailer tipped, full of heifers. M. Happel still unlucky: his wife gone to Europe, his trailer upside down in a ditch.

The hooked finger of Trapper Peak beckoned as it had since Ruthie was a girl. Pip motioned her over to the counter. She glanced around furtively, guarding a secret. All the other customers were engrossed in the continuing tide of goat talk. Satisfied, Pip rose from her stool. She cupped her hand over Ruthie's ear and whispered, "I'm pregnant."

All other sounds in the diner ceased. Ruthie nearly dropped the dirty plates in her hand.

"I went to Delilah's clinic in Spokane to make sure."

Ruthie had assumed she was off in the mountains. Her mind stumbled over itself with questions and possibilities. She felt overwhelmed. She'd known Pip wanted a child, but hadn't thought she'd actually do it. "Whose is it?" she whispered back.

Pip smiled. "It's mine," she said. "All mine."

A MAN AT THE SAWMILL BAR told Ruthie once about a button. You push it and half the world dies. Asked: Do you push it? She'd answered yes so quick it froze him, openmouthed. A new wariness in his eyes. Men always think they're the tough ones until they realize they aren't. Then they scramble around for their boots, underwear, mothers.

Cook rang the kitchen bell. He hummed to himself as he worked, as if goat-clogged roads and snowless mountains were common to his experience. Still dazed, Ruthie collected the dish of Denver omelet, bacon, and useless orange slice from the order window. *Pregnant?* She was surprised by how hurt she felt. Sitka had left, and now Pip was leaving, too, in her own way. Pushing a tiny, helpless version of herself out into the world, then leaving Ruthie behind to look after it for eighteen years.

The old men lined in through the café door. They tipped their puckered heads at the SPECIALS board: taco omelet and turkey chili, same as every other Friday. The streams of monosyllables issuing from their gummy mouths ran into one another. "Hep no snow for 'em don't know the last time I saw it. Bud's dog drug up warm clay." Blindly yapping, they took the long table in the center. "Warm clay? Caught Len's sheep at a phone pole licking sweat."

Ruthie felt like she was treading water. Remembering to breathe.

Pip swiveled toward the old men in her short pants, her white thighs beaming. She seemed emboldened, in a new fullness of herself. Ruthie felt a pang of jealousy. Pip nodded out at the goats now milling in the playground. "Gum their teeth down to nubs on the rocks," she said. "It kills them in the end." A flash of sadness darkened her eyes. "I saw one once, toothless on St. Mary's Peak, looking around for a place to die." The old men humphed and nodded, not wanting to glimpse themselves in this recollection.

Ruthie poured their coffee. Kept her attention on the cups. Aware of sliding glances, sweaty hat band indentations, dandruff. Suntanned wrists, upper arms white as cream, occasional turquoise jewelry. Gnarled fingers longing to nip her on the buns. Just a pinch, enough to get an old man through the long, hot afternoon. She fought to hold her face blank. *A mother*, she thought.

The goats had assembled by the jungle gym, oblivious. Licking the shining red paint. Searching for old palm prints and sweaty finger holds. A summer-come-early treat beneath the snowless mountains. Ruthie wondered if she could have lured them down, as she had with the otters when she was a girl.

THE TOURISTS HAD CLEARED, old men cleared, even Pip had gone on home. Only Badger persisted. Ruthie had left the coffeepot on the table at his elbow twenty minutes before, to go cold. But he'd been staring into the same cup. One arm hooked over his chair, hat on the table across from him, his sleeves rumpled, a digital watch that you couldn't buy anymore. He should've been out shooting road signs and pulling over blondes, like any other Montana cop.

"We could switch," Ruthie said, from her stool by the cash register. "You give me the badge and gun, I give you the apron. Sit there as long as you want. Just stick your ass out if anybody comes in. Cook'll do the rest."

He blinked at her. Rumpier than she remembered, and the bald spot growing. There'd been so much more of him in the chest back when, but his face had softened. Janine—with her suitcases full of Mary Kay makeup, pink bobbed hair, and endless projects—was turning him to mush. The type you'd find weeping between snowmobiles in the garage at night.

"I'm on goat patrol," Badger said. "You going to make me sit in the car?"

"You're the one with the gun."

He sighed, his mind stuck. "They shouldn't be down here, Ruthie." He bunched his lips and looked at her, trembly. "Think they're starving up there in the high country? Got no food left?"

Ruthie had her own problems. "Go on and check. See if the Goat-Mart closed. The Goat Bell, Goat Wendy's."

"Oh, you're a hard one." Badger lowered his head.

"Tell you what, I'll go as soon as you clear out. Bring them egg scraps and bacon fat, a whole bushel of salt. Whatever Cook allows." She kicked her heel back against the metal leg of the stool. A dull ringing sound. "Hear that? Catch the goat bus now."

"Oh sure," he said, unfolding himself from his chair. "A hard one, Ruthie Fear. You'll outlive us all." He reached for the crumpled hat and straightened his gun. Chucked a burr from his sleeve. Left a dollar and several dimes on the table and headed out to the goats.

WHITE TUFTS OF HAIR twitched on the gravel. Riddled up against the curb, effluvium of invisible tide. Goat smell, too, a deep musk. Not entirely unpleasant. Ruthie lifted her chin to the sun and let it wash over her. She looked up at the hitch of Squaw Ridge like a belt cinched against the belly of blue sky. How could she be mad at Pip? She wanted her to be happy. To have a love inexhaustible and never-ending. Something Ruthie had never found. A hawk knifed across the hills, caught an updraft, slowed to a float, and was carried up, up, up above the snowless peaks.

Her friend moving on while her own life stayed still.

Badger slumped in his cruiser across the road, fiddling with the radar gun. Cook came outside and stood beside Ruthie. He fished a crumpled pack of cigarettes from the pocket of his apron. Lit one and handed it to her. The thin curl of smoke was a comfort; the dry bitter taste. *I have a dog and a mansion*, she told herself, but it didn't help. Sitka had left a hole she didn't know how to fill. She exhaled, considering Badger's words. Was she hard? Did hard people feel soft?

She took another drag. Saw in the smoke a foggy mirror of the hair below. Hardly any snow, but enough pale things to go around.

"Perhaps they aren't starving," Cook said. "Go to the salt for the minerals."

Ruthie didn't see any difference. No food, no minerals, either one could kill you. "My dad says he used to skate across Lake Como when he was a kid."

Cook nodded. "Sure, back in Utah we used to skate all the time."

"It's hardly frozen solid in my entire life. Seems like there's a better chance it'll catch fire."

But Cook was drifting away, his mind on food. "Deer, squirrels, moose, sheep. All of them needs a lick. Not just goats." He patted the sides of his hair and smoothed back over the graying tail. "What do you suppose it tastes like, gasoline? Same as its smell?"

"Christ, Cook." Ruthie rubbed her eye with the heel of her hand. She could see him pondering a recipe. Car parts and antifreeze stewed in petrol, boat hulls over wet nails. He'd get himself a TV show. His maroon hairnet a wild attempt at fashion. She pictured him down on all fours in the road next to Pip. Ponytail flopped over, licking away. The whole town flabby-assed and panting, sucking up gas.

Push the button.

Enough. The loneliness was breaking her down. She tossed the cigarette aside and walked across the road. Rapped on Badger's window. His eyes widened as he hauled it down. "Come over tonight," she said.

ROSE PAINTINGS ON THE WALLS, rose bedspread, even a tall crystal rose Ruthie had paid too much for at the mall in Missoula. In her head, she still sometimes thought of herself as Rose. What kind of a father names his daughter after himself? Pharaoh bumped into her legs as she went from the kitchen to the bedroom. His whole butt wagged; he was unused to being in such a small house. "Yeah, yeah, yeah," she said. "You fend off intruders."

Pharaoh nodded at her, smiling, drooling, the least threatening guard dog in creation. In danger of besmirching the reputation of pit bulls everywhere.

Ruthie drew the curtains out of habit. She didn't worry about Len watching her anymore. She'd hardly seen him since Badger's beating, so carefully did he avoid her. She considered the brushstrokes of *Wild Woman with Tame Horses* as she unclasped her bra from under her work shirt. All hair and flanks swirling around her face, which was clearly based on a fantasy of the painter's: too perfect. A younger, better version of herself. Lips the color of roses. Ruthie shrugged out of the bra and savored the brief, cool weightlessness.

The teardrop mirror on the dresser reflected the sharpness of her face. New wrinkles, a vein in her forehead she had yet to reckon with. It was true what they said: you make an expression long enough, it sticks that way. But she found herself beautiful, too, when she tilted her chin up to the right.

She took off her jeans and sat in her underwear on the edge of the bed. The only time she cried at movies was when a horse ran in slow motion. Something about the grace of it. Body and mind working together so perfectly. A feeling she'd never quite achieved. She looked down at her knees. What exactly was the plan? Badger? Jesus. Like she wanted every step to be backward. Spend her whole life crawling in the muck while the diner men watched her ass fatten and her breasts sag.

But maybe this could be different, a change in the whole system. A correction. And in the one difference, a whole host of others to come, like pulling a plug.

•

BADGER PRESSED RUTHIE against her bedroom wall and tried to kiss her. She could feel his heart hammering beneath the years' accumulation of fat and longing. His hands trembled like a teenager's.

She pushed him back. "Stop it."

Badger withered. The form went from him like a popped balloon. He backed away. He looked down at his tented pants in shame. Apparently his difficulties in the bedroom didn't extend to hers. Ruthie wondered what he'd told his wife. Janine was known to keep close tabs on him, calling 911 when she couldn't reach his cell. "What'd you want me over for?" he asked.

"Don't pout. Take your boots off," Ruthie said. He sulked on the edge of the bed and did as he was told. Ruthie stood over him and stripped off the rest of his clothes. Uniform shirt, undershirt. His hairy breasts spilled forth. "Up now." He reddened but obeyed. Uniform pants, frayed boxers covered in peaches. She left his holey black socks on—his feet would be too much. Turned him around and shoved him, unwieldy, onto the bed.

The surprise took him a moment to register. He was naked on all fours. She watched him find himself there. The helplessness. The slight breeze on his asshole. His eyes widened in shame and pleasure and she felt a warmth in her own abdomen. "You going to get undressed?" he asked hesitantly, looking back at her through his legs.

"Shut up," Ruthie said.

Badger winced but didn't move. She saw him go breathless. His neck flushed red.

"You're going to do what I say," she said.

He sighed in relief, all his years of failure suddenly given deep and sensuous meaning. "Yes," he said softly.

Badger's belly drooped, bearish, toward the bedspread. His hairy shoulders were still somehow cop-like. His cock waved tentatively below him. His thighs quivered. Blue eyes fixed on her rose pillowcase. Pharaoh whimpered on the other side of the closed door, hating to be left out.

Ruthie nodded. It would do. "Good boy," she said.

Both man and dog went quiet.

A car passed on Whispering Pines Road. Headlights intruded. Badger swayed his ass gently from side to side. Ruthie set her hips against him. He moaned. She ran her nail down the gully of his spine. She imagined all men were much the same from this angle. Muscles widening around the shoulder blades, a smattering of freckles. Hair on the shoulders and then again on the ass. The nape of his neck imperfectly trimmed. The bald spot like a rear-facing eye. Arms straining to hold his weight. She felt a twinge of affection. So pathetic you could come all the way around to loving them. Men, that is. She slid her hand over the pouch of Badger's belly and down to pubic hair. He sucked in his breath, as if he might cry.

A BRICK CAME IN through the window. Janine close behind. Clairvoyant right to the bottom of her husband's wayward soul. She used the shotgun butt to clear away the remaining glass. Poked her head through the rose-covered curtain. Flinched at the scene, but her makeup held her face in place like a cast.

Behind the door, Pharaoh barked apoplectically.

Ruthie stared back at Janine. Both women motionless. An age-old connection between them: *Oh, is this one yours?* Badger was still planted on all fours, his chest heaving. *The door was unlocked*, Ruthie thought. *No need to smash the window. Pharaoh wouldn't hurt you.* She almost laughed at her lack of fear. She'd been thinking about the end of the world all day. Maybe this was it. A shotgun blast to white light. But no, Janine would never shoot her, not with all her projects left undone, so much makeup to sell, babies yet unborn. Badger ducked his head, his paradise despoiled.

Janine's jaw began to work. Veins appeared as ridges in the foundation on her forehead. Tendons strained to keep her head attached to her shoulders. Her eyes skipped over her husband and lingered on *Wild Woman with Tame Horses*. The shotgun was pointed ceilingward. Her legs were still outside.

"This?" she said. "Like this?"

Ruthie straightened and wiped her palm on her jeans. Clearheaded, cruel, more so than she could remember. She could walk over and put her lips around the shotgun barrel. Make eye contact. She could take her pistol from the bedside table and shoot them both.

Badger was frozen. As if he thought, by remaining motionless, his wife wouldn't be able to see him.

Glass shards shone on the floor, their wide-flung pattern percussive. Ruthie remembered walking across the desert in the night, the temperature of the air matching her body, the dry earth sinking below her bare feet.

Janine gave a last look and came to some decision. She leveled the shotgun and fired over Badger's back, neatly obliterating *Wild Woman with Tame Horses*.

Plaster showered down around the mangled canvas. Ruthie stared at the plate-sized hole in the wall. Dust rose. "Oh, come on," she managed. But Janine was already gone.

AFTER MIDNIGHT, the goats returned. They gathered in the road in front of the Montana Café. A fine place, lots of drippings. They lowered their heads and licked the salt. Young and old, thin and fat, whole families. Tongues searching between the tiny rocks and particles of tire rubber. Minerals traveling down their throats and through their bodies. Animating limbs, nerves, the whole living engine.

Ruthie climbed out through her busted window. She walked past the Whispering Pines Trailer Park and crossed the schoolyard. She thought of Pip when they were young. Running through the night, her legs white as snow. The fertility icon she'd found. All their plans for the creature. Ancient, flaring passions. Back in Len's time, both of them would've been burned as witches. Faced off above crackling brush on the courthouse lawn. No place in this country for passionate women, or Indians, or wolves, or buffalo, or . . . Ruthie approached the goats in the moonlight. All the houses were dark. Badger had gone away to his cruiser to drive out the night on endless patrol. The goats looked up but didn't move. Didn't seem to fear Ruthie. Why should they? She wanted nothing from them except to watch them live.

Snowless mountains, rising seas. Sitka floating in the ether like her mother. The beginning and the end. But here, briefly alive. She raised her hands in benediction. Walked among the shaggy heads. Felt anointed in the dry air, untethered and terribly free, like a ghost in a graveyard. Like a queen of spirits.

34.

Her father was in love and she was not. The unfairness of this settled squarely on Ruthie's shoulders, exacerbated every time she saw Rutherford in his high, glowing state. He pushed backward through the diner's door and spun in wearing his special red boots. He greased his hair down with Crisco. He bought seasonal flower arrangements from the stand in Super 1. Sylver Means had stuck with him for almost a year, and showed no sign of giving up. They were blossoming. A cousin of Terry's, she was as squat and tough as the engines on which she worked, several inches shorter than Rutherford, wide at the beam, with strong cheekbones and small hazel eyes always in motion, contrasting with her black hair sprayed so rigid it looked like cut glass. She had a daughter Ruthie's age, and two sons who worked on the oil fields of North Dakota. She'd done a stint on the fields herself, and in addition to knowing how to drive a semi, it was clear she could put a man out of her house, or set him down for good if she had to. She told Rutherford exactly where to put his shirts, and he delighted in it. "Oh, she's a battle-ax," he said to Ruthie, and whistled long and low.

Father and daughter went hiking up Bear Creek, between the great, tumbled draws of granite and sheer, glacier-cut cliffs. They walked a mile to where the exposed roots of a fallen spruce jutted from the hillside. Light wind from the north rustled Ruthie's hair. It still smelled of the controlled burns that had recently been extinguished. Three young bucks scattered into a stand of pine and she watched them with the out-of-season-hunter's idle curiosity. Her father stopped above a falls in the creek to catch his breath. Water gone turquoise poured over a series of small cliffs, foaming and swirling in the pools between. Rutherford was a week shy of fifty, with more gray than red in his beard. He squatted on his haunches on one of the flattened boulders in the top pool. Elbows to knees, looking off up the creek, he spoke in a tremulous voice, as if reverting to early, overwhelming boyhood, "I see three things here: the stillness of the rocks, the wild water, and the strength of the blowing trees."

Poetry. At first Ruthie thought he was losing his mind. That his physical brain simply couldn't handle the stimulation of being in love, and had turned to porridge. The strength of the blowing trees? She remembered stories of her customers' parents succumbing to Alzheimer's, forgetting their own names, shitting on carpets. Placated to infantile delight by one granddaughter while raging against all the others.

At least he was Sylver's problem now. She could change his diapers.

"Got some deer scat here on the trail, too," Ruthie said.

As they hiked on, Rutherford's mood shifted and he returned to familiar topics: the profligacy of the National Forest Service and the eternally rising price of gasoline. "By next year, if I take every cent

I have out of the bank, I'll barely make it to El Paso," he said. "The whole trucking industry's about to come down. Sylver's got her pension, but the younger drivers . . . Damn country's in the shitter."

Ruthie never watched the news unless it was on in the Sawmill, and even that was too much. She imagined if she listed all the endangered species now, she'd be awake all night. "I think they'd give you enough gas to get across the border," she said. "As long as you promised not to come back."

Rutherford smiled. "I don't even think they'd let me out of Montana."

FOR HIS FIFTIETH BIRTHDAY PARTY, Rutherford decided on a Native theme, acknowledging both his third-generation standing in the valley and the rich heritage of Sylver's people. Succumbing completely to this fit of nostalgia, he emptied out the storage shed (his beetles now lived in a large corrugated hut all their own) and arranged a sort of museum to himself around the yard. Tacking up old taxidermied heads, laying out various traps he'd made, his pencil drawings of wildcats, the box of eagle feathers, and the World War II grenades his grandfather had left, along with an old Navajo rug and two kachina dolls Ruthie had played with as a girl. It made her wonder how she'd survived her own childhood, and what Sylver's family would think when they came upon it.

The party also marked the opening of The Last Wolf, his great project since paying off the bank and owning outright his square acre of land at the mouth of No-Medicine Canyon. A private bar for him and his friends, where they could drink Busch Light and talk about whatever they wanted, free from the yuppies, scientists, students, and tourists who filled the Sawmill Bar in greater numbers every year ordering IPAs and discussing belay gear and the dying coral reefs.

The bar was another shed, really. The same model from which he'd hung the wolf so long ago, only upgraded, with fresh paint, a window on the back, and insulation and knotted-pine siding inside. Raymond Pompey had chain-sawed a custom bear to guard the entrance. It wore Rutherford's trademark jeans and black T-shirt. Through the door, two couches faced a sixty-inch flat-screen TV donated by Terry French from his pawnshop. A cedar bar ran along the back wall with four tall stools. Rutherford had made the bar with wood reclaimed from Darby's original mercantile, and glazed and sanded the top so lovingly that it had taken on a suspiciously womanly shape, with a knot between where the legs would be.

"Just don't want to walk in on him with a power drill and his dick out," Sylver said to Ruthie, the first time they saw it. It was the first time anyone had seen The Last Wolf, so secretive and proud had Rutherford been of his work. The two women stood side by side in the doorway; Rutherford waited anxiously behind the bar. A moose head he'd taxidermied watched over the couches, along with the old posters from Cancún and Las Vegas. A custom-made dartboard with a picture of Wiley King's face for a target hung by the single window, courtesy of Kent Willis, who forgave no one, not even the dead. The samurai sword was mounted over the TV. The wolfskin rug covered the floor. Rutherford had had it professionally cleaned, and the fur was as white as it had been when the wolf was alive. Even now, the rug made Ruthie want to lie down, curl up, and go to sleep.

"It's nice," she said. "Really."

"Good place for you to sleep when I kick you out of bed," Sylver said, but sweetly.

Rutherford blushed. "It's just for friends. Plan to be open Thursday through Sunday, and Mondays during football season. Dollar a beer, two dollars a drink. Lot cheaper than anywhere else. I hope you'll come around. It's not only for men." His eyes followed Ruthie's to the floor and his stance softened. He leaned forward over the freshly stained bar. "Your mother left me over that rug," he said. "Don't think I ever told you that. It was funny, she was never much for ani-mals, but one day she looked at it and just started packing up. Like it was too much. After that, it was the only place you'd sleep."

"I know," Ruthie said quietly.

Rutherford's pale eyes scanned the small room, as if searching for something more. His worn hands gripped the bar in front of his short, wiry body. He shrugged and his shoulders dropped. "Guess I've never known what to be proud of." He rapped his fist against the wood and looked away. "Except you."

The words lingered in the air, as naked as any he'd ever uttered. Ruthie was too surprised to answer. Poetry and open love. He was surely losing his mind. It wasn't until after he'd walked out from behind the bar and past her without meeting her eyes that a flood of feeling rushed up her throat and threatened to well into tears. His back looked old and bent as he crossed the yard, hardly filling his black T-shirt. His Wrangler jeans were snug to his bony hips. His big hands and feet remained slightly disjointed from the rest of him, the young man still visible in their constant reaching. The person he'd been when he filled up Ruthie's sky. He stopped and ran his forearm over his eyes before going into the trailer.

"I been married three times," Sylver said, beside her. "And do you know why I fell for your father? He's the simplest man I ever met. Wouldn't know a snake if it bit his nose. He loves you so much he doesn't know what to do with it." She touched Ruthie's arm, then fol-lowed Rutherford across the yard and into the trailer, her stiff black curls barely moving.

Ruthie found herself alone in the shed's doorway with tears on her cheeks. She remembered how her father had held her as he taught her to shoot. The steadiness of his hands flowing into hers. The smell of sawdust in his collar. His heart beating against her shoulder. She took in the room of his small dreams. Animals and beer and guns and a little bit of pride. She saw the edges of his life, and how much he'd wanted it to mean something. She wished she could have been more for him: that she'd married Sitka and become the rich wife of a football star, or won more trap-shooting competitions, or become a star herself in Las Vegas, like the showgirl on the faded poster. But she knew he didn't care.

The moose looked down on her from the wall. Its glassy brown eyes were calm. The long pugnacious snout both endearing and cruel. Lost shitkicker hooves that would've stomped her to pulp. Rutherford had shot it outside Cut Bank near the Canadian border. She tried to imagine how she'd see him if he wasn't her father, just another of her customers in the Montana Café. As a simple man, like Sylver did? Or a fool? One of many subsisting in trailers scattered across the Bitterroot Valley, struggling to find work, to keep their dignity, afraid and uncomprehending of the massive forces shifting around them. Rising waters and falling trees. All the mills moving to China. All the wealth moving to hard drives. Their beliefs becoming outdated and repugnant. She knelt and ran her fingers through the wolf's fur, stroking downward as if it were still alive. She imagined—as she always did—the muscle and bone beneath the skin. The lips relaxing over the bared teeth. The animal standing, shaking itself, and loping off into the woods.

Could it really be why her mother left? The reason she hadn't called once in thirty years? This spirit here on the floor, its name nailed in wood letters over the TV.

35.

Rutherford's party went late into the night. Dancing and drinking and shouting. People filled the yard and crowded in and out of The Last Wolf, carrying tallboys and boxes of wine. Pharaoh bounded around greeting everyone with his mouth open, spit flying, his butt wagging in a frenzy. The property was a second home to him. Freed from the responsibility of his death, Rutherford welcomed him as his own. Most days, Ruthie dropped him off here on her way to work.

The entire extended French family was present, including Delilah, visiting from Spokane. A mess of Pompeys also, Kent Willis, Danette and Judy, June and Reed Breed (old and quiet and seemingly content), Cook, Pip, Badger, Tracy Trimble and her twelve-year-old daughter, even M. Happel, alone and drinking determinedly from a handle of whiskey in the far corner of the yard. Pip was five months along and visibly showing. Her skin had a ruddy glow. Her pale legs had thickened to hold her new weight. She threatened Kent with her knife when he tried to get her to have a drink. Ruthie hugged her beside the firepit. She felt guilty for the way she'd pulled away when her friend told her she was pregnant, but Pip was smiling at her. "I want you to be the godmother," she said.

"Of course," Ruthie said. "Of course I will."

They played games of Stump and Cornhole, cursing back and forth in the night. Hand-rolled cigarettes, a bonfire, microwave taquitos; the smell of hair spray, spilled whiskey, and peppermint chewing tobacco. The long folding table was covered with chips and booze. Small bills changed hands. Badger slow-danced awkwardly with Pip to "Low Places." His chin grazed the top of her head; her arms reached wide around his shoulders. Ruthie danced with him to "Thunder Rolls" and he told her she looked beautiful, with no makeup and the hood of her sweatshirt raised against the chill night.

"You just tell me what to do," he whispered in her ear as the song ended. He now lived alone in the same apartment above the old mercantile where Ruthie had for years. He could lean from the window and yell for men fighting in the street to keep it down. Terry and Billy swayed by arm in arm. Billy held a burning torch from the bonfire in his right hand. He waved it at Ruthie, as if they might charge together into some unseen battle. His expression was loose and drunk. Dawn was off visiting her daughters in Ronan—she hated to be around drinking of any kind. Young Evers Pompey trailed the Frenches with a plastic Super Soaker full of tequila, threatening to burn the entire place down. Ruthie touched Badger's cheek. She felt a softness within, as if the sharp edges were finally wearing away.

"You owe me a painting," she said to Badger, and turned and walked off by herself to the corner of the yard, where Rutherford's topper trailer still stood, unused, rusting on its metal poles driven into stumps. Behind it, the nailed front boards were all that remained of her blind. The view of the Breeds' yard was completely blocked by dense brush that had grown up over the years. Moses's grave was covered also, his little bones somewhere underneath. Ruthie leaned back against the topper. She watched the people of her life together: laughing, dancing, shouting back and forth. Pharaoh charging around their legs.

Rutherford and Terry drank shots with Happel over a stump. In the way they leaned together—Terry much taller with his long black hair, Rutherford below, the eternal little brother, always going first— she saw a love that transcended logic. Shot through with starlight as it hurtled toward its demise.

THE PARTY WAS still in full swing when midnight struck. Things turned rowdier, louder, more prone to fighting—the mark of any quality gathering in the Bitterroot Valley. Kent Willis lumbered around the periphery, preparing to speak. The Breeds were sitting on folding chairs under the porch lights with Rutherford and Sylver. Pushing seventy, June stood and twirled in a full circle, her long orange dress flowing around her. The sight made Ruthie feel like a little girl. The moon overhead was tinged red, reminding her of the red in her childhood hair. She looked into No-Medicine Canyon beyond the yard. The great mystery that had always loomed on the edge of her life.

Perhaps all her visions had meant to tell her only one thing: You are not the center. There is more here than you can see.

Danette tugged Kent's shirt, begging him not to make a scene, but he ignored her and climbed onto the fence. Perched unsteadily on top, he began a speech about Rutherford that quickly transitioned to a screed on the Rocky Mountain Laboratories. The irreparable damage its scientists were doing to the water table, and how the weapons being made there would surely be turned on the valley's populace.

Danette stood below him with her arms outspread in her flower-print muumuu, as if to catch him. Everyone else went back to the party. Sylver turned up the music. Cook and Pip flail-danced in front of the fire. His hair, loosed from his hairnet, whipped around his face. She stomped her pale legs in the dust. Her body seemed to orbit around the faint rise of her belly. Badger watched from a camp chair with two beers in his lap and a dreamy smile on his face, as if in the one-bedroom apartment where he now lived beside them, he was finding a peace of his own.

Janine was already engaged to another cop in Stevensville. Ruthie figured she'd be pregnant before the wedding.

The wheel-turns of fate. Ruthie ran her fingers along the cool, corrugated side of the topper. She thought of how her father had slept out here when she started puberty. The memory made her sad. *This can't last*, a voice said in the back of her mind. Pharaoh came running out of the fray and butted against her legs. Sylver had tied a blue bandanna around his neck, giving him the dashing look of a sailor. Ruthie scratched his ears. He smiled up at her and flopped his pink tongue over her palm. "I know," she said. He licked her again, then lifted his head, sniffed, and bolted. He made a diagonal across the corner of the yard and ran headlong, without hesitation, into the mouth of No-Medicine Canyon.

Stunned, Ruthie stared after him into the darkness. She tried to comprehend how it was even possible that he'd gone inside. Over her lifetime of avoiding the canyon, it had taken on an impossible quality to her, as if it physically could not be entered. Another dimension, protected by a force field all its own. She wanted to laugh. Thirty years of her and her father's myths shattered in an instant by an idiot pit bull who ran straight inside.

And now she was going to go after him.

The moon echoed her sentiment with its reddish halo. Ruthie patted the front of her sweatshirt, hoping to find she was secretly armed.

There was nothing in her pocket except a cigarette and a plastic lighter. This struck her as even funnier. She laughed out loud as she walked along the edge of the yard in the shadow of the woods. She stopped briefly to look back at the dancers and the fire and her father. His eyes met hers, though she knew he couldn't see her in the darkness. He'd always been watching her, even when she was far away and felt alone. She realized how much more alone Pip had been, without a father. An earthy petrichor smell wafted out from the canyon and she heard a distant sound that may have been a bark or the warning cry of a waking demon. A cigarette? That was her protection? She shook her head, wished briefly for Sitka, and went in.

The walls towered damply around her. Ruthie was surprised by how much light the canyon held as soon as she was outside the fire's glow. All of its surfaces were reflective—the wet walls, the water trickling over the rocks on the bottom—and while it seemed to swallow light during the day, it now held the moon and starlight in harvest. The sounds of the party were replaced by silence. The air tasted ripe, fecund. By going into the canyon, she was also descending into the earth.

She passed the place where she'd seen the creature. She searched the shadows, as if it had been waiting for her.

The walls widened the deeper she went, an entire world opening up. She picked her way over boulders and skirted the softwood trees that lined the waterway. The sliding water seemed to reshape itself as Ruthie's perspective shifted. Shadowy specters moved around her, flickering from her periphery. The petrichor filled her lungs so deeply that her drunkenness fell away and she felt a heightened awareness, as if she could sense movement miles ahead and walk all night. She wasn't afraid. Her life in the valley had come to a place of acceptance. If the canyon held an entrance to the underworld, she wanted to find it. If there were spirits inside, she wanted to meet them. If five hundred years of Salish warriors waited for her in its depths, she'd surrender.

She opened her mouth but couldn't bring herself to call out, afraid her voice would shatter the canyon's spell. She sensed that Pharaoh was safe, ahead of her.

The night swam. A huge scree field filled with chunks of granite like cubes of ice tumbled down in the moonlight. House-sized boulders rose from the creek, with still pools in bowls carved from their surface. Water skeeters drifted across. Dead trees, charred black from an ancient fire, lifted their bare branches to the sky. Exposed roots reached down toward the heart of the earth. Ruthie walked and walked, letting her mind go still to match the night. Her life receded behind her. She'd always been here between these walls and always would be. Both she and her father. Along with the trappers and miners and generations of Salish and the People of the Flood. All held by their love of the valley, and its colossal, encompassing mystery.

The hood of Ruthie's sweatshirt was snug around her ears like fur. She hummed her favorite song. *My fellow lonesome rider. May you one day escape the darkness and experience the light.*

She suddenly felt giddily happy.

Pharaoh waited for her in a cathedral-like opening surrounded by western larch—the trees that lit the hillsides yellow in the fall. It was a clearing like Eden. Untouched. He stood directly in the center awash in moonlight, a broken rabbit in his jaws. The brown fur on his chin was stained with blood.

"Oh, you," Ruthie murmured, kneeling before him. He gently placed the animal at her feet, then stepped back, frightened and proud. Not knowing what he'd done or what it meant, but only that he'd done it. It was a feeling she understood. She was a hunter just as much as her dog, but it was the life of prey she loved above all else. The innocence of things that moved through the grass seeking only to live another day. She picked up the animal, feeling its last heartbeats, the muscles that had leapt toward the sky, and the bones that had propelled it across the earth. Its fleeting animation like the breaking of a wave.

When she looked up, a herd of elk stood shimmering in the clearing behind Pharaoh. Their translucent hides were marked by bullet holes. She saw the vacant-eyed cow and the helpless calf that had gotten caught in the fence, still trailing barbed wire from its hind leg. The bull stood apart from the others with blood caked across his neck. His antlers were raised to the sky. It was the same herd she and Badger had helped to slaughter. The valley's long and exacting memory. Spirits in the penumbra of the visible world. The bull looked into her eyes. His rack was silhouetted against the canyon wall, the tines stretching upward impossibly in extended shadow.

The cupped hand of his antlers seemed like it could hold a small planet, and she saw within it all her losses: Sitka, her mother, her childhood, the wild landscapes of her home. Her burdens held for her until she could bear the weight.

"I'm sorry," she said.

The bull flickered. Only the cupped hand of his antlers remained distinct above him. The rest of the herd began to disappear also, rustling against one another as they did, with the rippling memory of life. The bull raised his front hoof and by the time he brought it down he was gone. Ruthie knelt in the dirt with the dead rabbit in her arms. Sorrow and gratitude ran through her. She stayed this way, Pharaoh lying beside her, until the first rays of dawn impaled the eastern sky.

36.

The party was over when Ruthie returned. She walked silently across the can-and-butt-strewn yard with Pharaoh at her side. Cool mist around her, dew at her feet. She gently pushed open the door of The Last Wolf. The room was trashed: a patch of vomit in the far corner, stools overturned, and the satellite unplugged but the TV's blue screen glowing like a portal to another world. Kent Willis lay passed out facedown, shirtless, on one of the couches. His ass rose and fell, lifted well above the cushions by his girth. Danette was on the couch opposite him. Her muumuu was pushed up, revealing lacy black garters and stockings. A secret, sexy, wanting woman. Ruthie smiled. All of them just the same. She set the rabbit on the bar as an offering.

A dart was lodged between Wiley King's eyes. Another protruded from the moose's neck. Ruthie removed them and tossed them onto the floor. Then she knelt and gently shook the cans from the wolfskin rug. They clattered against the fallen stools. Willis grunted but didn't move. Danette looked like she might be dead; a bit of drool trembled between her lips. Ruthie smoothed down the fur, rolled up the rug, and held the bundle to her chest. She backed from the shed and jogged across the yard to her truck. Pharaoh jumped in beside her.

Back in her small house, below the replastered wall where *Wild Woman with Tame Horses* had hung, she unrolled the rug on her bed. She undressed, lay down upon it, and fell asleep. She slept for the entire day, more deeply than she had in years.

She dreamt of her father swimming in Lake Como, below the high rock teenagers jumped off, where Len had carved his chair. Sediment danced in the water around him. Bubbles streamed past his nose. He was turning slowly, sinking. His eyes were open and he smiled up at her atop the cliff, motioning for her to join him. His thin hairless legs kicked his body downward, as if there were something he wanted in the depths. His belly sagged over his ragged briefs. His thinning hair flowed above him. He outspread his arms and used his large hands to pull himself deeper. Ruthie wondered if she should be afraid, if she should save him, or let him find whatever he was looking for. She was surprised by his agility, his fearlessness in the water, as if secretly it had been his home all along. He stroked on to the silty depths, where huge silver fish traced S-patterns through the scintillating darkness. Ruthie saw other things moving down there, larger creatures, but they were too shadowy to make out. Her father reached down into the silt. He burrowed himself within it, wriggling deeper, until the only sign of him was a faint cloud among the silver fish.

Alone, Ruthie looked up. The sky rippled far above her. A summer sky she'd seen before as a little girl, the day she threw the rock at the boy. She saw herself atop the cliff looking down, with the green, kidney-shaped rock in her hand. On the edge of her life, on its precipice. All of it spread before her. She wanted to jump but she was afraid.

She wanted to swim but she was bound to the earth. She wanted to hurt no one, yet people had brought so much pain. Her cheeks were flushed red from the cold. Clouds framed the very tops of the trees.

"*Jump*," she heard her father say.

Ruthie did. Plunging down through the cold air, the rock in her hand pulling her like an anchor, rushing to meet her destiny, something warm and triumphant opening in her chest.

VI

37.

The creature lurched. There was no other word for it. It lurched on two long, bony legs out from willows on the edge of Jon Sitka's pond. Ruthie Fear crouched behind the duck blind, straining to see through the dawn mist rising off the water. A damp luminescence, the last remnant of night, made everything appear distant and unreal. She held her breath. Her heart thudded. She realized she'd been waiting for this moment for twenty-five years.

The ducks hadn't moved. They floated placidly between two bright green algae blooms, oblivious to the strange being behind them and the hunter in front. The Auto-5, old and hard-recoiling, was warm beneath Ruthie's fingers. It was the same gun her father had used. He'd given it to her for her thirty-second birthday. Her knuckles were white on the barrel.

The creature continued across the pebbly beach. It lurched softly, making no sound. At the water it paused, leaning forward, its legs like stilts in the soft light. It was even taller than Ruthie remembered, nearly twice her height. The sides of its kidney-shaped body were covered in grayish feathers. Tufted tail feathers rose from its rear. Its black underbelly gleamed like an eel. There were two joints in each of its legs and they wavered horribly, an awkward, deviant unsteadiness. But the worst part, the part that brought a sickness to Ruthie's stomach once again, was that it had no head.

The front of its chest continued in an unbroken plane over its collar and back along the ridge of its spine. Nothing protruded. No neck, no eyes, no mouth, no orifices at all that she could see. Yet still it was leaning forward over the pond as if it wanted to drink.

Slowly, Ruthie raised the shotgun to her shoulder.

The creature tipped to the left, like a deer cocks its head when sensing a predator. It faced Ruthie with its eyeless mask. She knew it was a new being, something never before seen, but she feared it, as she always had. Another blight on an earth that was becoming more blighted by the day. Toxic ponds, clear-cuts, extinctions, droughts, wildfires, disease. The bees dying. Her life marked by the steady progression of houses and stores across the valley floor.

It wouldn't escape this time.

Calm down, she told herself. But when the creature suddenly jerked upright, Ruthie jerked the shotgun to her eye in a mirrored motion. Her finger slid from the trigger guard. She remembered her father's words. "Only touch the trigger when you're going to shoot." She and the creature stayed like this for a moment, faced off across the fifty yards of water, the muzzle of Ruthie's gun and her gray eyes visible between the slats of the duck blind. Then the creature turned to flee, and Ruthie fired.

•

"I SHOT SOMETHING." Ruthie's voice shook. She was back at her truck, leaning against the cab, with her phone at her ear and the shotgun propped beside her. The sickness in her stomach had spread to her limbs. She felt, perhaps, that she'd done something terribly wrong. "I was out hunting ducks and I shot something."

"Who?" her father asked.

"Not someone. Something. At the pond. I killed it."

She heard Sylver's voice in the background. "An animal?" Rutherford said.

Ruthie nodded, chewing her lip. "I . . . I think so. It doesn't have a head."

The line was silent for several seconds. "You been drinking?"

"Jesus Christ, Dad. It's six a.m." Ruthie squeezed her eyes shut and then opened them. A red-tailed hawk winged overhead into the stand of pine trees around Sitka's house. "It's what I saw when I was a girl. When you didn't believe me."

The line went silent again. Then rustling as her father muttered something to Sylver and climbed out of bed. "Okay," he said. "I'm on my way."

Ruthie hung up. She looked through the trees and across the water to the rocky beach, where the humped feathered form lay motionless.

NEXT, SHE CALLED PIP. "It came back," she said.

"What?" Pip's voice was faint and sleepy on the other end of the line.

"The creature. It came back and I shot it." Ruthie was surprised by how difficult it was to keep from crying.

"Why?"

"I don't know." Ruthie paused. "I felt like I had to. I didn't want to let it get away again."

The line was silent. Adrian began crying in the background. Ruthie's goddaughter, named after Pip's uncle, she was a year old, with a thatch of black hair and bright brown eyes. Ruthie was astonished by the love she felt every time she held her. How tiny she was, the perfection of her hands and feet. Each digit so finely formed. Ruthie didn't know what the reappearance of the creature meant, but she was determined to send Adrian out of the valley. "I think you need to take Adrian and go," she said. "Just to be safe."

"What for?"

"I have a bad feeling. I can't explain it."

"Come with us," Pip said, hearing the fear in Ruthie's voice.

"I will," Ruthie answered. "But I want to make sure people see it first. I'll meet you in Missoula, at Bonner Park."

"Okay," Pip said. "But I want to see it, too."

"I'll take a picture."

The line was silent again.

"Please, for Adrian."

"All right," Pip said. "We're going."

Relief flooded through Ruthie.

SHE AND HER FATHER walked shoulder to shoulder along the water's edge, avoiding the branches strewn across the path. There'd been a windstorm the week before, and Ruthie had yet to clear the debris. The property was beginning to fall into disrepair: paint flaking off the mansion walls, weeds growing up through the deck. It was too much for her to take care of on her own. Each winter left new potholes in the driveway.

As they neared the corpse, Ruthie slowed, wondering again what she'd done.

"Looks like some kind of a bird," Rutherford said, hitching up the Smith & Wesson Governor holstered at his waist—his midlife crisis weapon: oversized and unreliable. "Maybe an emu got loose from Del's farm."

"That's what you said last time."

Her father went quiet for a moment. "If it is one we're going to have to sink it and not tell anyone it was here. You know how much an emu costs?"

"They were five thousand dollars twenty-five years ago," Ruthie said in exasperation. The pop of a gun across the valley interrupted her. Rutherford squinted after it, his brow furrowing.

"Everybody hunting in May now?"

The sun was high above them and the ducks had disappeared. Only the algae remained on the surface of the water. Its bright green was dulled by the sunlight. With the mist and luminescence gone, the pond looked like what it was: a sad little feed swamp seeping back into the hills around it. They stopped at the edge where an old bleached paddleboat lay half submerged. The thin willow branches above them swayed. A red hummingbird feeder hung over the water. Deer ran by, heading for the mountains. Pharaoh barked from the mansion below, no more a hunting dog than a guard dog. Ruthie forced herself to look at the creature. Its feathers weren't plain gray up close, but held a bluish incandescence, a shimmer. They were bunched at the sides like wings yet there was no sign of bones nor arms nor any way to raise them, any way to fly. The force of the bullet had knocked it backward and its legs lay splayed out on the rocks. They were bare, horribly so. Nothing but grayish bones held together by orange sinew at the two joints.

Rutherford let out a low whistle and walked gingerly toward it. He nudged the creature's chest with the toe of his boot. It flopped back into place. He leaned over to inspect its rear. He grunted. "Where's its head?"

Ruthie bit her lip.

The sound of more gunshots drifted across the valley. Rutherford nudged the creature again and a bluish ooze leaked from the wound on its chest and trickled over the rocks. A horrible smell, somewhere between sewage and melting rubber, wafted out. Ruthie covered her mouth with her forearm. Rutherford straightened. He reached down to his waist, touching first the butt of the revolver, then digging into his pocket for his phone. "Terry will know what it is," he said, fear in his voice.

"You sure we shouldn't just sink it?" Ruthie was suddenly desperate to be done with the creature. To go home, call in sick at the diner, and spend the rest of the day in bed under the covers. She needed a week off. Or a month. She felt herself fraying at the edges.

A branch cracked behind her and her father spun, dropped his phone, drew the revolver, and fired. The .410 shotshell exploded past Ruthie's arm. She leapt back and turned in time to see another of the creatures convulse, twist on its stilt-like legs, and topple into the underbrush.

"Goddammit," Rutherford said. He looked down in disbelief at the smoking gun in his hand. "It spooked me."

Ears ringing, Ruthie fought to return the air to her lungs. Her heart rattled her rib cage.

Dark tissue splattered the willow trunk behind the fallen creature. "What's wrong with you?" she managed, finally. "You could've killed me."

THE CREATURE WAS like an anvil in the back of Ruthie's truck. She could feel its weight when she toed down the accelerator. She could feel the specter of its presence in the cab. A doom, a pall. Carrying

them around the pond had been one of the most horrible experiences
of her life. They were fantastically heavy and slipped out of her fingers
like sacks of sludge. The hellish smell that steamed out of them was
so strong she kept having to set her end down to wipe her eyes. And
now her eyes burned.

Her father's enormous dual-cab bounced on the dirt road in front
of her, commandeering both lanes, weighed down by his own kill.
She slowed to keep from driving in the tornado of dust. Sitka's ranch
shrank in the rearview mirror. The fields on either side of Willow
Creek Road were newly harrowed, ready to seed. Their rich black soil
glowed in the sun. It reminded her of the creature's belly, and brought
a fresh wave of nausea up through her chest. Christ. If only she'd
missed. But she hardly ever missed, not since the fiery day her father
had taught her to shoot. She pushed her hair back from her forehead
and rubbed her temple.

Off in the distance, a man ran across a field carrying a long-stock
rifle. Ruthie rolled her window down to see more clearly. The crackle
of gunfire greeted her. What was happening? The old men in the
diner joked that a war might break out and they wouldn't hear about
it in the Bitterroot Valley until the bullets were snapping by their ears,
but not like this.

They passed Old Well Road and Whipple's and the new artisanal
bakery. Its clapboard sign advertised fresh biscuits and gravy. The
tables on the porch were empty, something Ruthie had never seen
before on a Sunday morning. Usually they were full of ranch wives in
church clothes nibbling scones and gossiping while their silent husbands looked across the wind-blasted fields and longed for football.

More houses appeared on the outskirts of Darby. Her father pulled
onto the grass by the entrance to the Whispering Pines Trailer Park.
Kent Willis was standing shirtless in jeans and cowboy boots smack-
dab in the center of his driveway with his Weatherby semiauto cocked
to the sky. He appeared to be making some kind of last stand. His face

was lit by excitement. The unkempt ring of hair on his head stood up crazily. He rose on his toes to look into the bed of Rutherford's truck.

"That's a smell I won't soon forget," he said. "Shot one of the fuckers off my back porch. It was staggering around the sprinkler in Danette's little flower garden and before I even knew what I was doing I'd killed it." He wiped his forehead. "Folks been shooting them all over."

"They creep up on you," Rutherford said.

Willis nodded. "Must be some kind of experimental creature. Got loose from the labs." His voice was exultant; he'd been waiting for this his whole life. He looked to the eastern horizon—the drones and fighter jets couldn't be far behind. "I been saying it for years, who knows what they're doing up there, messing around with all that government money. They got no more sense than pig shit."

"Anybody seen them do anything?" Rutherford asked. "The creatures, I mean."

"Like what?"

"I don't know, eat something or run or fight back."

Ruthie looked down at her fingers on the steering wheel. Long and thin and chewed around the nails. She wondered what else they were capable of beyond pulling the trigger. She wondered if many of the misdeeds in her life that she'd blamed on others had been her doing all along. "It was just out there sniffing for water," she said.

"Better not to find out what they want with it," Willis said, turning to her. "Last thing we need are some headless laboratory freaks contaminating our feed ponds." He gripped the stock of his shotgun. As if he'd ever had a feed pond.

"We're finding somewhere to dump these, be done with 'em," her father said.

Willis nodded. "Go on downtown. That's where everyone else is."

Rutherford pulled away. Ruthie followed, ignoring the shotgun wave Willis sent her. He lumbered off through the grass in her rearview mirror. Past the trailer park came the Super 1 and the Sinclair. Two men were shouting back and forth over the pumps. One of the creatures lay between them in a puddle of gas, its feathers shimmering in the sunstruck, viscous liquid. Ruthie wondered what had become of the one she'd seen as a girl. Or had it been a premonition, a ghost image of what was to come?

She imagined a wave of the creatures flooding out of No-Medicine Canyon. Silent, lurching in the dawn, like a biblical plague.

Trucks lined the curb on Main Street. Some were rolled halfway up on the sidewalk, as if the drivers had been in too much of a hurry to even fully stop before hopping out. The lone stoplight blinked red. Sheriff Badger's cruiser was angled out in front of Glacier Bank. Its flashers strobed wildly across the pavement and into the Montana Café, where Danette and Judy sat at the window table, hunched together over cups of coffee, wide-eyed, staring out at the street. Seeing them filled Ruthie with relief. The world might crumble but they'd meet it with the same cowlike wonder they reserved for every other event. She raised her fingers from the steering wheel. Danette looked up but didn't wave back.

"Don't even think about dumping those here," Badger called, as she and her father rolled to a stop. His wide ass was planted on the cruiser's bumper and his arms were crossed. "Air's hardly fit to breathe as it is. Folks been bringing 'em in all morning."

Rutherford started to speak but Badger cut him off. He was so mad he couldn't look at Ruthie. "I'll ask you the same question I been asking everybody else: What'd you shoot it for?"

Both father and daughter were silent.

"That's what I thought." Badger dropped his hand onto the butt of his Glock. "Like everybody's lost their damn minds."

"They don't have heads," Rutherford said.

"Just because you can't see a thing's head doesn't mean you can kill it, goddammit. Maybe they've got heads inside." Badger pushed off the bumper and took a step toward the grille of Rutherford's huge truck, as if the force of his indignation would be enough to hold it back. "Did it become new species hunting season all of a sudden? Is that what May is now? About fifty of them have come through in the last half hour, all shot to hell." Badger wiped the spittle from his chin and rubbed his hand on his rumpled beige uniform. "What am I supposed to say when the news gets here?"

"Hell, just tell 'em they're aggressive," Rutherford said.

"Aggressive?" Badger slumped back down on the bumper and the rear axle creaked. He looked around helplessly. "I don't see how they can even walk on those spindly legs, let alone hurt somebody." Bits of paint were flaking off the decal on the side of his cruiser. It had an old CB radio on the dash instead of a laptop. None of the new bike path and brewery money had trickled down to the sheriff's department. "Don't any of you people know how to keep your guns holstered?"

"It spooked me," Rutherford said.

"Yeah, I'll just tell that to CNN." Badger sighed dejectedly and waved on down the road. "Head out to the dump, that's where everybody else is. Fire department, too. I guess they're gonna burn 'em up."

THE DEAD CREATURES were piled in a massive, glistening mound, more than fifteen feet high and thirty wide. Behind them, the trash pit stank and rotted. Dishwashers and nail-studded plywood, pink rolls of insulation, and reams and reams of moldy bread and vegetables. Flies swarmed these, but none touched the leaking corpses. Apparently some things were too foul even for flies.

The corpses were bent and sprawled and crammed together. A crowd of men and women stood around two fire trucks and a forklift, looking up at them. A regular massacre. Pulling past, Ruthie felt sick, like a cavalryman bringing in scalps for gold in the Indian days. Senseless, cruel. It had just wanted a drink. She found a spot in the corner of the lot. Her father's truck wouldn't fit and he circled twice before finally coming to a stop in the lane, boxing her and two other trucks in.

"We're not staying long," he said, hopping down off the runner.

"You shot one, too," Ruthie said.

"I know that. You think I don't know that?"

The gravel crunched beneath their boots as they heaved the first creature down and staggered with it over to the pile. Whipple Jr., Tracy Trimble, and Dalton Pompey parted to let them through. "On three," her father gasped. They heaved the creature onto its fellows. They were all different, Ruthie saw. Every one. Some grayer, some bluer, some with a greenish tint to their bellies. One was nearly double the size of what she and her father had brought. Ruthie had no idea how anyone had managed to carry it. Even the forklift didn't seem big enough.

Tracy nodded to her with tight lips. "Hell of a Sunday," she said.

"I might start to think I'm going crazy," Ruthie answered, turning back for the second corpse.

The fire chief was talking on his cell phone, his right arm draped through the ladder on the back of the fire truck. "Yeah, we set a couple aside," he said. "Should be in good shape, other than the bullet holes." He laughed into the phone, his teeth as stained as his suspenders.

Had it been fear that caused her to pull the trigger, or anger? Carrying the second creature, Ruthie felt it was important to know. The skin of the belly was still warm. It felt like rubber, with fine downy tendrils that clung to her fingers then suddenly slipped away, causing her father to curse and heft his end of the load. Her eyes watered. The muscles in her shoulders strained. She searched for signs of an internal head, or teeth, claws, anything that might make the creatures dangerous. The legs bent over her arm and dragged in the dust. They did have spiky little prongs at the end, but she didn't see how they could raise them high enough to do any damage. You'd have to let one walk right over you. Harmless. Yet even now as she slung the creature onto the pile, she felt a twinge of hatred at its lumpy, foreign shape. She decided that fear and anger equaled more or less the same thing, in the end.

The fire chief snapped his phone shut and turned to the crowd. "All right, we got the go-ahead," he said. "Let's light 'em up."

Dalton went to his truck and came back carrying gas cans with his seven fingers. Ruthie'd been at the 4-H parade when he lost the other three, caught up in a float rope. Ever since, his face had swollen like a sad, mottled balloon. She remembered how alive he'd been rubbing against her thigh after the homecoming dance, the night her childhood ended. She felt something else ending now. The fire chief took one of the cans and Hose Corwin took another and all three went to a different corner of the pile. They shook and spewed the gas up over the bodies. The sharp benzene smell was nothing but a slight tang in the air, thoroughly overpowered by the dead creatures' stink. Ruthie longed to plunge her nose into one of the cans, huff the fumes until her head swam. Forget everything.

"Let's get out of here," her father said.

But Ruthie didn't move. She felt they should watch. That it was the least they could do after shooting them down. "You think they've got heads inside?" she asked.

He grunted. "Must be something in there. Don't know if I'd call it a head."

"You're not curious?"

"My stomach's twisted. And I can't think straight in this goddamn smell. It's worse than the old mill."

Ruthie nodded, dimly remembering coffee-colored smoke belching from the plant where her father had worked for her earliest childhood. During the winter, inversions had been so bad she couldn't see ten yards in front of her hand, but it had never made her eyes burn like this.

Rutherford rocked back on his heels and spat in the dust. "Sylver makes omelets on Sunday morning, you know that? I'd be eating a goddamn omelet right now." His belly looked ready to pop out of his shirt and catch a tan. Sunlight gleamed off the handle of the Governor. Ruthie was glad he'd shot one of the creatures, too. Glad it hadn't just been her. A vulture slowed overhead, circled, then changed its mind and carried on south across the sky. Ruthie stared after it, expecting more to follow.

Instead, from the crest of the mountains, a phalanx of planes appeared, flying east. Twelve private jets with gold stripes along their sides. Ruthie had forgotten Angel's Landing. It jarred her to think of this hidden town now. Castles around a man-made lake in the roadless woods. A private chef, a private school. The silly fantasies she'd had as a little girl. The jets flew in a slant, like ducks, and disappeared over the Sapphires. Their parallel contrails streaked across the sky.

"Where the hell are they going?" her father asked.

"Fuck 'em," the fire chief said. "They clear out every time the wind changes. You know they've got their own fire department?" He shook his head in disgust. "Bunch of asshole commandos."

He lit a match. "Everybody stand back." He dropped the flame to the trickle of gas at his feet. A pulsing thread of blue fire jumped forward, growing and turning yellow as it rushed toward the corpses. It leapt up the sides and immediately burst into a wild orange ball. Sparks shot to the sky. The flames crackled. Heat radiated outward and the crowd began to back away.

"Goddamn," the fire chief said, also stepping back, surprised by the fire's strength.

A plume of black smoke funneled up from the center of the pile. The smell sharpened, growing harsher, taking on a cutting edge that caught in Ruthie's throat. Holding her breath, she watched the flesh melt. Ooze poured forth in popping gusts. It sizzled, smoking mightily. The flames roared and churned, something gleeful in them, as if the creatures had been meant to burn. The fire grew, quickly engulfing the entire mound.

"Come on," her father said, taking her arm, a sudden urgency in his voice. Ruthie felt it, too. The heat was too strong, too sudden. The smoke too harsh. Dalton began to cough. His shoulders shook. Tears streaked down his cheeks, mixing with sweat. Wide-eyed, he looked at Ruthie, hacked again, then ran.

Ruthie raised her arm over her mouth and followed. She weaved between the bumpers. Her heart banged in her chest. Her father leapt into his truck as Hose shouted for him to get the fucking thing out of the way. The tears in Ruthie's eyes made it difficult to see. Fingers shaking, hacking and coughing, she opened her door. The big wheels of her father's F-350 screeched on the gravel as it peeled away. She pitched into the driver's seat and slammed the door shut. The air was better inside, but it still felt like a giant fist was squeezing her lungs. She turned the key in the ignition, put the truck in reverse, then joined the crush of traffic exiting the lot.

The last thing she saw in the rearview mirror was the firemen desperately spraying jets of water onto the flaming pyre. Then they, too, turned to flee, two of them dragging the prone body of the chief between them, the black smoke billowing over their heads.

DANETTE AND JUDY had abandoned their coffee and stood in the sunlight in front of the diner watching the growing black cloud. Their wide faces were slack-jawed in disbelief. Kiley Pompey sat on the curb beside them with tears in her eyes. Terry and Billy French leaned together in front of the bank, still and silent. Sorrow was written on Terry's face. Something darker on his brother's. Parents and kids in church clothes clustered on the sidewalk. Homeless men gaped on the corner. All of them transfixed, heads upturned to the fingers of black smoke reaching across the valley.

Repent, Father Mike should have said.

The streets were empty; everyone had left their cars to watch on foot. Rutherford pulled up beside Ruthie, rolled his window down, and shouted that he was going home to check on Sylver. Ruthie nodded and gunned through downtown, thinking of Pharaoh alone in the mansion. She passed the high school, her house, the trailer park—Kent Willis gone from his driveway—and Whipple's, back to Willow Creek Road. The new-harrowed fields flashed by. They were deserted also. The whole valley empty as its residents streamed toward the pyre.

Ruthie prayed that Pip was far away.

She slammed to a stop in front of the mansion. Dry leaves were scattered across the porch. The paint-flaking columns spoke grandly of ruin. Still Wiley King's as much as Sitka's or hers. She stumbled to the door. Pharaoh was waiting inside, panting. He tried to jump up on her legs but fell down weakly. Ruthie locked the heavy door behind them and leaned back against it. "It's okay, boy," she whispered, barely able to speak. Pharaoh followed her slowly from room to room as she closed all the windows. Even here, miles away, the acrid smell polluted the air. She touched her chest, hoping the pain and tightness would fade. She sank down on one of the leather couches and stared across at the open mouth of the fireplace. The gold records gleamed above it. She rested her hand on Pharaoh's heaving ribs. What was happening?

The pain in her throat intensified. It took on a searing, acidic quality, as if the tissues were being eaten away. She tried to swallow some moisture and found it catching, dripping, falling straight down to her stomach. A siren wailed in the distance. Cold fear seeped up through the tree of her limbs. She had to leave. Drive to Missoula, a hospital. She'd promised to meet Pip. But she felt exhausted. Pharaoh whimpered.

Slowly, she pushed herself up. Supporting her weight on the wall, she made her way to the kitchen. She almost collapsed, but caught herself and regathered her strength. Something warm would help. Hot water with lemon like for a sore throat. She set the kettle to boil and looked at the clock in the knot of sunlight above the stove. Only ten a.m., still three hours before she had to be at work. She leaned forward and peered through the window. The black cloud blocked out the mountains. It billowed and pulsed, a faceless beast, still growing. So much smoke, but she remembered how dense the creatures were, and how readily the fluid in their bodies had burned.

A tickle began at the base of her chest and worked its way up into a wracking cough that knocked her forward over the sink. Pain seared her throat. She spat, wiped her eyes, and then looked down in horror at the pale tissue in the large red glob stuck to the drain.

Ruthie gagged, beginning to panic. She gripped the edge of the counter and spat again. Blood came, and more tissue. She saw the creature as she had at dawn, its lurching, helpless path. The way it had leaned over the water. She felt sick. What had she done?

Sweat dampened her palms. She stared desperately out the window. The morning was silent. No more sirens or gunshots. Nothing stirred in the trees. Only a single contrail divided the blue sky, moving much too fast for a regular plane.

Military. She wondered if everyone else had already left; if they'd fled like the rich. If she was the last woman in the valley. Then on the driveway far below her she saw a man running. Large and staggering in his beige uniform, his cruiser wrecked behind him. He weaved up the cracked pavement, barely able to stand, driven by a last desperate strength. He nearly made it to her front walk before pitching forward to lie motionless on the edge of the grass.

Ruthie stumbled to the door. The effort made her dizzy. She could barely unlatch the bolt. Blindly, she ran down the walk to where Badger lay. She fell to her knees beside him. He looked up at her. His wide face was contorted. Sweat poured down his cheeks. The remains of his brown hair was mussed back from his high forehead. *Ruthie*, he mouthed.

She touched his chest. Felt the desperate kick of his heart within. It was a song she'd listened to many times as a girl. One she'd longed for, loved, feared, loathed, and then come to feel something else: the knowledge that it was only that—a man's heart, a bloody motor always running down, a soft and scared and changing thing. She heard in its music Sitka's also, and her father's. Always her father's. With Sylver now, she hoped.

She wiped the sweat from Badger's cheek. His lips worked, trying to form a word.

I know, she mouthed.

The pain left Badger's face. It was all he wanted. Pharaoh crawled outside and lay beside them. Ruthie held both their heads in her lap. She couldn't speak. Something had melted away: her voice box, her trachea. She looked across the valley. The shadow of the black cloud advanced over the shining path of the river and the turn for Red Sun Road. The teal dot of her trailer disappeared. The patchwork of farms and trailer parks on either side. Only the white tip of Trapper Peak rose from the blackness to the sky.

Ruthie looked up at the hooked finger for the last time. She saw a bald eagle streaking toward it like a fresh-shot arrow. Then the eagle dropped, suddenly, into the smoke.

38.

Ruthie Fear's spirit lingered in the sky above the ranch. As spirits often do, wanting to see how things turn out. Time became fluid. Days and weeks passed like the river that divided the valley below. All was still, all was silent. The black smoke cleared. Ranchers lay in the fields beside their dead cows. Cars littered the roads, their drivers slumped over the steering wheels, their engines turning until they ran out of gas. The lights in the stores blinked off one by one. The bodies on the sidewalk reached out for one another. When night fell, a darkness as pure as ink covered them.

Innumerable stars punctured this curtain. Dawn brought a glistening radiance. Weeds and vines grew up the sides of the buildings. Grass appeared in a crack on the roof of Whipple's Feed Store and spread steadily outward.

Ruthie was waiting for something, but she didn't know yet what it was.

A convoy of military trucks entered the valley from the north. She saw them spread out on roads through Darby, Hamilton, Corvallis, Stevensville, all the little towns where she'd spent her life. She saw men in white hazmat suits take readings with handheld instruments. She saw them walk through the high school. She saw them converge on the labs, and she saw the equipment they carried out. She saw them drive past her father's trailer, and walk into No-Medicine Canyon. She saw Rutherford's face in the window, pale and empty beside Sylver's.

None of it held much interest for her. Even when they came for her body, zipping it along with Badger's and Pharaoh's into polyurethane bags and taking them away to be buried under concrete with all the others, she watched with little emotion. She knew the flesh now held no more of her than the rocks and the trees.

She waited in a haze. Unthinking but present.

Some months later, after the first snow had fallen, when all the hazmat men had gone and only huge barricades remained behind them, blocking the roads into and out of the valley, sealing it off as the ice dam had once sealed off Lake Missoula, she saw a black speck moving on the snowy ridge near Skalkaho Pass. It wakened her fully. She flew toward it without knowing why. The rising ground blurred beneath her. It was the first time she'd moved this way, and she was amazed by how quickly she shot through the air. The speck took on fur as she approached. Legs and paws, a long bushy tail. The sloping back, heavily muscled neck, long muzzle, and powerful jaws of a wolf. Its coat was black as charcoal, as if it had spent the past thirty years running through a fire.

It raised its head as she drew to a stop above it. Its ears twitched forward. It looked up at her. Its eyes were like light on water—alive with twin flames. Its lips rested over its teeth. Muscles shifted beneath the black fur. It sniffed, unconcerned, greeting her as it did all the other spirits that moved through the air of the West.

Then it lowered its head, turned back to the mountainside, and loped over the snowy ground and down from the Sapphire Mountains into the Bitterroot Valley.

Acknowledgments

To Dave Wallace, as always, for setting me on this path. To Chris Clemans, for his tireless wisdom, and the memory of his mother, Anita Shreve. To Tom Mayer, for believing in this book before it existed. To my readers Panagiotis Gavriiloglou, Grant Munroe, Kurt Pitzer, Mikkel Rosengaard, and Janie Taylor, for their kinship in words. To my old friend Brian Furey, for first showing me the Bitterroot Valley. To my parents, Candace and Doug Loskutoff, for their enduring love. And to all those who walk with light in a darkening world.

Special thanks to the Corporation of Yaddo, MacDowell Colony, Brush Creek Foundation, Playa, Jentel, Sitka Center for Art and Ecology, Joshua Tree Highlands Artist Residency, Willapa Bay AiR, Oak Springs Garden Foundation, Monson Arts, and the James Merrill House, where sections of this book were written, and the *Chicago Tribune*, *Narrative*, and *Distinctly Montana*, where sections first appeared, in different form.

Aho, the wolves have returned.